PENGUIN BOOKS

The Nightingale Daughters

Donna Douglas lives in York with her family. When she is not busy writing, she is generally reading, watching Netflix or drinking cocktails. Sometimes all at the same time.

Also by Donna Douglas

The Nightingale Girls
The Nightingale Sisters
The Nightingale Nurses
Nightingales On Call
A Nightingale Christmas Wish
Nightingales At War
Nightingales Under the Mistletoe
A Nightingale Christmas Carol
The Nightingale Christmas Show
A Nightingale Christmas Promise
Nightingale Wedding Bells

The Nurses of Steeple Street
District Nurse on Call

The
Nightingale
Daughters

Donna
DOUGLAS

PENGUIN BOOKS

PENGUIN BOOKS

UK | USA | Canada | Ireland | Australia
India | New Zealand | South Africa

Penguin Books is part of the Penguin Random House group
of companies whose addresses can be found at
global.penguinrandomhouse.com

Penguin
Random House
UK

Published in Penguin Books 2023
001

Copyright © Donna Douglas, 2023

The moral right of the author has been asserted

Typeset in 10.4/15pt Palatino LT Pro by Jouve (UK), Milton Keynes
Printed and bound in Great Britain by Clays Ltd, Elcograf S.p.A.

The authorised representative in the EEA is
Penguin Random House Ireland, Morrison Chambers,
32 Nassau Street, Dublin D02 YH68

A CIP catalogue record for this book is available from the British Library

ISBN: 978–1–804–94368–7

www.greenpenguin.co.uk

MIX
Paper | Supporting
responsible forestry
FSC® C018179

Penguin Random House is committed to a
sustainable future for our business, our readers
and our planet. This book is made from Forest
Stewardship Council® certified paper.

In loving memory of Jacqueline Linda Quennell

21 January 1947–9 June 2022

Chapter One

I know you.

Matron Helen McKay stared at the girl sitting across the desk from her. It was three o'clock and she was the last of the prospective students to be interviewed that day. Helen had seen at least twenty girls since that morning; all those bright, eager faces, with neat hair and clipped accents, brandishing their school certificates and gushing about how honoured they would be to train as nurses at the famous Florence Nightingale Hospital in Bethnal Green.

She had already crossed through most of the names on her list. Girls she could tell would be too fragile to make it through the rigorous training. Overconfident girls who probably wouldn't take instruction. Girls who fancied themselves mopping fevered brows and flirting with young doctors.

But this girl, the last on her list, was different.

She didn't simper about how she had always loved caring for babies, or her pets. But there was a genuine warmth in her intense blue eyes.

She seemed awkward as she sat across the desk from Helen, her long limbs folded into the chair as if she did not

1

quite know what to do with them. She'd made an attempt to clip back her unruly dark curls, but Helen could never imagine them sitting neatly beneath a starched nurse's cap.

But she emanated practical good sense, and Helen could imagine her keeping a calm head on the ward.

I know you.

There was something tantalisingly familiar about her. Helen searched for the memory, but it remained elusive, just out of her reach.

She turned her attention back to her notes. The girl had an excellent report from her school, along with a handful of O Level certificates.

'I see from your application you've been working for the past two years in an office?' she said.

'That's right, miss – I mean, Matron,' the girl corrected herself. Her accent was as East End as a plate of jellied eels. 'I worked in the Accounts department at the town hall.'

'I don't see a reference?'

The girl's face clouded over. 'It wouldn't be worth reading, I daresay,' she muttered.

'And why's that?'

'I got the sack.'

'I see.' Helen blinked at her forthrightness. The girl stared back at her, bold and defiant. Helen picked up her pen and wrote a question mark beside the girl's name. 'May I ask why?'

'It was personal. Nothing to do with my work,' she added quickly. 'I was a hard worker, and I was good at my job.'

'Then why were you dismissed?'

The girl's eyes flickered for a moment, then her mouth set in a grim line and she reluctantly said,

'I had a disagreement with someone.'

'Who?'

'My supervisor.'

'What about?'

'I told you, it was personal.'

Helen blinked, taken aback at her tone. It certainly wasn't what she would usually expect from a prospective student.

'I see,' she said. 'I feel I have to point out, this hospital runs on a strict hierarchy. That means junior nurses taking orders from their superiors.'

'I don't mind taking orders.'

'And yet you had a disagreement with your supervisor?'

Her chin jutted obstinately. 'I told you, that was personal.'

'Perhaps you'd like to tell me what it was about?' The girl stared back at her, stubbornly silent. 'I'm afraid I can't consider taking you on unless you tell me what happened.'

Defeat and disappointment flickered in the girl's eyes.

'In that case, I'm sorry I've wasted your time.' She stood up and started to put on her coat. Helen stared at her in astonishment. She had never known a prospective student walk out of an interview before. She usually had trouble getting them out of her office.

She looked at the girl's stubborn face, and suddenly it struck her. The spark of recognition kindled and caught into flame.

How could she not have noticed it before? It was the height and the dark colouring that had thrown her. She had her father's looks but her mother's determination. Not to mention that East End pride that had always landed her in so much trouble.

Helen reached for the documents the girl had given her and found the birth certificate. She had barely glanced at it before, but now she studied the names carefully.

Winifred Rose Riley. Father's name, Nicholas Albert Riley. Mother's name, Dora Elizabeth Doyle . . .

'Dora Doyle,' she murmured.

The girl looked wary. 'What about her?'

'I know – knew her,' Helen corrected herself. She stared down at the name on the birth certificate. They had once been as close as sisters. But they hadn't seen each other for more than ten years, and somehow those bonds had loosened, the memories fading. 'We trained together. I was Helen Tremayne in those days,' she said.

Winifred smiled. 'Oh yes, she told me all about you. You used to be good mates.'

Used to be. Helen felt a twinge of guilt at their lost friendship. Dora had been at her side through her happiest and saddest moments, but now all that was left were the Christmas and birthday cards they exchanged.

'You were a child when I last saw you.' She looked Winifred up and down. There was nothing small about her now. She must have been five feet ten, at least. 'You have a twin brother, don't you?'

'That's right. Walter. And there's Danny, too. He's only ten.'

Helen nodded. Dora had invited her to the baby's christening, but it was just after the war and she was living in Scotland with David at the time.

'How is your mother?' she asked.

'Just the same as when you knew her, I expect. Taking care of everyone and bossing us all about!'

'That certainly sounds like her.' Dora was the one they had all turned to when they were in trouble. Helen had certainly had reason to be grateful to her over the years. 'I'm surprised she didn't come to the interview with you?'

'I'm sure she would have if she knew I was here.'

'You didn't tell her you'd applied?'

Winifred shook her head. 'I didn't want to get her hopes up, just in case I didn't get accepted,' she said quietly. 'I've already let her down once. I didn't want to do it again.'

Helen looked at her across the desk. There were so many reasons why she should not give her a chance. There were other girls on the list to see the following day, promising candidates with better qualifications, excellent references and none of Winifred Riley's truculent attitude.

She looked down at the note she had scribbled. *Disagreement with supervisor. Personal matter.* She could just imagine how that would go down with the ward sisters. It would be madness to even consider taking on a troublemaker like her.

A picture of Dora Doyle came into her mind. Just like her daughter, she had come to the hospital with a belligerent attitude and a shadowy past. But she had turned out to be one of the best nurses Helen had ever worked with, as well as a trusted friend.

Helen took her pen and crossed out the question mark she had written beside her name.

'I'm going to send you for a General Education test,' she said. 'If you pass, then I will consider you for training.'

She expected the girl to thank her, or at least to smile. But Winifred Riley eyed her warily.

'Is something wrong, Miss Riley?' Helen asked.

'I don't want you to give me a place here just because you know my mum.' Winifred's jaw jutted stubbornly. 'That wouldn't be right.'

Helen stared back at her, caught between admiration and feeling insulted. She had her mother's pride, that was for sure.

'I can promise you, Miss Riley, I do not hand out places simply on the basis of friendship,' she said tightly.

'I'm sorry, I didn't mean to offend you—' The girl's face flushed with embarrassed colour.

'You'll earn your place like any other applicant to this hospital.' Helen scribbled a note on a piece of paper and handed it to her. 'Take this down to the Nurses' Training School.' She looked at her watch. 'With any luck there'll still be time for you to take the test this afternoon.'

'What, you mean – now?' Winifred looked shocked.

'Why not? The sooner we get the results, the sooner we can decide what to do with you. Well, hurry along,' Helen prompted her, 'before the office closes.'

'Yes – thank you.'

Winifred left the office, still clutching the paper, a dazed expression on her face. Helen smiled as the door closed behind her.

Like mother, like daughter, she thought.

Chapter Two

'You? Matron wants *you* to take the test?'

The woman stared at Winnie in disbelief. She was in her late thirties, very smart in her navy-blue dress, her attractive, sharp-featured face framed by carefully coiffed fair hair. Her voice was so posh, she could have been an announcer on the BBC Home Service. She looked Winnie up and down and clearly did not like what she saw.

Winnie lifted her chin. She had thought Matron was intimidating enough, but this Miss Cheetham took the biscuit. Even the poor office girl didn't dare to catch her eye. She sat at the desk in the corner, typing frantically, her head down.

But Winnie remembered what her mother always told her. She was just as good as anyone else, no matter how many airs and graces they put on.

'That's what she said,' she replied.

Miss Cheetham looked down at Matron's note in her hand, then back at Winnie. Her pale pink lips were a tight line.

'You'll have to wait,' she said shortly. 'The other girl is just finishing. Sit over there.' She indicated a line of chairs in the corridor.

A toothless old woman in a moth-eaten coat sat in the furthest seat, grinding her gums, her gaze fixed firmly on the closed door with a sign on it saying 'Test in progress'. She looked up and gave Winnie a terse nod, then turned her attention back to the door.

Surely she wasn't waiting to take the test too, Winnie thought.

She sat in the seat furthest away from the old woman, beside the window. Outside was a square of lawn, edged by a gravelled driveway. In the centre of the lawn was a small pond with a fountain. Two girls in navy-blue capes perched on the edge of the fountain, laughing and sharing a cigarette.

Winnie felt a sudden pang. She so wanted to be like them. They seemed so sure of themselves.

The office door opposite was still half open, and beyond it she could hear Miss Cheetham complaining to the office girl.

'Did you hear the way she spoke?' she was saying, her voice carrying over the clack of the typewriter keys. 'Honestly, I can't imagine what Matron is thinking. Her sort has no business being here.'

Anger rose up inside her, tingling through her feet and legs, and it was all she could do to stay in her seat. Fortunately, before it had had a chance to take hold of her brain, the door to her right suddenly opened and a red-haired girl came out, clutching what looked to be a test paper. She was done up to the nines, with scarlet lips, high heels and a pencil skirt so tight it was a wonder she could even walk.

At the sight of her the old lady hauled herself to her feet. 'Well?' she said. 'How did you get on?'

'I did my best, all right? Keep your wig on.'

'You'd better not have mucked it up on purpose.'

'As if I would!' The redhead laughed, then turned to Winnie. 'Your turn next? Don't worry, it ain't as bad as you think.'

Miss Cheetham threw open the office door. 'Don't talk to each other, it's not allowed!' She held out her hand. 'Give me your test paper.'

The girl handed it over. 'Here you are, miss. Since you asked so nicely,' she added under her breath, which made Winnie smile.

'I daresay Matron will be writing to you in due course,' Miss Cheetham said.

'I daresay she will.' The redhead winked at Winnie. 'Good luck,' she mouthed. Then she sauntered off down the corridor, her curved hips swaying in her tight skirt. The old lady hobbled after her, still talking, even though the girl didn't seem to be listening to a word she was saying.

'I don't suppose we'll be seeing her again, thank God,' Miss Cheetham's sharp voice interrupted her thoughts. Then she looked at Winnie. 'Your turn,' she said. 'Come on, I haven't got all day!'

When her test was finished, Winnie crossed Victoria Park along Grove Road, then turned left on to Roman Road to visit her friend Judith, who worked at Woolworth's.

Judith was behind the sweet counter. She looked a bit like a nurse herself in her overall and white cap emblazoned

9

with a red letter 'W'. She was at the till, chatting to a customer as she served them with a five-penny bag of pic'n'mix, but she quickly ended the conversation and handed over their change when she saw Winnie.

'There you are!' Her eyes lit up behind her owlish pink NHS spectacles. 'I've been watching the clock all afternoon, wondering when you might come in.' She closed the till drawer. 'Well? How did you get on?'

'Not bad,' Winnie shrugged, fighting to keep the smile off her face.

'Not bad? What does that mean?'

'I think I might have got in.'

It was the first time she had said the words aloud, but she could scarcely believe they were coming out of her own mouth. None of it seemed real.

'I knew it!' Judith squealed, jumping up and down with excitement. 'Oh, Win, I said you could do it, didn't I?'

'Watch it, your boss has got her eye on you.' Winnie glanced over to where the supervisor was watching them sternly.

'I'd best get back to work. Look, we're closing in ten minutes. Can you wait for me outside? I'll be as quick as I can, I promise.'

Winnie stood on Roman Road, her arms folded against the September chill. It was past five o'clock, and the market traders were all packing up for the day. Winnie watched them loading their goods into the back of their vans and wrapping up their canvas covers, leaving behind the skeletons of their stalls and gutters strewn with broken wooden crates, bits of cardboard and rotten fruit.

Judith appeared around the corner. She was a slight little thing, much shorter than Winnie, but then so were most people, even the boys. Winnie felt herself stooping as usual as they fell into step beside each other, heading back along Roman Road towards the Regent's Canal.

'Go on, then,' Judith urged, linking her arm through Winnie's. 'Tell me everything!'

'Well, I had to take a test – English and maths and general knowledge, all that kind of thing.'

'Was it very hard?'

Winnie shook her head. 'They just wanted to make sure I could read and write, I suppose.'

Actually, the test had been much harder than she let on. Winnie had silently sent up a prayer of thanks that her dad insisted on listening to the BBC Home Service instead of the Light Programme that Winnie and her brothers preferred.

'What about the interview?' Judith asked. 'Was the matron very terrifying?'

'Not at all. She was very nice, as a matter of fact. But I didn't think I was going to get through, especially when she asked me why I'd been fired from the town hall.'

Judith sent her a sideways look. 'What did you tell her?'

'Nothing.'

'But surely she wanted to know why you—'

'I told her it was personal.'

'And she didn't ask any more?'

'Not really.'

Winnie still couldn't believe it. She'd really thought it was all over for her when Matron asked about her previous job. She'd had her coat on ready to go and everything.

'Perhaps you should have told her?' Judith ventured. Winnie shook her head.

'It's in the past,' she said firmly. 'I don't want to bring it all up again.'

'But—'

'It's over, all right? I don't want to talk about it.'

Judith was silent as they crossed the bridge over the canal. As they turned right on to Bonner Street, Winnie said,

'She mentioned Mum. Turns out they knew each other when they were students.'

'Did she? That was lucky.'

'I know.'

'D'you think that's why she gave you a chance?'

'I don't know. I hope not.' The thought still weighed heavily on Winnie's mind. She hated unfairness of any kind. She would rather miss out completely than not be accepted on her own merits.

Judith must have read her expression because she said, 'Even if she did, at least it means you got your foot in the door. Now it's up to you what you make of it.'

'That's true,' Winnie said.

It suddenly dawned on her what she had taken on. Was she really up to becoming a nurse? All that training, those years of study . . .

'I wonder what your mum will say about it?' Judith interrupted her racing thoughts.

'I expect she'll be relieved,' Winnie shrugged. 'She's been telling me ever since I lost my job how I'll never find another one. "How do you expect anyone to take you on with no references?"' she mimicked her mother's angry tones.

But deep down, she was hoping for much more. She knew she'd let her mother down, and even though she would never admit it to herself, she wanted to make it up to her, to show her she wasn't the disappointment she imagined she was.

Chapter Three

Winnie would have chosen a better time to tell her mother, preferably when they were on their own. But that never seemed to happen in the Riley household.

As usual, she walked in to find the house in chaos. Her two young cousins, Shirley and Joyce, and her youngest brother Danny sat at the kitchen table eating bread and jam while Winnie's Aunt Josie and grandmother Rose sat opposite, peeling potatoes and stringing beans.

Winnie's mother stood at the stove, still in her district nurse's uniform with an apron tied over the top. Her frizzy red curls were caught up in a messy knot at the nape of her neck. As usual, she was doing three things at once, stirring mince for a shepherd's pie in a pan while talking to her mother and sister and half-listening to *The Archers* on the wireless.

Winnie couldn't remember ever seeing her sit still. If she wasn't doing the washing, Dora Riley was cooking, or sweeping, or polishing. The only time she sat down was when she was at the table, peeling vegetables or rolling pastry. Even when one of Winnie's aunts came round for a natter, her mother would be doing the ironing, cleaning the floor or getting on with her mending.

'All right, love?' Her mother gave her a distracted smile over her shoulder, then went back to her cooking before waiting for an answer.

Winnie hesitated, looking around the room. It was now or never. 'Mum—'

'Your nan's just been telling me about Eric Finch from down the road,' her mother went on. 'He was making a bit of a show of himself last night, by all accounts.'

'Drunk as a lord, he was,' her grandmother said as she painstakingly peeled a potato. Her stroke six months previously had left her with a useless right hand, but she was still determined to do her bit. 'Singing and shouting the odds. I'm surprised you didn't hear him, Dor.'

'You know me, Mum. I'm asleep the minute my head touches the pillow. What about you, Win? Did you hear anything?'

'No, I didn't. Mum, can I talk to you?'

'I'm surprised the police didn't take him away,' Aunt Josie said.

'If the rozzers turned up to everyone who got drunk round here, they'd have half of Bethnal Green locked up. Including my old man!' Dora grinned. 'Honest to God, can you imagine it? They'd never get anything else done—'

'I went to the Nightingale,' Winnie blurted out.

All three women stared at her blankly.

'Whatever for, love?' her grandmother asked. 'You ain't ill, are you?'

'I'm fine, Nan.' Winnie looked at her mother. 'I had an interview with the matron,' she said. 'I've applied to be a nurse.'

A long silence followed her words.

'A nurse?' her mother said slowly. 'You?'

Winnie laughed nervously. 'It ain't such a daft idea, is it?'

Her mother didn't reply. She just stared at Winnie with a blank expression on her face.

'Well, I think it's lovely,' her aunt said, breaking the tension. 'Imagine that, Dora. Our Winnie, following in your footsteps.'

'I remember when our Dora got accepted,' Nanna Rose joined in. The right corner of her mouth turned down, leaving her smile lopsided. 'We really celebrated that day, didn't we?'

'Mum don't seem to be putting out the flags,' Winnie muttered, still looking at her mother.

'I'm just surprised, that's all,' Dora said, going back to her stirring. 'It's a lot to take in.'

'When will you find out if you've got in?' Aunt Josie seemed determined to show an interest, at least.

'Not until January. But I did all right on the test, so I should get in. Matron sent you her regards, by the way.' Winnie's eyes never left her mother, still desperate for a reaction. 'You'll never guess who it was?'

'Helen McKay.' Dora's voice was flat, her eyes still fixed on her cooking. 'I heard she'd taken over as Matron.'

'Is that the one who was related to the royal family?' Nanna Rose asked.

'No, Mum. That was Millie, my other room-mate.'

Winnie stared at her. 'Well? Ain't you got anything to say about it?'

'What do you want me to say?'

'Well done might be nice.'

16

'Well, I think it's wonderful,' once again Aunt Josie broke the silence. 'Come and sit down and tell me all about it.'

Winnie took a seat at the table. Aunt Josie asked all kinds of questions about her interview, and the test she'd taken. Winnie tried to answer them, all the while aware that it should have been her mother taking an interest.

But Dora stayed stubbornly silent, her back turned to them as she went on with her cooking.

'She's probably still taking it all in,' Auntie Josie whispered. 'You know your mum, she likes to think about these things.' She beamed at Winnie. 'But for what it's worth, I reckon you've done the right thing. It's just the new start you need, love.'

'I hope so.' Winnie stared at her mother's turned back, bitter with disappointment. Would it have killed her to give her a smile or a kind word?

All the way home, she had been picturing the scene in her mind, imagining the pride and delight on her mother's face when she heard the news. But instead all she got was a sullen silence.

Aunt Josie was wrong, she thought. She had never known her mother to take time to think about anything. If she had an opinion about something, she spoke up straight away.

And if Dora Riley was staying silent on a subject, it was never a good sign.

The shepherd's pie was ready and in the oven by the time her father and twin brother Walter came home. Winnie heard them laughing and joking together as they took off their boots outside the back door, before coming into the kitchen.

They were strikingly alike, father and son, both tall and lean, with a shock of black curls and intense blue eyes. Winnie had also inherited the same height and dark colouring. Only their younger brother Danny had their mother's fiery red hair and freckles.

'You're late,' her mother snapped.

'Yes, but I'm worth waiting for.'

Nick Riley came up behind his wife and wrapped his arms around her.

'Get off!' Her mother tried to shrug him away. 'You reek of sweat.'

'You've never complained before.' His arms tightened around her, and he nuzzled her neck. Her mother tried to protest, but soon she was laughing in spite of herself.

Winnie exchanged a grimace of embarrassment with her brother.

'Look at them,' Aunt Jodie said fondly. 'Like a pair of teenagers.'

'Do you mind?' Walter said. 'I don't act like that.'

'Chance would be a fine thing,' Winnie muttered.

Her father finally released Dora and looked around at the faces gathered round the kitchen table. 'The gang's all here again, I see,' he commented.

'Bea was called into work, so she left the kids here,' Dora said.

'And there was me, thinking we'd adopted them.'

He laughed when he said it, but Winnie caught the long, meaningful look that passed between them. Her cousins spent more time at their house than they did at their own, thanks to Aunt Bea being such a poor excuse for a mother.

'Your daughter's got some news,' Aunt Josie piped up.

'Oh, Sis. What have you done this time?' Walter wandered over to the stove and went to pick a crispy piece of potato crust from the shepherd's pie, but their mother slapped his hand away. 'Here, you ain't in the family way, are you?'

'Don't talk about your sister like that!' Her father turned to her. 'What's going on, Win?'

'I've applied to be a nurse at the Nightingale Hospital.' She kept her eyes fixed on her mother as she said it.

'Have you now? And how did you get on?'

'I reckon they'll offer me a place.'

'Of course they will. You're a bright girl. They'd be lucky to have you.'

'That's what I thought,' Aunt Josie said.

Walter laughed. 'You, a nurse?'

'What's so funny about that?' Winnie snapped.

'I can't see you mopping brows and wiping backsides, that's all.'

'There's a lot more to it than that,' Aunt Josie said. 'Ain't that right, Dor—'

They all jumped as her mother dropped a handful of cutlery on to the table with a clatter. 'Make yourselves useful and set the table,' she grunted. 'Josie, you can serve the tea.'

'Why, where are you going?'

'Out.'

19

Her mother retrieved a packet of cigarettes from behind the biscuit tin and went outside into the yard, slamming the back door behind her. Walter watched her from the scullery window.

'She's smoking,' he said. 'You know what that means, don't you?' He turned to Winnie, a grin on his face. 'I reckon someone's in trouble!'

Chapter Four

Dora stood in the alleyway that ran along the backs of the row of houses and opened her cigarette packet with trembling fingers. She used to smoke all the time when she was nursing, but now she hardly ever did it. The last time she could remember reaching for her cigarette packet was when her mother had had her stroke six months earlier. Now her hands were shaking so much she could hardly hold the match steady.

There was a nip to the September evening, and Dora wished she'd had the presence of mind to pick up her cardigan before she flounced out. Her uniform and pinny were no match for the cold, but she would not allow herself to set foot back inside that kitchen until she had given herself time to calm down.

She looked back across the yard towards the house. They had lived there on Old Ford Road for the past ten years, ever since her youngest, Danny, was a baby. Nick had wanted to move into one of the new flats the Corporation was building at Weaver's Fields. He had worked on them himself and he reckoned they were lovely, with inside toilets and bathrooms and everything. But Dora hadn't fancied being cooped up in a flat, mod cons or not. She liked being able to escape outside, even if it was just a little patch of yard which hardly ever saw the sun.

At least it gave her somewhere to calm down.

'I thought you'd stopped smoking?'

She swung round. Nick stood behind her, leaning against the open back gate. She took a defiant puff on her cigarette, then turned away again.

'I might manage it if everyone didn't keep driving me mad,' she muttered.

She turned away from him, the wind making her shiver. The next moment she felt the weight of his jacket around her shoulders, enfolding her in the warmth from his body and the musky smell of his skin.

'Thanks.' She glanced sideways at him. At forty-three, Nick was still an attractive man, with his greying dark curls, intense blue eyes and flattened boxer's nose. When they were kids growing up in Griffin Street, everyone was wary of him. He had a reputation as a tearaway, as vicious and unpredictable as a junkyard dog.

Nearly twenty years of marriage and three children had tamed him, but Dora knew that legendary Riley temper still simmered somewhere below the surface. And woe betide anyone who threatened his wife or his children.

Nick took the cigarette from her and drew on it, then handed it back. They stood in silence for a moment, staring up at the darkening sky.

'I take it you don't agree with this idea of Winnie's?' he said at last.

Dora let out the sigh she had been holding in ever since her daughter had made the announcement, feeling her ribs relax at last.

'I don't know what to think,' she admitted. 'She's never

mentioned wanting to be a nurse to me before. How about you?'

Nick shook his head. 'It's the first I've heard of it. Perhaps your Josie's right, and she wants to follow in your footsteps?'

'I doubt it.' Dora took the cigarette from him and dragged on it, sending a smoke ring up into the darkening sky. 'Can you imagine Winnie looking up to me?'

'You'd be surprised.'

'I'd fall down in a dead faint if she ever agreed with anything I said or did.' Winnie had always been a contrary one, right from when she was a little girl. While her twin brother was easy-going and biddable, Winnie was forever arguing. And she always had to be right, too.

'So why do you think she's done it?' Nick asked.

'I dunno,' Dora sighed. 'But I reckon she's made a big mistake.'

Nick turned his head to look at her. 'How do you work that out, then?'

'I don't think she understands what she's let herself in for. Nursing is hard work. It takes it out of you up here, as well as physically.' She tapped her temple. 'If her heart's not in it she won't last five minutes.'

And even if her heart was in it, she would end up getting it broken far too often. Even now, after twenty-five years of nursing, Dora still hadn't got used to the pain her work sometimes brought with it.

She would never wish that on Winnie.

'You never know, it might be the making of her,' Nick said.

'I wish I could believe that, I really do.'

They stood side by side in silence for a moment. 'I don't think she'd have any trouble with the training,' Nick said at last. 'She's bright enough.'

'Not bright enough to know where she's well off!' Dora shook her head. 'I really thought she was set for life when she got that job at the town hall. She was doing so well, wasn't she? But she still managed to get herself fired.'

She was still angry and frustrated about it. She'd been so proud when Winnie got that job in the Accounts department. There was even talk of her becoming a trainee book-keeper. She was happy and settled, and that was all Dora had ever wanted for her.

And then, out of the blue, she'd come home and said she'd been fired. Dora still hadn't got to the bottom of it, and Winnie wouldn't say why. Dora could only assume it was because she'd lost her temper and was now embarrassed about it.

'Perhaps it wasn't her fault?' Nick said.

'You saw the letter that supervisor sent. "A poor attitude", it said. She probably answered back once too often. You know what she's like.'

'She takes after her mother.'

Dora opened her mouth to protest, but then she saw her husband's grin.

'Maybe,' she conceded ruefully. Nick might be the one with the tempestuous reputation, but Dora was no blushing flower, either. Growing up in the slums of Bethnal Green, she'd had to learn to stand up for herself.

'A poor attitude won't get her very far as a nurse,'

she said to Nick. She shuddered at the thought of Winnie answering the ward sisters back and questioning everything she was asked to do.

'She might surprise you.'

'More likely she'll be thrown out on her ear! You know as well as I do, Winnie won't listen to anyone because she thinks she already knows it all.'

Nick laughed. 'She definitely sounds like you!'

'I'm serious, Nick.' Dora took a long drag on her cigarette. 'I only managed to get through the training because I had a real passion for the work, and because I knew it was my only chance to better myself.'

She had left school early, without any certificates or exams. But she'd had to support her widowed mother and all her siblings, so she'd taken a job in a garment factory. Being accepted to train at the Nightingale was like a lifeline for her.

Perhaps that was the problem, she thought. Perhaps Winnie should try sewing trousers for twelve hours a day in a cramped, dimly lit backstreet basement. That might make her realise where she was well off.

'If you can do it, then maybe Winnie can do it, too?' Nick argued. 'Especially if she knows this is her last chance.'

'I hope you're right,' Dora said. 'But this has to be something she wants to do with all her heart, or she'll fail again.'

And she didn't want to see her daughter fail. Winnie had put on a good front when she lost her job at the town hall, but Dora knew her confidence had taken a bad knock.

'Time will tell.' Nick put his arm around her. 'You're freezing. Why don't you come in and have something to eat?'

'I ain't hungry.' Dora blew another smoke ring into the sky. 'Bad day?'

Dora shot him a sidelong look. They rarely talked about her work as a District Nurse. Dora preferred to leave her troubles on the doorstep.

But today had hit her especially hard.

'I lost a patient today,' she said. 'We all knew it was coming, but I'd been looking after him for so long, I'd got to know him and his family quite well.'

Rule number one of nursing – don't get emotionally involved. She'd given up on that one a long time ago. The reason she was so late home was because she'd sat with his poor wife, hugging her close while she sobbed her heart out. They were an elderly couple whose only son had been killed in the war. All they had was each other, and now she had no one.

That was another reason why she didn't want Winnie to go into nursing. For every joyful moment, there was also heartbreak. And those were the ones that stayed with you.

'Oh, Dor.' Nick held her close to him.

'Take no notice of me, I'm just being silly.' Dora pulled away from him, dashing at her eyes with the back of her hand. 'A good night's sleep will soon sort me out.'

'You shouldn't take on everyone's troubles,' Nick said. 'Look at that lot in there. You're looking after us, and nursing your mum, and you're still taking in waifs and strays.'

'They're family,' Dora said. 'I can't just turn my back on them, can I?'

Her sister Josie got so lonely living on her own, no wonder she was forever coming round. And she could hardly turn away Bea's little girls when they showed up on her doorstep starving hungry because their mother had spent all her wages on a perm and a new dress.

'You don't turn your back on anyone,' Nick said. 'That's your trouble.'

'Like I said, they're family. And family means everything to me.' Dora straightened up and patted her hair, smoothing a stray curl back behind her ear. 'Anyway, I'd best go in and make sure Mum ain't taken it upon herself to clear the table. She will have it that she can manage, even though she's got no strength in her hands—' She saw her husband's face and stopped. 'What?' she said. 'What is it?'

'It's nothing,' Nick said quietly, not meeting her eye.

Dora confronted him, her hands on her hips. 'Don't you give me that, Nick Riley. I know you. And I know when something's on your mind, too. So what is it?'

He raised his gaze slowly to meet hers. 'It's Walter,' he said.

'What about him? Oh lord, don't tell me he's in trouble now too?'

'Depends what you mean by trouble, don't it?'

Dora took one look at her husband's face and felt the blood drain to her feet. 'Tell me,' she said, even though she already knew what he was going to say.

Nick looked sombre. 'Have you still got those ciggies? Only I think you might need another one . . .'

Chapter Five

'Take no notice of Mum. You know her bark's worse than her bite. I bet she didn't mean half of what she said.'

'I know what I heard, Wal.'

Eavesdroppers never heard any good of themselves, so everyone said. And overhearing her mother discussing her with her father in the back yard had hurt Winnie more than she could admit, even to her twin brother.

I reckon she's made a big mistake . . . She won't last five minutes . . . She'll be thrown out on her ear.

She hadn't heard every word they'd said, but she'd heard enough to let her know exactly what her mother thought about her.

'She doesn't think I can do it,' she said.

'Don't be daft. You got accepted on the training, didn't you?'

'Yes, but she doesn't think I'll get through it.'

'Then it's up to you to prove her wrong,' Walter said.

Winnie looked rueful. 'Mum's never wrong. You ought to know that by now.'

'I reckon you can do it,' Walter said.

'Then why did you start laughing when I mentioned it?'

'I was just surprised, that's all. You've never mentioned wanting to be a nurse before.'

Winnie was silent. How could it be that none of them remembered? It had always been in the back of her mind that one day she would follow in her mother's footsteps, just like Walter had followed in their father's. She had listened to Dora's stories as a child and thought how wonderful it would be to be like her.

But her mother had made it clear she had a different path in mind for her daughter. She had wanted Winnie to stay on at school, to get her A Levels and perhaps even go to university. When Winnie said she wanted to leave at fifteen, after her O Levels, Dora had encouraged her to go to night school and take shorthand and typing instead.

Winnie had done it all to please her mother. But all the time in the back of her mind she had wondered why she couldn't train as a nurse.

And now she knew why. Her mother did not believe she was up to it.

'Anyway, you're the clever one, you can do anything if you set your mind to it,' Walter said.

Winnie smiled at her brother. She and Walter were twins, and that gave them a special bond. Of course they still fought like cat and dog at times, but they were still best friends.

As far as temperament went, they couldn't have been more different. Walter was placid and even-tempered. He had gone straight from leaving school to helping his father on the building sites. He had stuck at it and now, nearly three years on, he had a decent trade.

Sometimes Winnie wished she had been born a boy. Then her life path might have been a lot simpler.

It would have been an advantage in other ways, too. It wasn't easy being a girl of nearly five foot ten. While Walter was practically fighting off the girls, she'd more or less given up hope of ever finding a boyfriend.

'You're right,' she said. 'I'm going to get through this course and become a nurse if it's the last thing I do. Just to spite Mum, if nothing else!'

'I'm not sure that's the right attitude, but I suppose if it helps . . .' Walter gave an expressive shrug. 'When do you start your training?'

'January, when I turn eighteen. If I get in, of course.'

'January? Oh no!'

'Why? Don't tell me you'll miss me?' Then she saw his crestfallen expression and her smile faded. 'What's wrong?'

'That's when I'm going, too.'

'Going? Going where?' Then realisation dawned and her stomach dropped. 'You got your letter?'

He nodded. 'It came in the afternoon post.'

He didn't need to say any more. They had been expecting the envelope to arrive every day. No one said anything, but Winnie could feel her mother's trepidation every time she heard the letterbox rattle.

National Service. Every young man had to go through it, but somehow Winnie had hoped that her brother would be forgotten.

'So you've finally been called, then?'

'Couldn't really avoid it, could I?' Walter gave her a lop-sided grin, but she could see the apprehension in his eyes.

She could understand why. Two months earlier, Colonel Nasser had nationalised the Suez Canal Company, and the

British and French armies had been mustering ever since. An invasion was imminent, and all their boys were bound to be sent over.

'Does Mum know?' Winnie asked.

'What do you think?'

Winnie already knew the answer to that one. If her mother knew her son was getting called up, she certainly wouldn't have been thinking about Winnie's career prospects.

'Dad knows,' Walter went on. 'He was here with me at dinnertime when the letter arrived.'

'What did he say?'

'Oh, you know Dad. He doesn't say much. But he looked a bit upset. I s'pose it brought back memories of his time in the army.'

'Poor Dad.' Her father talked little about his experiences during the war. But Winnie knew he'd been shot and wounded, and her mother had thought for months that he wasn't coming home. 'He'll miss you,' she said to her brother. 'You've been working together for so long, I don't know how he'll manage without you.'

She felt a pang as she said it. Sometimes she envied her brother his relationship with their father. She wished she could have been as close with their mother, but she and Dora were both too proud and too prickly.

'Anyway, they won't be calling me up until I've turned eighteen,' Walter said cheerfully. 'I've still got a couple of months of freedom yet.'

'Me too.'

'Better make the most of it then, hadn't we?'

They looked at each other, and suddenly it struck her that everything was going to change for both of them. 'We'll be all right. Won't we, Wal?' she whispered.

''Course we will, Sis.' For a moment she thought her brother was going to break the habit of a lifetime and hug her, but instead he reached out and gave her arm a friendly punch. 'Anyway, you never know. This might be the making of both of us!'

Chapter Six

December 1956

Christina Cheetham was the Head of the Nursing School. She was around five years Helen's junior in age, as well as rank. But somehow she still managed to make her feel gauche and inadequate.

Helen could feel Miss Cheetham's cool grey gaze on her as she sat behind her desk, going through the list of students starting at the nursing school the following month.

'Bernadette O'Dowd and Philomena Flanagan,' she read out. 'I recruited them on my last visit to Dublin. They've both completed a year's pre-training at St Anthony's Fever Hospital—'

'So no doubt they'll think they know everything,' Miss Cheetham murmured under her breath.

Helen ignored her and continued, 'We also have two girls from the West Indies. Louise Charles has been staying with her family in London for a few weeks, but Frances Andrews will be coming straight from Barbados, so she will probably need some help settling in . . .'

She addressed herself to Miss Coulter, the Home Sister, who was in charge of the nurses' home and looked after the girls' well-being. Unlike other Home Sisters of Helen's experience, Margaret Coulter was a very motherly person, and the students warmed to her instantly.

Unfortunately, the same could not be said of the Assistant Home Sister, Miss Beck. With her stiff manner, hawkish nose and beady eyes, she was far more like the old-fashioned sisters Helen had known during her own training.

'I'll do my best, Matron.' Miss Coulter made a note on her list. Miss Cheetham shifted in her seat and rolled her eyes heavenwards.

'And then we have Maya Kumar, who comes from India, but is also staying with family over here—'

Miss Cheetham let out a heavy sigh. Helen set down her pen.

'Is there something you wish to say, Miss Cheetham?' she asked.

Christina Cheetham did not hesitate. 'I know it's hardly my place to say, but I must tell you I'm troubled by the number of foreign students you're taking on,' she said.

'What about them?' Helen said.

'As you know yourself, Matron, gaining a place to train at this hospital used to mean something. We only ever took the best at the Nightingale. But now it seems as if we're taking anyone. Irish, black, girls with scarcely a qualification to their name. If we're not careful, this hospital will lose its excellent reputation.'

Helen stared at her. 'How do you know these girls are not the best?' she asked.

'I daresay they are – where they come from,' Miss Cheetham replied with a slight sneer.

Helen glanced at the two Home Sisters. They looked

back at her, their faces frozen with embarrassment. And no wonder; once upon a time it would have been almost blasphemy to argue with Matron.

But Helen was new, and clearly Miss Cheetham had sensed a weakness in her.

She regarded her across the desk. Christina Cheetham sat looking poised and unruffled in her stylish grey two-piece and heels, one silk stockinged leg crossed over the other. Even her lack of uniform seemed to set her above the rest of them.

'I'm not sure if you're aware of this, Miss Cheetham, but since the National Health Service was introduced, there has been a shortage of nurses in this country,' she said, holding on to her patience. 'Yes, we are fortunate that our reputation means we can attract girls wanting to train. But we still have to cast our net further afield to find them.'

Miss Cheetham's perfectly shaped brows rose. 'Do you mean to tell me we don't have enough British girls to fill the places we have available?'

'You said yourself we only ever take the best,' Helen reminded her.

'Yes, but surely foreigners—'

'Girls from the Commonwealth are not foreigners, Miss Cheetham. They are British, like you and me. Surely you know that?'

Delicate colour rose in Miss Cheetham's cheeks. But before she could open her mouth to reply, the door opened and William Tremayne, the Chief Surgical Consultant, walked in.

'Sorry, am I interrupting something?'

His appearance had an almost magical effect on the three women. Miss Coulter blushed, Miss Cheetham flashed a smile, and even Miss Beck started fussing with her short grey hair.

No wonder, Helen thought. He was in his mid-forties but still boyishly good-looking, tall with twinkling brown eyes and dark hair that still managed to be unruly in spite of its short cut.

She was probably the only woman in the hospital immune to his charms. But only because he was her older brother.

'Hello, ladies.' He greeted them all. 'Miss Coulter and Miss Beck, how delightful to see you. You keep yourselves hidden away in that nurses' home far too much. And Miss Cheetham—' He turned to the Head of Nursing with a flirtatious smile. 'I hope you're keeping those students of yours in line?'

'I do my best, Mr Tremayne.' Miss Cheetham simpered like a schoolgirl under his twinkling gaze.

Oh, William. Helen stifled a sigh. He simply couldn't help himself.

The meeting ended shortly afterwards.

'And not a moment too soon, judging by the look on your face,' William remarked, as he took the seat Miss Cheetham had vacated.

Helen sighed. 'Miss Cheetham gets on my nerves.'

'She's rather a corker though.'

'Will!' Helen screwed up a piece of paper and threw it at him. 'You're a happily married man, remember?'

'I can still look, can't I? Besides, Miss Cheetham is also spoken for, from what I've heard.'

'Oh, really? Who's the lucky man?' Helen couldn't imagine anyone being good enough for the haughty beauty.

William tapped the side of his nose. 'Privileged information, Helen. Anyway, I thought you didn't approve of gossip?'

'I don't approve of you calling me Helen while we're on hospital premises,' she told him shortly.

William grinned. 'Sorry, *Matron*.'

'That's better.' Helen consulted the open desk diary in front of her. 'Anyway, I have a meeting with the Building Maintenance Manager at eleven, so whatever you've got to say, you'd best make it quick.'

'What are you doing for Christmas? Only Millie wants to know if you'll come down and spend it with us at Billinghurst.'

'I'm not sure if I'll be able to.' The excuse was on her lips before she'd even given herself time to think about it. 'I'll probably be on duty over Christmas . . .'

'Come on, Helen. It's so long since you've seen Millie, she's pining for you. So are the children. You used to see them all the time.'

'Yes, well, things have changed, haven't they? It's more difficult to get away now I'm in London . . .'

'So you won't come?'

'I really think it's better that I don't.'

He sent her a long look. 'This is nothing to do with work, is it? It's because of David.'

The sound of his name made her flinch. Helen took a

37

deep, steadying breath. 'You must see how difficult it would be, having both of us there?'

'Fine. I won't invite him.'

'You can't do that!'

'Why not? He's not family. You are.'

'He's your friend, Will. And he's Lottie's godfather.'

'And you're my sister.'

Her gaze dropped. 'He'll be on his own.'

'So will you.'

'I don't mind, honestly.'

'You still care for him, don't you?'

'Of course I still care for him. We were married for a long time.'

Helen picked up her pen and dipped it into the inkwell. She could feel her brother's steady gaze on her.

'He misses you,' he said.

'I'm sure he'll get over that soon enough. And no doubt there would be any number of women willing to console him.' The surgery waiting room was always full of them, hair done and reeking of perfume. They must be having a field day now David was a free man.

'Is that why you left him?' William pounced. 'You thought he was having an affair? Because I can assure you it would never cross his mind—'

'It wasn't that.'

'What, then?'

'It's our business.'

'If that's the case, perhaps you should tell your husband? Because I think he's still trying to work out what went wrong.'

Helen stared down at the blank sheet of paper.

'He knows,' she said. Just because he couldn't accept it wasn't her fault.

A drop of ink fell from the end of the nib, splashing on the list. Helen snatched up a piece of blotting paper as William got to his feet.

'The invitation for Christmas still stands, anyway,' he said. 'It would be nice if you could come.'

'I'll try.'

'Liar.' He smiled at her. 'You can't avoid this situation forever, Helen.'

No, Helen thought, dabbing savagely at the spilt ink. *But I can certainly try.*

Chapter Seven

'I do love the Christmas lights, don't you?'

Judith sighed happily as she looked around her. It was a late Saturday afternoon in the middle of December, and she and Winnie had caught the number fifteen bus from Aldgate up west.

Oxford Street had put on a fine show, with strings of lights festooned across the road, and giant illuminated snowflakes suspended in the sky above them, their colours reflecting off the rain-washed street. Every store window was a feast for the eyes, with lavishly decorated Christmas trees everywhere they looked. Hundreds of eager shoppers filled the broad thoroughfare, hurrying in and out of the shops laden down with Christmas shopping, or just stopping to stare at the festive displays.

But for once Winnie was in no mood to gawp.

'Come on,' she said, nudging her friend. 'We've got to get to Clarks before they close. I still haven't found a decent pair of shoes.'

Auntie Josie had given her money for Christmas early, so she could buy what she needed for her nursing course, which started the following month.

She had received her formal letter of acceptance two weeks earlier. Even though Mrs McKay had already told her she had a place, Winnie had not allowed herself to believe it until she held the letter in her hands and read the type-written words on the paper.

'What do you think of that, then?' She had tried hard to keep the pride out of her voice as she'd handed the letter to her mother. Dora had barely looked at it before handing it back to her.

'I hope you know what you're doing,' was all she'd said. Then she'd bustled off into the back yard to hang out the washing.

'She is pleased for you,' her father had said. 'You know your mum. She's never been one for showing her feelings.'

Strange how she had no trouble showing her feelings about Walter, Winnie thought. Her mother had been a bundle of nerves ever since he'd got his call-up papers. She never seemed to stop fussing over him.

Of course Winnie understood why. She was just as anxious for her brother. After his basic training, Walter could end up being sent to Egypt, or Cyprus, or anywhere in the world. None of them had ever been further than Margate, let alone to a foreign war zone. She couldn't bear to think of him in danger.

But she still wished her mother could have shown some interest in her. It would have been nice if she had offered to come up west with her this afternoon, to offer some advice about what bits and pieces to buy.

She won't last five minutes. Her mother's unkind words came back to her. Dora probably couldn't be bothered to go with her because she knew Winnie wouldn't make the grade.

As it was, it was Judith who had come with her. They had been busy all afternoon, buying stockings, hairgrips, collar studs, tie pins and exercise books. They had just emerged from C&A, where they had purchased a navy-blue raincoat and a cardigan.

'Why don't we go to Dolcis?' Judith asked, pointing across the street. 'They've got some lovely shoes in there.'

'I'm not after lovely shoes,' Winnie reminded her. 'They've got to be stout and serviceable, remember?'

'They sound delightful,' Judith said with twisted smile.

The crowds of shoppers had increased since they had been in the last store, and Winnie had to jostle her way determinedly through the tide of bodies and bags, Judith trailing behind her.

Finally they made it down to Clarks. The fashionable young assistant smiled in anticipation when she saw them, only to look faintly horrified when Winnie told her what she needed.

Winnie tried on several pairs of black shoes, each one uglier than the last.

'You'll certainly get the boys running after you in those!' Judith giggled, as Winnie walked up and down the length of carpet in the latest monstrosities.

'I don't think that's the point,' Winnie replied, slightly cross at her friend. 'I can hardly strut down the ward in a pair of stilettos, can I? Anyway, I'm used to flat shoes. When you're a giant like me you can't wear heels.' She looked down in despair at her polished black leather feet. 'But should I buy these, or the brogues? I've no idea which to choose.'

'Tell you what,' the assistant said. 'My manager's daughter is a nurse. Why don't I go and ask her what she thinks? She'll know which shoes are the most suitable.'

The assistant went off and they sat side by side and waited for her to return.

'What's up with you?' Judith asked. 'You were in a good mood earlier, but you've suddenly got a face as long as a fiddle. Why?'

Winnie looked at her. 'What if I'm wasting my time?' she said.

'Eh? What are you talking about?'

'This nursing course. What if I ain't good enough?'

'Of course you're good enough. They wouldn't have taken you on otherwise, would they?'

'I suppose not.' Winnie stared at her bare stockinged feet. There was a small hole in the toe of her right stocking.

She couldn't help worrying that her mother was right. What if she couldn't make the grade? She wasn't sure she could face the humiliation of going home and telling her family she had failed again.

'Oh no,' Judith said.

Winnie looked up. 'What? What is it?'

'Don't look now, but that old cow Wendell's just walked in!'

Winnie stared at the tall, bespectacled woman who stood in the doorway. Their former office supervisor looked as rigid and unapproachable as ever in her stiff tweed coat with a scrap of fur around the collar.

As if she knew she was being watched, Miss Wendell turned her head and caught Winnie's gaze. There was a flash of recognition in her pale eyes before she turned away.

'Look,' Judith said in disgust. 'She can't even look you in the eye.'

'Let's go,' Winnie said, scrabbling to put on her shoes.

'What? No, Win, you can't!' Judith grabbed her sleeve. 'What about your shoes?'

'I can come back for them another time. Come on.'

She hurried out of the shop, nearly stumbling over the outstretched feet of the other customers as she hurried to get away.

It wasn't until they were back outside that she could finally breathe again. The cold, bracing December air cooled the blood that burned in her cheeks.

Seeing Miss Wendell again had brought back all kinds of horrible memories. Just looking at her made Winnie's heart race in her chest.

You're nothing but a liar and a troublemaker, Winifred Riley. We don't need your sort here.

Winnie risked a glance back through the window. Miss Wendell was fiddling with her gloves as she waited to be served. She was a skinny stick of a woman, in her late fifties, with a narrow face, pinched mouth and prominent, lashless eyes.

'Look at her,' Judith said. 'She knows what she did. She knows she was in the wrong.'

'Of course she does,' Winnie replied. 'But she'll never admit it, will she? Anyway, it's over now.'

'That's right,' Judith said, tucking her arm through Winnie's. 'And it might turn out to be a blessing in disguise for you, eh? You're going to be a nurse, Win. That's better than working in a boring old council office for the rest of your life, ain't it?'

Winnie looked down at the paper carrier bags in her hands, containing all her purchases for her training. She had been so excited when she'd bought them, but now she just felt foolish.

Her mother's words came into her mind, mingling with Miss Wendell's cruel remarks.

She won't last five minutes . . . She'll be thrown out on her ear . . . We don't need your sort here.

Perhaps they were all right, she thought. Perhaps her dreams, like her, would never come to anything.

Chapter Eight

Christmas 1956

It had been six months since Helen had left the little Kent village of Billinghurst, her home for the last six years. She thought she'd put enough time and space between herself and her past. But when she stepped out of the train on to the platform of the tiny country halt on Christmas Eve, memories and emotions came rushing at her like a torrential flood, nearly knocking her off her feet.

This was the place she had once called home. She remembered her cosy cottage, warm fires, long country walks, her friends and family . . .

And David. Helen closed her eyes, steeling herself against the emotion that rose up inside her whenever she allowed herself to think about him.

She opened her eyes again, looking around her. It was a bright wintry day, and the countryside looked picture perfect, like a Christmas card, the bare trees and hedgerows laced with sparkling frost.

She should never have come here, she knew that now. Safe behind her desk at the Nightingale, she had imagined she could cope, but now she realised it was too soon, the pain still too raw.

But she was here now, and all she could do was grit her teeth and get through it as best she could. She picked up her suitcase and marched through the five-bar gate that separated the platform from the lane.

Millie had promised William would pick her up, but there was no sign of the car. Helen looked up and down the deserted lane, and was just wondering whether she should start walking when she heard a voice behind her.

'Mrs McKay?'

Oh God, not her. Helen turned round, a bright smile pasted on as she faced the dumpy middle-aged woman who stood before her.

'Mrs Bratton. Fancy seeing you here.'

Of course, the local gossip would be the first face she saw. By teatime there would not be a single soul in the village who didn't know that dear Dr McKay's wicked wife had returned.

'I was just up at the farm, visiting old Mrs Aston. She's bedridden again, poor dear. It's quite a walk, but I thought it was the neighbourly thing to do. She doesn't get much company, except for me, and the vicar, and – the doctor, of course.' Hilda Bratton looked carefully at Helen as she said it. 'He's such a dear, comes up to check on her every day. But I'm sure I don't need to tell you what a good man he is?' Helen did not reply. 'I suppose you've come to visit your family?' Mrs Bratton went on.

'Yes.'

'I'm heading past the big house myself. I'll walk with you, if you like?'

'No, thank you. Someone should be picking me up shortly.'

Please God, she added silently, as she looked in despair up and down the empty lane.

She willed Mrs Bratton to take the hint and leave. But she was not the type to give up on the promise of potential gossip that easily.

'We haven't seen you around in a while?' she commented. 'Is it true you've taken a job up in London?'

'That's right.' Helen stared up the lane. *Come on, Will*, she urged.

'I was so sorry to hear you and the doctor had parted. I must admit, when I first found out I didn't think it could be true,' Mrs Bratton went on. 'You always seemed such a devoted couple . . .'

Thankfully, at that moment a car horn blasted out. Helen turned in time to see a bright red open-top MG Midget barrelling down the lane towards them, her sister-in-law grinning away behind the wheel.

Millie jerked to a halt and leaned out. She was wearing a fur coat, corduroy trousers and wellington boots, with a headscarf over her blonde hair.

'Hello,' she sang out. 'Sorry I'm late. We had a bit of a crisis up at the house.'

'Oh dear, Your Ladyship. Nothing serious, I hope?' Mrs Bratton leaned in, eager for more news.

'It was nothing, Mrs B. Just a door fell off one of the barns and I had to help the estate manager round up the cows.'

'That hardly seems fitting for someone in your position, Your Ladyship.'

Helen saw her sister-in-law wince at the title, but her smile did not dim. 'Someone's got to do it, haven't they?

Can't have half the herd wandering the countryside.' She turned to Helen. 'Put your suitcase in the back and get in. I'm not sure we've caught them all. I left Mr Willis searching for one of our Lincoln Reds.'

As Helen climbed in beside Millie, Mrs Bratton said, 'Will you be attending the carol service this evening, Your Ladyship?'

'I should think so, since I'm supposed to be reading one of the lessons,' Millie replied.

'And will you be joining us, Mrs McKay?' Mrs Bratton turned her eager gaze to Helen.

'I – I'm not sure—'

Another memory flooded her mind, catching her unawares. The annual Christmas Eve carol service, the church beautifully illuminated by the glow of candlelight, the smell of incense and burning wax, listening to the voices of the choir rising into the rafters, feeling David's gloved hand in hers as they huddled in the pew to keep warm . . .

'Well, it would be nice to see you. And I'm sure the doctor—'

'Anyway, we'd best be off.' Millie started up the engine and roared away, leaving Mrs Bratton open-mouthed in mid-sentence.

'I'm sorry,' she said to Helen as they rounded the next bend. 'I didn't mean to leave you in that awful woman's clutches for so long. Can you forgive me?'

'I suppose so.' Helen smiled grudgingly. 'But I thought William was supposed to be picking me up?'

'So he was. But he had to go back up to London. Some emergency at the hospital, apparently.'

'What kind of emergency?' Helen was immediately alert.

'Don't look so alarmed, darling, the place hasn't fallen down without you!' Millie laughed. 'He just went haring off last night to deal with one of his private patients. I thought he might be coming back on the same train as you, actually. I hope he's home by this evening, otherwise we'll be having Christmas without him!'

Helen looked at her sister-in-law. Millie took everything in her stride – nothing seemed to faze her at all.

She had settled into country life so well. But then again, she had been born to it. As the only child of the Earl of Rettingham, she had inherited five thousand acres of Kent countryside as well as the beautiful house of Billinghurst.

It was wonderful to see her so happy and settled after all the heartache she had suffered. Her first husband, Sebastian, had been killed flying missions over the Channel when the war began. Millie had retreated to Billinghurst with their young son, Henry, only for her beloved home to be requisitioned by the RAF shortly afterwards.

Helen could only imagine how painful it must have been for Millie to watch the same planes that had killed her husband taking off from her very own front lawn.

But all those years of struggle had been worth it when Millie was reunited with Helen's brother William, who was stationed at the house. They'd had a brush with romance at the Nightingale when Millie was a student and William a junior doctor. But neither of them had been really ready for true love until they met again towards the end of the war. Now they had been happily married for more than ten years, and had two beautiful children together. And while

William divided his time between Billinghurst and his work as a consultant at the Nightingale, Millie was content to be lady of the manor.

Millie might have matured in the years since they'd studied at the Nightingale, but her driving had certainly not improved at all. She bowled through the country lanes with no regard for speed or whatever was coming towards her. Helen clung on for dear life as they sped into the village, scattering locals before them.

But Millie seemed blissfully oblivious as she chattered away about what had been happening in the village since Helen had been away.

Helen noticed her friend stuck to the back lanes through the village. She wondered why until it dawned on her that Millie was taking care to avoid driving past the village green and Lowgill House, where she had lived, and where David still had his surgery.

Helen was all at once grateful but slightly disappointed. There was a part of her that longed to see the place again, even though she knew how much it would hurt.

It had been their first real home together. From the moment they saw the graceful Georgian house, they had both fallen in love with it. They had explored the elegant high-ceilinged rooms hand in hand, working out which room would become David's surgery, and stood at the French windows overlooking the large, sunny garden, imagining their future children playing on the lawn . . .

She turned her mind away from the thought. She couldn't allow herself to think about that life, not any more. Those broken dreams were all in the past.

But all the same, she could not stop herself looking back over her shoulder as they drove through the village, hoping to catch a glimpse of the house.

'The children are very excited to see you again,' Millie broke into her thoughts. 'They've missed you.'

'I've missed them too.'

'You're always welcome to come and visit, you know.'

'I'm here now, aren't I?'

'Yes – at last!' Thankfully Millie changed the subject. 'So what's it like, being back at the Nightingale after all these years?'

'Very strange,' Helen admitted. 'I hardly recognise the place now. I keep getting lost with all the new buildings they've added. But in other ways it doesn't feel very different from the days when we were students.'

Millie laughed. 'I can't believe that! You're in charge now. That must make a big difference, surely?'

'It might if I remembered from time to time!' Helen said. 'Do you know, the other day I was walking down a corridor to do my rounds and I met a ward sister coming towards me. I immediately forgot who I was and stood to attention – and she did the same thing!' She shook her head. 'I'm sure she laughed about that with the other sisters. I doubt if I'll ever live it down!'

'Old habits die hard,' Millie said. 'I'm sure you would have despaired of me if you'd been in charge when I was a student.'

'You would have been on the first train home,' Helen said. Then she added, 'That reminds me. Does the name Winifred Riley mean anything to you?'

'Dora's daughter?' Trust Millie to know straight away. Unlike Helen, she had kept in touch with her old friends. 'What about her?'

'She's coming as a student in January.'

'How lovely!' Millie exclaimed, her face lighting up. 'Dora must be terribly proud. Have you seen her since you got back to London?'

Helen shook her head. 'Not yet, although I'm sure our paths will cross sooner or later.'

'It would be nice to catch up with her again, anyway. Perhaps we could all meet in town the next time I'm visiting?'

'I'll mention it if I see her.'

The three of them had once been inseparable. They had studied together, laughed together and cried on each other's shoulders. Dora had helped Helen through some of her most painful moments.

It was partly down to Dora that she had ended up marrying David. They might never have got together at all if Dora had not convinced her to give him a chance.

But was that a reason to be thankful to her old friend? Given what had happened to their marriage, Helen wasn't so sure.

Chapter Nine

No matter how many times she visited, her first sight of Billinghurst always took Helen's breath away.

It sat square and solid at the end of the half-mile stretch of drive, like something out of an Arthurian fantasy, with its crenellations and mullioned windows, its thick stone walls burnished gold by the wintry sunshine. The drive was flanked on either side with broad, perfectly manicured lawns and intricate rose gardens.

'What a glorious house,' Helen sighed. 'You're so lucky to live here.'

'I know,' Millie said. 'If only it wasn't falling apart at the seams. The roof's past the point of no return, we've got dry rot in one place, and wet rot in another, and all sorts of other rot in between. It costs every penny we have just to stop it collapsing about our ears.' She smiled fondly. 'But it's stood firm for the past four hundred years, so I suppose it'll last a while longer.'

She swung the car around carelessly in front of the house and screeched to a halt, skittering an arc of gravel from the wheels. Almost immediately the imposing front door opened and three dogs and two children spilled out, running towards them.

One of the Labradors was the first to reach Helen, closely

followed by a rather disreputable-looking Border collie with a tattered ear and mismatched eyes. They greeted Helen enthusiastically as she stepped from the car, barking joyful greetings.

'Auntie Helen!' Lottie and Timothy clamoured with them for her attention, while another, more elderly Labrador hobbled towards them on stiff legs, her tail wagging.

'For goodness' sake, you lot. Let your poor aunt breathe!' Millie laughed.

'It's fine, they're just excited.' Helen pushed away the collie's cold wet nose as it snuffled at her handbag.

'They're hooligans. And the dogs are just as bad. Except you, Biddy.' Millie stroked the elderly Labrador's head. 'At least you have some dignity.'

'Only because she's too old to jump up like the rest of them!' Lottie cried. At eight years old, she already had her mother's delicate blonde beauty, combined with her lively, sunny nature.

As Helen kissed and hugged her niece and nephew, a footman appeared out of nowhere and discreetly spirited away her suitcase, carrying it back into the house. Millie followed him, the dogs at her heels, while the children clung to Helen.

'Can we play chess?' Lottie begged.

'Of course,' Helen replied.

'I'm warning you though, I'm very good.'

'Have you been practising?'

'Uncle David's been teaching me some tricks. He says I'm practically a grand master! He says—'

'Do stop showing off, Lottie,' Millie interrupted. 'Now go off and find Miss Clark. I'm sure she'll be looking for you. And if I find out you've locked her in a cupboard again I shall be very displeased!' she called after them as they thundered up the stairs.

She watched them go and turned to Helen. 'I'm sorry,' she said. 'Lottie does rather idolise David.'

He has that effect on women, Helen thought. 'And so she should. He's her godfather, after all.'

'She adores you, too, of course. She keeps asking why you and David aren't both going to be here for Christmas. I don't think she's quite grasped the situation yet, and I hardly know how to explain it to her. I'm not quite sure I understand it myself,' she added in an undertone.

Helen looked at her. She wished her own unhappiness had not spilled into their lives, but they had always been so close, it was inevitable.

'I did tell William I was happy for David to come here for Christmas instead of me,' she said.

'Nonsense, you're family. Anyway, David has made other arrangements.'

'Oh?'

'He said he was going to stay with a friend.'

'I wonder who?'

'I have no idea.' Millie regarded her carefully. 'Why do you want to know?'

'I was just curious,' Helen said, a bit too quickly.

'I don't think it's another woman, if that's what you're wondering—'

'I'm not,' Helen cut her off. 'What David does is nothing to do with me.'

'Isn't it?' Millie sent her a searching look. 'You know,

I still can't quite fathom why you left him. It was all so sudden, I think even poor David is confused—'

'Well, he has no reason to be,' Helen interrupted her. 'I made it quite clear to him. And I don't need to explain it to anyone else,' she added firmly.

Anyone else might have reacted badly to such a snub. But Millie was too good-natured to bear a grudge.

'As long as you know what you're doing,' she said. 'Now, shall we have some tea?'

It was early evening when the family set off to the local village church for the carol service. But there was still no sign of William.

Millie did not seem unduly concerned, but Helen was peeved at her older brother.

'This is so typical of him,' she fumed, as they got out of the car outside the church. Thankfully Millie's driver had brought them in the Bentley, so she did not have to endure her sister-in-law's haphazard driving again. 'And after all the fuss he made about me not coming! I hope he doesn't miss the last train.'

'I'm sure he'll be fine,' Millie said airily. 'You know what Will's like. He gets so caught up with his patients he completely loses track of time.'

'I suppose it must be a new admission?' Helen said.

'Oh no, he's been back and forth with her for ages. I gather she's quite demanding,' Millie smiled. 'I just hope she's paying him well for his time. I've told him, I don't mind how often he has to go up to see her, if it means we can stop the roof leaking!'

Before Helen could reply, the curate appeared and ushered them into the church, where they took their place in Millie's family pew.

Once again, Helen was transported by the simple beauty of the country church, illuminated by candlelight. The whole village had gathered, and she felt the weight of their curious gazes.

She ignored them and picked up her prayer book. She started to flick through the tissue-thin pages, trying to distract herself. But she could not stop the troubled thoughts that crept into her mind.

As far as she knew, there were no private patients on any of the women's wards. Which meant her brother was lying to Millie about his frequent trips to London.

And when a man started lying to his wife, there was usually only one reason why.

No, she thought. *Not Will.* He might be an incorrigible flirt, but he would never do that to Millie. He loved her far too much.

She glanced sideways at her sister-in-law, her beautiful face bathed in the golden glow of the candles. She was such a pure soul; Helen would kill William if he ever hurt her . . .

And then something else drew her attention. A tide of whispers behind her, growing steadily louder and louder, until—

'Look!' Timothy piped up. 'It's Uncle David.'

Helen swung round at exactly the moment David McKay drew level with their pew. Before she had a chance to glance away they were suddenly eye to eye. It was hard to tell which of them was more startled by the encounter.

David recovered first.

'Helen,' he greeted her in his quiet Scottish burr. 'It's nice to see you.'

Helen was glad of the dim candlelight to hide the heat that burned in her face. She was uncomfortably aware of rows and rows of avidly watching eyes behind her.

'Hello, David,' she managed at last.

She tried not to look at him, but she was acutely aware of every detail of his appearance, from his dark wool overcoat to the lemony scent of his aftershave.

'I thought you were going away for Christmas?' Millie said.

'I am. But Mrs Bratton called this afternoon and asked if I'd read one of the lessons before I left. Apparently Mr Morris has gone down with an attack of laryngitis.'

'Couldn't they get anyone else?' Helen did not realise she had blurted out the words until she caught the look of amusement on her husband's face.

'I suppose they must have been desperate,' he said.

Desperate for gossip, you mean. Helen wouldn't have put it past Mrs Bratton to engineer the whole situation knowing Helen would be there.

'Nonsense, you have a beautiful speaking voice,' Millie said. 'Don't you think so, Helen?'

'I—'

Luckily she was spared from finishing her sentence as Lottie piped up, 'I beat Auntie Helen at chess this afternoon, Uncle David.'

'I'm not surprised. You're an excellent player. You've learned from the best, after all.'

'And yet I used to beat you more often than not,' Helen replied without thinking.

He turned to her, a twinkle in his dark brown eyes. 'How do you know I didn't let you win?'

Helen was about to reply when the spell suddenly broke. She turned away sharply, her gaze dropping to the prayer book in her lap.

'Where's William?' David asked.

'He'll be here later. He's in London, with a patient.' Once again, Helen felt the prickle of sensation at the back of her neck. But then Millie shocked her by adding, 'Do you want to sit with us? The church is rather crowded.'

Helen flashed her a look of panic. 'That's very kind of you,' David said. 'But I think we'd all be more comfortable if I sat somewhere else. Don't want to give Mrs Bratton and her friends anything else to gossip about, do we?' He smiled at them both. 'Merry Christmas, Millie. And you, Helen.'

'Merry Christmas, David.'

His gaze lingered on her a moment longer than was comfortable. And then he was gone.

Chapter Ten

'It's so good of you to come and see me on Christmas Eve, love. Especially when you must have so much else to do.'

'It's my job, Mrs R. Now then, how are you feeling?'

'Oh, you know me. Can't complain.' Elsie Roper smiled weakly. Her frail little body was racked with rheumatoid arthritis, but she would never let on how much she was suffering. She reminded Dora of her own formidable grandmother, Nanna Winnie, who had remained stoical until the very end of her life two years earlier. That was always the way with East End women.

'Let's see if we can't make you feel even better, eh?'

Dora applied the hot poultice she had just prepared to the old lady's knees, and Mrs Roper closed her eyes and sighed.

'Oh, that's such a relief. You get so used to the pain, you almost forget what it's like not to have it.'

'You can always get your son to make you a hot water bottle, if you find it helps?' Dora suggested.

'Oh no, love, I wouldn't want to trouble Gordon. He's too busy for all that sort of thing.'

Too busy to look after his own bedridden mother? Dora thought. She had only met Gordon Roper a couple of times, but she had already formed a dim view of him. He was a middle-aged bachelor, living in his mother's house, and yet he couldn't be bothered to look after her.

Not only that, he seemed to resent Dora's efforts, too. On the couple of occasions he had been home during her daily visits, he had been surly to the point of rudeness. He hadn't even bothered to ask how his mother was recovering from her last bout of fever.

There was so much Dora could have said, but instead she bit her lip and went on applying the poultices to the old lady's swollen, arthritic limbs. She saw so much hardship on her daily district nursing visits, it was sometimes very hard not to let herself get involved.

'I bet you'll have a houseful this Christmas, eh?' Mrs Roper said, as Dora worked.

'Our house is never empty!' Dora laughed. 'I sometimes wish I could have a bit more peace and quiet.'

'Be careful what you wish for, love. I daresay you'll miss it when your kids have gone.'

Her words pierced Dora like a dart to her heart. It had been preying on her mind for weeks, ever since Walter got his call-up letter. This would be the last Christmas they would have together as a family for at least two years.

'I'll have to make the most of it then, won't I?' she said quietly.

She had already made all her preparations. The house was decorated from top to bottom, with a big Christmas tree lit up in the window and brightly coloured paper chains festooned everywhere. That morning, she'd collected her Christmas Club money and gone shopping for food and presents. Now all she had to do was finishing wrapping them when she got home.

'You do that, girl. I remember what Christmas used to be like when mine were little. I used to long for a bit of peace and quiet. Now look at me.' She smiled wistfully.

Once again, Dora felt a pang of pity for her. Mrs Roper had been a widow for ten years. She had lost one of her sons at Dunkirk, and her daughter had moved with her own family to the new town of Harlow after the war ended. She had invited Elsie Roper to go with them, but as she'd explained to Dora, she was too set in her ways to make the move.

Dora sometimes wondered if she regretted her decision, now she was stuck with only her son to keep her company. Much good he was to her!

'Are you sure you wouldn't be more comfortable recovering in hospital?' she said. 'I could have a word with your doctor—'

'Oh no, I wouldn't want to trouble anyone in that way. Besides, I ain't got the money for hospitals.'

'You don't have to pay any more, Mrs R. That's what the National Health Service is for, remember?'

'So it is.' The old lady shook her head. 'You know, I still can't credit it. It used to be only the well-off could afford this sort of looking after.' She gave Dora an uncertain smile. 'To be honest, love, I feel a bit guilty, you coming in to see me every day. I'm sure you must have better things to do than fuss over a silly old biddy like me.'

'I happen to like fussing over you.' *Especially since I'm the only one who seems to bother*, Dora added silently. 'And don't tell anyone, but you're my favourite patient.'

'I don't believe that for a minute. I bet you say that to everyone!' Mrs Roper chuckled.

'I mean it. And just to prove it, I brought you this—' Dora reached into her nursing bag and pulled out a small, brightly wrapped gift.

'For me? Oh, my dear!' It was only a little box of Milk Tray, but from the way the old lady's face lit up when she unwrapped it, it might have been the Crown Jewels.

'We must open them straight away,' Mrs Roper declared. 'You'll stop for a cup of tea, won't you?'

'I—' Dora hesitated, her eyes on the clock. It was nearly six and she still had one more call to make before she could go home and make a start on her Christmas preparations. There were presents to wrap, vegetables to peel, and she'd promised Nick she wouldn't be late home . . .

But then she saw the beseeching look behind the old lady's smile. 'Why not?' she said. 'I'll pop the kettle on, shall I?'

Dora brought the tea up on a tray and they chatted for a while. She found herself telling Mrs Roper about her plans for Christmas, and the gifts she had bought for everyone. The old lady asked lots of questions and listened avidly, enjoying every detail.

She was especially interested when Dora told her about the present she had planned for Winnie.

'I thought I'd give her my old fob watch,' she said. 'She needs one for her nurse training, and mine's still going strong, so it seemed a shame not to use it . . .'

She trailed off, embarrassed by her own sentimentality. She had dithered about it for ages, going back and forth about her decision. She wanted to do something special for Winnie, to show that she supported her decision to go into nursing. But she wasn't sure how her daughter would take it. Things had been so prickly between them over the past few weeks, even more than usual. Dora knew Winnie was hurt that she hadn't been more enthusiastic about her idea to go into nursing, but it had come as such a shock. And she couldn't help having her reservations. It was a tough job, and only the most determined got through the training. Dora didn't want to see her daughter rejected again.

She was also guiltily aware that Walter had been occupying most of her thoughts over the past few weeks. He might be a strapping young man, but he was still her little boy, and the thought of him going off to a hostile foreign land was more than she could bear as a mother. She was so preoccupied that she had almost forgotten Winnie was facing a daunting adventure of her own, moving out of her home for the first time.

Not that Winnie seemed to need or even appreciate her interest. Unlike Walter, she shrugged off Dora's attention in her usual huffy way.

Dora wanted to mend the rift between them, but she did not know how. She wasn't one for gushing sentiment, and apologies never came easily to her. She hoped her gift would help convey the pride she felt.

'Well, I think it's a lovely idea,' Mrs Roper said. 'I'm sure she'll be honoured to wear it.'

'I don't know about that,' Dora muttered, embarrassed. She couldn't imagine Winnie being honoured by anything her mother did.

Dora finished her tea and prepared to leave.

'Thank you for stopping, love. I really appreciate it,' Mrs Roper said, as Dora packed up her bag. 'I don't get that many visitors, and it's a long day without company while Gordon's at work.'

'I could ask a neighbour to pop in?' Dora suggested. But the old lady shook her head.

'Gordon don't like strangers in the house.'

'Yes, but surely—'

'He's dead against it. He don't like everyone knowing our business.'

Dora tried again to persuade her, but Mrs Roper seemed adamant that she did not want to upset her son, so in the end she gave up.

Chapter Eleven

Christmas Day in the Riley house was a riot, as usual. Dora's sister Josie turned up first thing in the morning, closely followed by their younger sister Bea and her two daughters.

As usual, Josie made herself useful straight away, rolling up her sleeves and helping to prepare the Christmas dinner. Bea, meanwhile, moaned about the lack of decent alcohol in the house before unearthing a dusty half-bottle of sherry from the back of the sideboard that had been there since the previous Christmas.

'I'm drowning my sorrows,' she announced, as she filled her glass for the second time. 'Billy promised me we could spend Christmas together, but his wife said he had to be with her and the kids.'

'I ain't surprised.' Dora had little time for her sister's romance with Billy Robbins. He called himself a gangster, but he was nothing more than a local meathead who did other people's dirty work for them. 'I've told you before, you're better off without him, Bea.'

'But I love him!' Bea whined.

Dora looked at her without sympathy. Bea was in her mid-thirties and old enough to know better, but she insisted on acting like a lovesick teenager. She was also a mother and she owed it to her daughters to make sure they had a good home and some stability. But instead she spent her whole time chasing unsuitable men and leaving the little girls to fend for themselves.

'You should never have married that Billy,' their mother put in. 'His eyes are too close together.'

'We ain't married, Ma,' Bea muttered. 'That's the point.'

Dora shot her a warning look. Their mother's stroke had left her confused at times. She could remember events from years ago perfectly clearly, but anything more recent tended to get muddled.

'I don't blame his wife,' Josie said. 'Christmas is a time for families, after all.'

'Yes, but they're not a family!' Bea turned on her sister. 'He don't even love her,' she said, refilling her glass. 'If I was her, I'd have more pride than to go running after a man who's not interested.'

'Says the woman who's getting drunk because her boyfriend would rather spend time with his wife,' Dora muttered.

Bea glared at her. 'You know nothing about it.'

'I know you're wasting your time if you think he'll ever leave her for you,' Dora said. 'How long has it been now? A year? If he was going to pack his bags he would have done it before now.'

Bea gulped down the rest of her drink. 'It's all right for you, just because you've got a decent bloke. I'm still looking.'

'Your Malcolm was decent,' Josie pointed out.

'He was boring,' Bea said, refilling her glass. 'That's why I divorced him.'

'He was a nice man,' Josie insisted.

'And what do you know about men?' Bea snapped.

Josie fell silent. Dora glared at Bea. Her sister could be very cruel at times. Josie might not have managed to find a husband, but she had made a better life for herself than Bea could ever hope for. She had a good career as a school headmistress, a nice house and enough money to live on. She certainly didn't need to waste her time on a worthless piece of nothing like Billy Robbins.

At least everyone had cheered up by the time Dora put dinner on the table. By then, her youngest brother Alfie had joined them. He was a big, beefy lad – 'all brawn but no brains', as Nick called him. But he was good-natured with it, and he soon had them all laughing at his antics.

But even amongst all the laughter, Dora could not help feeling a pang of sadness as she looked down the table at her family and realised that this would be the last time they were all together for Christmas.

It did not help that Alfie had just finished his two years in the army and was telling them all outrageous stories about his time abroad. Walter was laughing along with the rest of them, but Dora could sense her son's apprehension behind his smile. Poor kid, as if he wasn't nervous enough!

Nick must have sensed her mood because he said, 'That's enough talk of National Service, I reckon. Let's have another drink, shall we?'

After dinner was cleared away, it was time to open their presents. They all gathered in the front room around the Christmas tree to exchange their gifts. There was much noise and laughter, especially when Walter presented his Christmas gift to his twin sister – his beloved bicycle.

'Mind you, it's more a loan than a gift,' he warned her. 'I'll need it back when I come home on leave.'

'Blimey, what are you going to do with that?' Bea wanted to know. 'As if you'll be able to ride that great big thing!'

'It suits me,' Winnie replied. 'I'm so tall I can't ride a dainty girl's bike without my knees ending up under my chin!'

Dora was touched when Walter and Winnie handed over the beautiful silk headscarf they'd bought for her.

'Win chose it, not me,' Walter said cheerfully. 'You can blame her if you don't like it.'

'I love it,' Dora said quietly.

'It's real silk,' Winnie blushed as she said it, as if she was embarrassed by her own gift. Dora understood perfectly. Winnie was every bit as bad as her when it came to not wanting to appear soft, or sentimental.

But she could feel the love behind the gift. And Winnie's faltering smile touched her heart more than any gushing words ever could.

'I'll take it upstairs so it doesn't get ruined,' she said.

She hurried upstairs and put the scarf in her dresser drawer, then took out the watch she had wrapped for Winnie and slipped it into her pocket. She had already given her a couple of small gifts but this was going to be her big surprise.

As she was coming down the stairs, she heard Josie saying to Winnie, 'You haven't opened my present yet.'

'But you've already given me money for Christmas,' Winnie replied.

'Yes, but I wanted to give you something to open.'

Dora could hear the sound of ripping paper and then loud exclamations all the way round the room.

'What's going on?' she asked, as she entered the room.

Winnie swung round to face her, her face alight with excitement.

'Look what Aunt Josie got me! Isn't it wonderful?'

Dora stared at the shiny new fob watch dangling from her daughter's fingers.

'It – it's beautiful,' she managed to squeeze the words out from lips that suddenly did not want to move.

'I wanted to get you something special. To let you know how proud I am of you.' Josie beamed.

'Did you know about this, Mum?' Winnie asked.

'I had no idea,' Dora said faintly.

'I know I probably should have consulted you, but I wanted it to be a surprise. It is the right sort, isn't it?' Josie looked anxious.

'Mum?' Winnie prompted, as Dora took her time to speak.

'Yes. Yes, it's perfect.' Disappointment nearly choked her, making it hard for her to say the words.

She caught Nick's sympathetic eye. He was the only one who knew what she was planning, thank God. She wasn't sure she could have stood the humiliation otherwise. She knew her husband wouldn't say anything. He understood her too well for that.

'I'll just go and put the kettle on,' she said. 'I think we've got some chocolate brazils somewhere, too.'

She hurried out of the room, leaving them all still oohing and aahing over her sister's wonderful present.

I shouldn't resent her, Dora thought as she rifled in the larder, searching for the chocolates. Dora had always encouraged Josie to think of Winnie, Walter and Danny as her own children. It was only natural she would want to treat them.

'You could still give her your watch, you know.'

Dora started at the sound of Nick's voice. He stood in the kitchen doorway, watching her.

'Shh, someone might hear you,' she warned.

'So what? I think Winnie would appreciate it.'

'Who'd want an ancient second-hand watch when they could have a nice new shiny one?'

'It's the thought that counts.'

Dora shook her head. 'No, it's all right. She's better off with a new watch. A new start, ain't it? Besides, I wouldn't want to hurt Josie's feelings.'

'And what about your feelings?'

Dora smiled sadly. 'My feelings don't matter,' she said.

Chapter Twelve

January 1957

Preliminary Training School
Week 1

The Florence Nightingale Hospital was a solid Victorian building, three storeys high, its lines of windows overlooking Victoria Park. It was separated from the road by a narrow stretch of grass lined with bare trees, their branches rimmed with January frost.

There was a gap in the trees where there had once been a pair of high ornate iron gates, but they had long since been removed to build Spitfires. Winnie took her feet off the pedals of her bicycle and freewheeled through the gateway to come to a halt outside the porter's lodge.

Two men in brown overalls sat inside the lodge. The older one was reading the *Daily Mirror*; the younger one was picking mindlessly at his spots while he waited for the kettle to boil.

They both looked up when Winnie appeared in the doorway.

'What can we do for you, miss?' the older man asked, putting down his newspaper.

'I've been told to report to the Preliminary Training School.'

'One of the new girls, eh?' The boy looked her up and down, leering. 'You're a tall one, ain't you? Bet you have trouble finding dance partners.'

Winnie stared down at the skinny young man. Even with his artfully Brylcreemed quiff, he barely came up to her shoulder.

'Even if I did you'd still be right down the list,' she said.

The older man guffawed. 'That's right, love. You tell him. Thinks he's God's gift to women, don't you, Tez?'

I can't think why. If the faint stink of BO didn't put anyone off, then the crop of festering acne that covered his weak chin certainly would.

'You'll find the nurses' home round to the right of the main building, love,' the older man told her. 'Just follow the drive all the way round, then take the path off past the dining room. You can't miss it.'

'Thank you.'

'And there's a shed where you can leave your bike,' the man called after her.

As Winnie kicked off from the pavement and started pedalling up the drive, she heard the young man mutter sourly, 'I ain't interested anyway. Did you see the size of her? She even has to ride a bloke's bike!'

'Beggars can't be choosers, Tez,' the older man said, going back to his newspaper. 'As you know only too well.'

As Winnie made her way up the drive, a car swept past, nearly knocking her off the road and causing her to wobble dangerously towards the verge.

'Here, watch it!' Winnie called after them. The girl in the back seat turned to look through the rear window at her, and Winnie could have sworn she saw her smirk.

Seeing the older couple in the front seat of the car gave Winnie a pang. She started to wish she had let her mother come with her after all.

Dora had offered to be there, but Winnie had refused. She was determined to do things her own way, and her mother had not argued with her. Besides, Dora was so distracted by Walter leaving for his training camp, she barely had time to involve herself in Winnie's plans.

She's probably just glad I'm off her hands, Winnie thought sourly.

Despite her determination, Winnie's nerves fluttered up like a flock of startled birds in her stomach as she rounded the path to the right and the nurses' home came into sight.

It was an odd-looking building. Looking at it one way, it was a slightly shabby Victorian gothic house. Chunks of ornate stonework along the eaves were missing, and the chimney stack at the gable end listed precariously – another victim of Hitler's bombs, Winnie guessed.

But from the back of the house there emerged another building, modern and functional-looking, with beige stucco walls and two floors that overlooked a half-demolished wall.

Winnie remembered her mother talking about the old nurses' home, and how grand it had seemed to her. Was her heart racing too when she first saw it? Winnie wondered.

The car that had passed her had pulled up outside the nurses' home. Winnie watched the couple get out, followed by a slim girl with shiny brown hair.

The man unloaded various bags from the boot, while the two women made their way confidently up to the front door. She saw the affectionate way they linked arms, and the older woman's smile of pride as she looked down at her daughter.

Once again, she thought of her own mother. All Winnie had got before she left was a quick swipe of her mother's hand to straighten her curls and a brisk warning for her to try not to get into trouble.

Winnie wheeled her bicycle round to the back of the home and found the bicycle shed. It was a dilapidated-looking wooden structure, with a patched tin roof and a door hanging wonkily off its hinges. Winnie wrestled it open and pushed the bicycle inside.

She propped it against the wall and then paused for a moment to look at it.

'Look after her, won't you?' Walter had said when he handed it over. 'Don't let her get into any scrapes while I'm gone.'

'I will,' Winnie had promised. But her brother had smiled and said,

'I was talking to the bike, Sis.'

Walter had only been gone a couple of days and Winnie already missed him dreadfully. It was a good thing she had her training to keep her busy, or she might have ended up moping about the house.

She left the bicycle and walked back around the side of the home to the front door. No sooner had she tugged on the bell pull than the door was opened by a jolly-looking woman in a navy-blue uniform. She reminded Dora of a country milkmaid, with her rounded figure and merry blue eyes.

'Hello!' she cried in a sing-song Scottish accent. 'I'm Miss Coulter, the Home Sister. And you are . . . ?'

'Winnie – Winifred Riley, miss.'

'You must address me as Sister.' The woman picked up a piece of paper from the table just inside the door and consulted it. 'Ah, here we are. Winifred Riley, Room Twelve. Right at the top. We like to keep the new girls on the upper floors. Makes it harder for them to abscond, you see.' She chuckled at Winnie's horrified look. 'Only joking, my dear. Come on, follow me. I hope you don't mind a climb?'

Winnie had been too nervous to eat anything before she left the house, and she began to feel quite light-headed as she followed Miss Coulter's bulky frame up one staircase after another.

'The front door is locked at ten o'clock sharp every night,' the Home Sister said over her shoulder as she led the way. 'You are expected to be in by then unless you have a late pass. And there's no point in asking for one of those because PTS students never get them. We have a maid, but you will be expected to keep your own room clean and tidy, and it will be inspected regularly to make sure you do. Likewise, you must make sure your laundry is put out every Tuesday morning in a bag labelled clearly with your name. Your uniform has been supplied, but it is supposed to last you for the three years of your training, so you won't want to be losing anything.' She paused on the landing for a moment to catch her breath, then continued, 'Classes and practical sessions will take place every day in the Preliminary Training School, which is at the far end of the path behind this building. Meals will be taken in the hospital dining room, but otherwise you will not need to go into the main building at all. Unless you've been summoned to Matron's office, of course, in which case God help you.' She looked over her shoulder at Winnie. 'Ach, I'm teasing you. She's not going to eat you alive, hen. Although I might, if I catch you wearing make-up or trying to sneak boys into your bedroom!'

She finally reached what Winnie thought must be the top floor, and led the way along the landing.

'This way, if you please. Now, you'll be sharing with two other girls, but they haven't arrived yet.'

'I didn't realise I'd be sharing,' Winnie blurted out.

Miss Coulter stopped so abruptly that Winnie almost cannoned into the back of her.

'This isn't the Savoy, you know! Anyway, you'll only have to put up with it for twelve weeks. Then if you're lucky you'll move over to the new building and then you'll probably get a room of your own. Well? Are you coming, or have you changed your mind already?'

Winnie stared up at the narrow flight of steps that Miss Coulter had started to ascend. They were steep, leading to a single door half-hidden in the shadowy eaves.

It couldn't be. 'The attic,' she whispered aloud.

Miss Coulter was already jingling the ring of keys that hung from her belt, selecting the right one.

'Don't let that put you off,' she said cheerfully. 'It's actually a rather nice room, especially when the sun's shining. And you've got a nice view over the rooftops, if you crane your neck a bit. Although I expect a tall lass like you will have no trouble seeing out of it. Mind, you'll have to be careful not to bump your head on the low ceilings. We should have checked your height when we assigned the rooms, I reckon!'

But Winnie wasn't listening. She was too busy staring around her at the long room with its sloping walls and strangely angled eaves.

Was it just fate that had put her in the very room where her mother had stayed when she trained at the Nightingale? Dora had often told her stories about her days as a student, sharing a room with Helen and Millie. She had laughed about the antics they'd got up to, climbing the drainpipes after dark and standing on the beds to smoke out of the high windows so the Home Sister wouldn't smell their cigarettes.

And now it looked as if history was about to repeat itself.

'You see? It's more than big enough for three,' Miss Coulter said, looking around.

Winnie looked around. It was just as her mother had described it, with three beds tucked into the eaves, one on either side of the room and another in the middle. There was a wardrobe at one end of the room and a chest of drawers at the other.

Back in her mother's day there had been bare boards on the floor and wind whistling through a gap in the window frame. But now at least it was cosy, with yellow curtains at the windows and a nice thick rug.

Each of the beds was made up, with a neat pile of folded clothes on top.

'That's your uniform, all ready for you,' Miss Coulter said. 'You don't have to wear it tonight, but you might want

79

to try it on later, just to make sure the sewing room got your measurements right. Most girls can't wait to see themselves in uniform, in my experience.' She turned to go. 'Putting the cap on can take some doing, but I daresay you'll be able to find someone to help you. Now, is there anything I've forgotten?' She paused, her finger pressed to her plump cheek. 'Oh yes, lunch will be served in the dining room at half past twelve. And there's a list of the rules on the noticeboard downstairs, in case you've forgotten anything I've told you. I'd advise you to study them carefully, in any case. You don't want to make any mistakes, do you?' She smiled at Winnie. 'Now, I'll leave you to unpack. Welcome to the Nightingale, Riley.'

And with that she was gone. Winnie set down her suitcase and sat on the bed. Miss Coulter's list of rules had left her head spinning, and she needed time to take it all in.

She looked around the room. Wait until her mum heard she was in the same room! Once again she felt a pang, wishing Dora was with her.

She glanced warily at the crisply folded uniform lying on the bed next to her.

'Most girls can't wait to see themselves in uniform,' Miss Coulter had said. But the idea of putting it on filled Winnie with absolute terror.

I don't suppose she'll last five minutes as a nurse.

Her mother's words came back to her. It was only the thought of her disappointed face that stopped Winnie fleeing there and then.

Chapter Thirteen

Dora watched from the corner of the main building as the front door to the nurses' home closed behind her daughter.

Winnie had told her not to come but she couldn't help herself. She had to be with her, if only from a distance.

Her heart ached to see her daughter's forlorn expression as she entered the nurses' home, and it was all she could do not to rush from her hiding place and wrap her arms around her. It was only the thought of how furious Winnie would be that kept her rooted to the spot.

She wished she had prepared her daughter for what was to come. But Winnie had made it clear she did not need her help or advice. So Dora had thrown most of her energies into helping Walter instead. Now she regretted not pushing it further. There was so much she wanted Winnie to know, and now it was too late.

She stood for a while, the January cold seeping through her coat, staring at the old nurses' home. She remembered how terrified she had been the day she arrived, how she had hidden her fears behind a brave face, and wondered if Winnie was doing the same.

Tears rose in her eyes. Not for her daughter, but for herself. What was she going to do now? Nick and the kids had been her whole life for the past eighteen years. How often had she heard them rampaging around the house and wished for five minutes' peace? Now they were gone, she could scarcely face the thought of returning to the house without them.

'Dora?'

She swung round. A tall, elegant-looking woman in a stiff black Matron's uniform stood before her. It took a moment for her to recognise her face, framed by the starched white headdress.

'Helen!'

The woman smiled. 'I wasn't sure you'd recognise me. How long has it been since we last met?'

'At least twelve years, I reckon.'

It seemed so strange to see Helen as a middle-aged woman, with lines around her brown eyes and threads of grey in her dark hair. And she was sure her friend must be thinking the same thing.

They stared at each other for a moment. Then they both laughed and the next moment they were hugging as the years fell away.

'Oh Dora, it's so good to see you.' Helen clung to her tightly. 'I hoped we'd run into each other. I suppose Winifred told you I was here?'

'She did.' Dora went to release her but Helen held on a moment longer, as if she was reluctant to let go of the embrace. 'But I wish you'd written to let me know.'

'I meant to, but I've been so busy settling in. You know what it's like.'

Dora nodded. She could hardly blame her friend for being a bad correspondent, when she had scarcely put pen to paper for years, apart from Christmas and birthday cards.

And then, when she did think of writing, there was so much to say she hardly knew where to start.

'I suppose you've come to see Winifred off?' Helen said. 'Has she settled in all right?'

'I'm sure she'll be fine.' Dora did not want to tell Helen that Winnie hadn't allowed her to go with her. She had too much pride for that.

'It must be hard, saying goodbye?'

Helen's eyes were so full of sympathy, Dora had to steel herself not to break down in tears on her shoulder.

'She's not a million miles away,' she said briskly.

'That's true.' Helen looked back at the nurses' home. 'I remember my first day, don't you? I was utterly terrified, but excited at the same time. There seemed to be so many rules to remember.'

'At least we had Miss Sutton to make sure we stuck to them,' Dora reminded her.

'Oh God, yes! And that dreadful little dog of hers – what was his name?'

'You mean Sparky?' Dora pulled a face. 'He was always snapping at our ankles, wasn't he? I nearly kicked him a few times, nasty little thing.'

'I think we all did!' Helen smiled at her. 'I don't suppose you'd like a cup of coffee in my office? It would be so nice to catch up properly.'

Dora looked past her towards the main building. 'I don't want to disturb you if you're busy . . . ?'

'I can always make time for an old friend.'

Dora hesitated. It was her day off, and the thought of going back to a silent house was hardly appealing.

'That would be lovely,' she said.

Helen led the way through the hospital, pointing out all the new buildings that had been constructed since they had trained there.

'It's all very smart,' Dora said.

'Not all of it,' Helen said. 'If you look carefully at the old building, you can still see where the plaster's missing from Hitler's bombs. There's a deep crack right across the ceiling of my office, but the Building Maintenance Inspector has assured me that the roof is unlikely to fall in on my head.'

'Unlikely? Blimey, that's encouraging.'

'I know!' Helen grimaced.

'Mind you, we've had worse, ain't we? Do you remember when we used to work in the operating theatres during heavy bombing?'

'You mean holding an umbrella over the surgeon's head as the plaster rained down on us?' Helen said. 'Those were the days, eh?'

She walked through a frosted glass door bearing the words 'Matron's Office' in gold lettering. A woman sat in the outer office, tapping away on a typewriter. Helen instructed her to make some coffee for her and her guest, then led the way into the inner office.

Out of sheer habit, Dora found herself hesitating on the threshold.

'It's all right,' Helen said. 'You can come in.'

'I'm not sure I want to!' Dora looked around the book-lined room, dominated by a heavy mahogany desk. How often had she stood here as a terrified student nurse, on the receiving end of yet another reprimand?

Helen laughed. 'I know! I still have to remind myself sometimes that I'm the one in charge.'

There was a soft tap at the door and the secretary brought in their coffees on a tray.

'Where should I sit?' Dora eyed the chair on the other side of the desk dubiously.

'It's all right, you're not being interviewed! Let's sit here, shall we?' Helen indicated two armchairs on either side of the fireplace.

Dora sat down, still looking nervously around her, as Helen poured their coffee. She tried to imagine how Winnie must have felt, coming here for her interview. Once again, she wished she could have been with her to offer her support. If only Winnie had told her what she was doing . . .

But there had to be a reason why she hadn't. Dora felt guilty that her daughter had not been able to share something so important with her. What did that say about her as a mother?

'Do you remember when you came here for your interview?' Helen's voice broke into her thoughts.

'Like it was yesterday,' Dora said grimly. 'I had a hole in my stockings, and I was convinced Matron would notice and think I was too slovenly!'

'I was terrified too,' Helen said. 'All I could do was sit there while my mother did all the talking. Although I suppose it wouldn't have mattered what I said anyway, since she was on the Board of Trustees,' she added ruefully. 'I don't think Matron would have dared to turn me down.'

'You would have got in with or without your mother's help,' Dora said. 'You were so clever, and the perfect student.'

'Oh, I don't know about that,' Helen looked embarrassed. 'I was never good enough for my mother.'

Dora thought about the formidable Constance Tremayne, and how she had ruled poor Helen's life for so long, until she found the confidence to finally break free.

'I wonder what she would have made of you now?' she said.

'She probably would have thought I didn't deserve it.' Helen looked down at her coffee cup, her expression wistful. Then she summoned a smile and said, 'She would certainly have told me to sit up straight and stop slouching!'

'I'm sure she would,' Dora laughed. 'I'm always saying the same thing to my Winnie. I suppose it's what comes of being so tall—'

Thinking of her daughter made the words catch in her throat, and she sipped her coffee to hide her sudden rush of emotion.

'So what made you decide to come back to the Nightingale?' she asked, when she could trust herself to speak again.

'I needed a job,' Helen said simply.

'Has David moved to London, then?'

Helen's gaze dropped to her cup again. 'David and I have separated,' she said.

'Oh!' Dora stared at her in shock. 'I'm sorry, I had no idea . . .'

'There's no reason why you should. It's still very recent.'

'I'm sorry to hear it. You always seemed like such a perfect couple—' Dora saw Helen's expression stiffen. 'But it's none of my business,' she said quickly. 'I mean, no one knows what it's really like, do they?'

'No,' Helen said. 'No, they don't.' When she looked up again her smile was back in place. 'Anyway, let's talk about you. What are you doing with yourself these days?'

'Much the same as usual,' Dora shrugged. 'We're living on Old Ford Road now. Nick's got his own building business, and I'm working on the district.'

'You're still nursing, then?'

'For my sins. I gave it up for a couple of years after Danny was born, but I always seem to go back in the end.'

'If you ever wanted to come back to the Nightingale I'd be glad to have you.'

'Oh no, not me.' Dora shook her head. 'I don't think I've got it in me any more to work on the wards. I'm much happier doing my rounds, thank you very much!'

'So now it's your daughter's turn?'

'Let's hope so,' Dora said quietly.

Helen sent her a curious look. 'You don't sound very sure about it?'

Dora took a mouthful of hot coffee. She had to be careful what she said to Helen. She might be her old friend, but she was still Matron of the Nightingale. The last thing she wanted to do was to ruin Winnie's chances before she had even started.

'I'm sure she'll get on all right.'

'I'm sure she will. She struck me as a very bright, capable girl.'

87

Too bright for her own good sometimes, Dora thought.

She set down her cup. 'Anyway, I'd best get off. I told Mum I'd only be gone half an hour, and I don't like to leave her alone too long.'

'It was nice seeing you,' Helen said, as Dora stood up. 'Perhaps we could get together again soon?'

Dora saw the silent appeal in her friend's brown eyes. 'You know where I am,' she said. 'You're always welcome to come round for a cuppa.'

'I'll take you up on that.'

'I hope so.'

'Millie wondered if we could get together the next time she's up in London?'

'That would be lovely.'

For a moment they looked at each other. Once again, Dora felt a surge of regret at all the years they had allowed to slip by. How could they have let their friendship fade away like that? She hoped it wasn't too late to rekindle it.

Chapter Fourteen

'We have a maid, but you will be expected to keep your own room clean and tidy, and it will be inspected regularly to make sure you do. Likewise, you must make sure your laundry is put out every Tuesday morning in a bag labelled clearly with your name. Your uniform has been supplied, but it is supposed to last you for the three years of your training, so you won't want to be losing anything . . .'

Beth hardly dared look at Grace as they followed the Home Sister up the stairs. She knew she would be pulling a face.

'Classes and practical sessions will take place every day in the Preliminary Training School, which is at the far end of the path behind this building,' Miss Coulter went on. 'Meals will be served in the hospital dining room, but otherwise you will not need to go into the main building at all. Unless you've been summoned to Matron's office, of course, in which case—'

Beth risked a quick sideways glance. Grace was mimicking the Home Sister, opening and closing her mouth as she was speaking. She caught Beth's eye and they both started laughing.

Miss Coulter swung round. 'Is something amusing, Bradshaw?' she demanded.

'No, Sister.' Beth quickly arranged her features into a sober expression, while Grace stared down at the floor.

'I should think not. These are rules you need to learn and obey if you're going to study here. Now, it's this way . . .'

She led the way up a narrow flight of stairs.

'A garret!' Grace whispered in delight. 'Now you can truly be a starving artist.'

'Hardly starving,' Beth whispered back. 'Meals are served in the hospital dining room, don't forget.'

Grace pressed her hand over her mouth, but her eyes still lit up with laughter. She really behaved disgracefully, Beth thought, considering she was supposed to be in such a responsible position.

'Now, one of your room-mates has already arrived . . .' the Home Sister said as she opened the door to reveal an empty attic room. 'Oh, where's she gone? Not run away already, I hope?'

'She can't have gone far, her suitcase is still on the bed,' Grace observed.

'So it is.' Miss Coulter indicated a neat pile of clothes on the bed in the middle of the room. 'Your uniform is there, all ready for you. You don't have to wear it, but I'm sure your mother will want to see you in it before she goes—'

'She's not my mother,' Beth said quickly.

'I'm just the housekeeper,' Grace said. 'And chauffeur, and general dogsbody,' she added cheerfully.

'I see.' Miss Coulter looked from one to the other, a frown creasing her plump face. 'Well, you're very welcome to stay and help your – Miss Bradshaw – settle in,' she finished. 'Lunch will be served in the dining room at half past twelve, so you'll have a chance to meet the rest of your set then. You're all in the same boat, so you can help each other.' She smiled at Beth. 'Welcome to the Nightingale, Bradshaw. I'm sure you'll settle in very well.'

The door closed, and Beth looked around. Everything felt distinctly unreal.

'She seems nice,' Grace said.

'Yes,' Beth agreed.

'And you'll be sharing with two other girls. That will be fun.'

Poor Grace. Beth could almost feel her desperation. All she wanted was for her to be happy.

How had the Home Sister thought she was her mother? She was only ten years older than Beth.

But in another way it made sense. Grace had been every bit as close and loving as a mother to her, especially over the past couple of years.

'You don't have to stay,' she said.

'But I want to make sure you're settled in all right,' Grace replied, taking in the surroundings. 'Your mother was so disappointed she couldn't come with us today. But you know what she's like when she gets one of her headaches.'

'Yes, I know.'

They both looked around the room, not meeting each other's eye. Grace knew her mother's sudden illness was an excuse, just as Beth did. But neither of them wanted to admit it.

Beth knew she should have been used to it by now. But she couldn't help the wave of bitter disappointment that threatened to engulf her.

A shriek of raucous laughter rang out from downstairs.

'Sounds like someone's having fun,' Grace commented. 'I suppose I'd best go, give you a chance to go and meet your new friends.'

She turned around and suddenly pulled Beth into her arms, hugging her fiercely. 'You will be all right, won't you?' she said, her words muffled as she pressed her face into Beth's hair. 'You're sure this is what you want?'

'Of course.'

'Really?' She held her at arm's length, her gaze searching. 'Because you know you don't have to do this—'

'It's what I want. Honestly.'

The door opened and a tall, dark-haired girl entered. She stopped in her tracks when she saw Beth.

'Oh, sorry,' she said. 'I didn't know—' She looked from one to the other. 'I'm Winnie,' she said.

'I'm Beth.'

'And I'm just leaving,' Grace added with a grin. She leaned in and planted a kiss on Beth's cheek. 'Look after yourself, sweetheart. I'll see you soon.'

'I'll come and visit when I can.' Beth followed her to the door, suddenly unwilling to let her out of her sight. 'And I'll write.'

'Make sure you do,' Grace wagged her finger at her, mock serious.

'Look after Mother, won't you?' Beth called after her as she left. But Grace was already heading down the stairs, her heels clattering.

Beth waited until she couldn't hear her any more, then reluctantly closed the door.

'Have you come far?' Winnie's voice broke into her thoughts.

'Kensington.' Beth turned to face her. She was sitting on the bed, nursing her uniform in her arms. 'How about you?'

'Bethnal Green. Just across the park.' Winnie looked around her. 'This used to be my mum's room,' she said.

'She trained here?'

Winnie nodded. 'Funny, ain't it? I never expected to end up here.'

Neither did I, Beth thought.

She looked around the room. Alison would have loved it, she thought. She would probably be already wearing her uniform by now, parading up and down, knocking on all the doors and introducing herself.

'I wonder who the other girl is?' Winnie spoke up again, nodding towards the bed on the far side of the room. 'She's late, whoever she is. If she don't arrive soon she'll miss lunch.'

'I suppose we'd better unpack, or we'll miss it too.'

They unpacked in silence, only speaking to share out the coat hangers in the wardrobe, and to discuss how they would divide up the drawers. Beth moved around the room, putting away her belongings, still feeling as if she was caught up in a strange dream.

Winnie seemed lost in her own thoughts too. Beth watched her out of the corner of her eye as she arranged a collection of photographs on her bedside table. She seemed to have a very large family. Beth was shocked she hadn't remembered to bring a photograph of Alison or her mother. How strange that they had both slipped her mind.

After she had unpacked all her belongings, Beth noticed a flat package at the bottom of her suitcase, wrapped in brown paper.

'What's that?' Winnie asked, as she took it out.

'I don't know.' It must be a present from Grace, she thought. She unfastened the string and unfolded the paper wrapping.

'A sketchbook and pencils?' Winnie said, from the other side of the room. 'Are you an artist?'

'I used to be.'

A typed note fell out and fluttered to the floor.

To dearest Beth. Don't forget who you really are.

She opened the sketchbook and ran her hand over the thick, unblemished white pages, each one full of possibilities. Faces, landscapes, flowers, trees, just waiting to be captured.

She slammed the book shut and threw it back into her suitcase. As she turned, she caught sight of her reflection in the dressing table mirror. A sad, lost face looked back at her.

Grace was wrong. That wasn't who she really was. It couldn't be.

Not any more.

Chapter Fifteen

After they'd finished unpacking, Beth and Winnie headed to the dining room for lunch with the others.

The dining room was bright and noisy with the clatter of crockery and the high-pitched chatter of voices. It was the size of a gymnasium, and laid out with several long tables. Around each table sat a group of young women, all wearing different coloured uniforms – some pale blue, some striped, some lavender.

'Everyone sits at different tables, according to their seniority,' explained Nurse Foster, the first-year student who had been assigned to their table – their 'babysitter', as she had introduced herself when she met them by the door. 'The first years sit over there –' she pointed to a table of girls in royal-blue uniforms like her own, 'the second years sit over there, and that lot are the seniors, or third years.'

'But all the students are wearing the same blue uniforms,' an Irish girl, whose name was Bernadette, spoke up. 'How are we supposed to tell them apart?'

'You see the belts they're wearing? The second years wear white belts, and the seniors wear blue. But you won't have to worry about that,' she said. 'You'll soon know if you get it wrong, believe me. Just remember not to try to speak to anyone above you. And you'll never see a third year scrubbing a bedpan, either. They leave all the dirtiest jobs to us juniors!'

'I suppose that will be us when we start on the wards?' Bernadette said.

'I can't wait!' Foster grinned mischievously.

'Do we have to talk about bedpans?' The girl beside Beth pushed her plate away from her in disgust. She had sleek brown hair and a sharp-featured face, with a nose that seemed permanently tilted up in the air. 'It's putting me off my lunch.'

'Oh, you'll get used to it,' Nurse Foster said cheerfully through a mouthful of food. 'You get so hungry on the wards you'll be eating the patients' leftovers in the sluice room. Although don't tell anyone I said that,' she added hastily. 'It's not really allowed.'

'I don't think I could bear to eat someone else's leftovers, could you?' Beth's neighbour whispered. 'But I suppose it's how you were brought up, isn't it?' She looked meaningfully around the table.

Beth turned her attention to Lou, the Jamaican girl on her other side, who was pushing her food around her plate.

'Aren't you hungry?' Beth asked.

Lou sent her a pained look. 'How can you eat this? It doesn't taste of anything.'

'Well, I'm afraid you'll just have to get used to it,' the girl beside Beth declared. 'This is our country and this is what we eat.'

'Lucky you,' Lou muttered.

As they ate lunch, they went around the table and introduced themselves. Besides Lou, there were two other girls from the Commonwealth – Frances from Barbados, and a quiet Indian girl called Maya, who said little but sat watching everything around her with wide dark eyes.

Then there were two Irish girls, Bernadette – or Bernie, as she introduced herself, and Philomena, who liked to be called Phil. It turned out they had known each other back in Ireland and were already firm friends. They chattered away nineteen to the dozen, unlike the girl opposite them, who did not say a word all through the meal, apart from whispering that her name was Susan, and asking if someone would pass the salt.

The girl beside Beth with the brown hair was called Camilla. Unlike silent Susan, she seemed to enjoy talking about herself. She quickly let everyone know that her father was a GP, that she had a horse, played tennis and her mother had once been a ward sister, so she more or less knew everything there was to know about medicine.

Then there were two other girls, Peggy and Alice, who seemed to have quickly become friends and didn't really speak to anyone else.

'There's one missing, isn't there?' Phil said, counting heads around the table. 'I thought there were meant to be twelve in our set?'

'Our room-mate hasn't arrived yet,' Winnie spoke up from the far end of the table.

'Where's she from, I wonder? Timbuktu?' Camilla's mouth curled.

Beth caught the look Frances and Lou exchanged down the table.

As she looked back, she suddenly caught a glimpse

97

of a familiar face out of the corner of her eye. She was sitting on the second-year table, amid a group of chattering girls.

Alison?

As if she had said the name aloud, the girl looked up. Their eyes met and suddenly Alison was gone, and the only voice Beth could hear was Camilla bellowing in her ear.

'Beth? Are you listening to me?'

She looked round. 'I'm sorry, were you saying something?'

Camilla laughed. 'What happened to you? You looked as if you were a million miles away. I was just saying, was that an American car you arrived in?'

Beth nodded. 'An Oldsmobile.'

'Is your father American?'

'My father is dead. The car belongs to my mother. Alfred Hitchcock gave it to her.'

She hadn't meant to let it slip. Suddenly she seemed to be the centre of everyone's attention.

'Gosh,' Camilla looked impressed. 'Is she famous? Would we have heard of her?'

Beth hesitated. It was too late now; the cat was already out of the bag.

'Her name is Celia Wells,' she said quietly.

There was a chorus of gasps from around the table.

'Celia Wells? The film star?' Camilla goggled at her in disbelief.

'We've seen all her films. Haven't we, Phil?' Bernie said.

Phil nodded. 'We loved her in *The Blonde*.'

Suddenly there seemed to be a thousand questions, all at

once. What was her mother like? Did they live in Beverly Hills? Did she know Rock Hudson? How about James Dean?

They seemed rather disappointed when Beth told them she had never even been on an aeroplane, let alone to Hollywood, and that she had spent most of her childhood in boarding schools while her mother was away working.

'I don't think I'd be here if my mother was a movie star,' Alice laughed. 'I think I'd be lounging by a swimming pool and eating caviar.'

'I certainly wouldn't be learning to scrub bedpans!' Peggy agreed.

Beth looked around at the ring of faces that surrounded her. 'I'm here because of my sister,' she said. 'She had just started training to be a nurse here when she died. I want to finish what she began.'

There was a general murmur of sympathy and approval.

Frances sighed. 'What a lovely thing to do for your sister.'

'I'm sure she'd be very proud,' Winnie said.

Thankfully, the conversation moved on and Beth stopped being the focus of all the attention. She was glad – neither she nor Alison had ever liked the limelight. They preferred to leave that to their mother.

Lunch ended and they headed back to the nurses' home, chatting as they went. Camilla made a beeline for Beth as they were leaving the dining room.

Beth's heart sank, waiting for more questions about her mother. But all Camilla wanted to know was, 'Which boarding school did you go to?'

'Benenden.'

'I went to Wycombe Abbey,' she said. 'The headmistress

was very keen for me to apply to Cambridge, but my mother thought nursing would be better for me. She trained at the Nightingale herself, you see. Although it's all changed since her day. It seems they'll take anyone these days.' She glanced around her.

'What do you mean?' Beth asked, genuinely perplexed.

Before Camilla could reply, a motorcycle suddenly came out of nowhere, roaring up the road behind them.

'Look out!' Phil shrieked as it ploughed through them, scattering them like skittles.

'Is everyone all right?' Bernie asked. 'Maya?'

They rushed to help the slight girl, who had tripped and fallen backwards on to the verge.

'I – I think so,' she stammered, as Winnie hauled her to her feet.

'Wretched road hog!' Camilla muttered. 'It could have killed us!'

'It's stopped outside the nurses' home.' Phil pointed to where the motorbike had skidded to a halt outside the door, sending up a wave of gravel and dust.

The engine cut off and they all watched as the pillion passenger swung herself off from the back. She wore rolled-up denim jeans, a tight black jumper and red lipstick.

As they stared, transfixed, she unfastened the scarf from under her chin and let her head roll back, shaking out luxuriant waves of auburn hair.

Then she turned to them with a radiant smile.

'Wotcha, girls!' she called out in a cockney accent even broader than Winnie's. 'Lovely day, innit?'

Chapter Sixteen

Winnie recognised her instantly. It was the redheaded girl she'd met the day she'd sat her test. She was about to say something when the front door was flung open and Miss Coulter emerged, followed by a tall, thin woman in a navy-blue sister's uniform.

'Who's that?' Maya whispered.

'Miss Beck, the Deputy Home Sister,' Nurse Foster said in a low voice. 'She's in charge of the Infirmary. She's a nightmare.'

'What's going on?' Miss Beck demanded, her gaze shooting between the girl and the motorbike. 'What is this?'

'It's a motorbike, lady.' The rider took out a packet of cigarettes and lit one up. He looked like a Teddy Boy version of James Dean, with his drape jacket, quiffed hair and sulky good looks. 'Do you want a ride?' He winked at her.

'Roy!' the girl giggled. Everyone else tittered nervously. Even Miss Coulter looked as if she was fighting to keep the smile off her face.

'Most certainly not,' Miss Beck retorted. 'Get it out of here. And you can go with it.'

'You mean I can't come in for a cup of tea?' The boy aimed a smoke ring insolently into the air.

Miss Beck's cheeks turned puce. 'Men are not allowed in the nurses home.' *Especially not your sort*, her look said.

The young man put down his cigarette and turned to the girl. 'Looks like I'll be seeing you, sweetheart.'

He pulled the laughing redhead into his arms, and kissed her passionately.

Winnie looked around her. The other girls were divided between those who did not know where to look, and others who could not tear their eyes away. The Irish girls were staring avidly, while Camilla looked horrified.

Miss Beck and Miss Coulter seemed to be divided over it, too. Miss Coulter hid a smile behind her hand, while Miss Beck seemed as if she might faint from the shock of it all.

'That's enough of that!' she finally managed to splutter.

The young man released the girl. 'See you later, darlin',' he said. He revved up the motorbike, circled it around and then sped off, his cigarette dangling precariously from his lower lip.

The redhead watched him until he had disappeared out of sight, then she picked up her suitcase and turned to Miss Beck.

'All right, love? This way, is it?'

Then, without waiting for an answer, she disappeared inside. Miss Coulter darted after her, leaving Miss Beck speechless on the step. She stood for a moment, staring as if she could not quite believe what had happened. Then she recovered herself and called out,

'Don't just stand there gawping, girls! Go to your rooms and try on your uniforms. You need to make sure they fit properly before Matron carries out her inspection later.'

'I reckon that must be our new room-mate,' Winnie whispered to Beth as they climbed the stairs back to their room.

'I think you're right.' Beth looked apprehensive at the prospect.

Sure enough, there was singing coming from beyond the attic room door.

'I've never felt more like singing the blues—' the girl broke off from her humming as Winnie and Beth entered. 'Oh, hello. Is it you two I'm sharing with? I'm Vivien – you know, like Vivien Leigh, the film star? But you can call me Viv. Everyone does. And you are . . . ?'

'Beth Bradshaw.'

'Winnie Riley.'

'Winnie? Like Winifred Atwell? I love her music, don't you?' Viv gave them a dazzling smile that dimpled her cheeks. She was a beautiful girl, Winnie thought, with her shiny auburn hair, green eyes and knockout figure. 'Right, I'm guessing this is my bunk—' she dumped her suitcase on the bed at the far side of the room. 'So where do I put my stuff?'

Beth showed her the spare hangers in the wardrobe and the spare drawer they'd left for her. Viv regarded them apprehensively.

'I'll never get everything in there!' she laughed. 'Oh well, I daresay I can find a place to put everything . . .' She looked around her.

'The Home Sister says we're to keep the room tidy,' Winnie reminded her.

'Not much chance of that with me around!' Viv laughed. 'My gran says every room I'm in turns into a bombsite.' She turned to Winnie. 'You sound local, like me. Are you from round here?'

'Just the other side of the park.'

'I'm from Clapton myself. Queensdown Road, if you know it?' She moved around the room as she talked, unpacking her belongings from her suitcase into the chest of drawers. 'Here, that Miss Beck is a bit of a dragon, ain't she? But she can't be any worse than living with my gran . . .'

Winnie said nothing. She was too transfixed by the array of frilly underwear Viv was taking out of her suitcase. She had never seen anything so fancy. It certainly put her plain old bras and knickers to shame.

Viv must have noticed her looking because she smiled and held up a pair of lacy pants and said, 'My mum says a girl should always have nice underwear on.'

'Why? Who's going to see it?'

Viv gave her a knowing look. 'You never know, do you? That's the point.' She folded the pants and tucked them into her drawer. 'Have either of you got a boyfriend?'

Winnie and Beth both shook their heads. Beth looked positively terrified at the idea.

'I'll have to ask my Roy, see if he can fix you up with someone. He's got loads of friends, I'm sure one of them is bound to take a fancy to you two.' She produced a packet of cigarettes from her handbag and offered it to them.

'No thanks. And I don't think we're supposed to smoke in our rooms, either,' Winnie added. Although Miss Coulter had reeled off such a long list she could hardly remember them all.

'Yes, well, I like to break the rules!' Viv grinned. 'Granny Trent says I get that from my mum.' She took a long, defiant drag on her cigarette. 'Anyway, let them throw me out if they like. The sooner the better as far as I'm concerned.'

Beth stared at her. 'Don't you want to be here?'

'Are you joking? I'd still be working at Clarnico's if my gran hadn't forced me to apply to this dump. She said I needed to make something of myself, before I came to a bad end. Threatened to throw me out if I didn't, mean old cow!' She rolled her eyes. 'Mum says she was just the same with her when she was a kid. Mind you, she was pregnant with me by the time she was eighteen, so I s'pose she might have had a point!'

Winnie recalled the grumpy-looking old lady sitting outside the test room.

'I think I saw your gran, when I came for my interview,' she said. 'We met just after I took my test.'

'So we did!' Viv's face brightened. 'I thought you looked familiar. Yes, that was Granny Trent,' she grimaced. 'She insisted on coming with me. I reckon she would have sat by my side during that test if she could. She was convinced I was going to make a mess of it on purpose.'

'Why didn't you?' Beth asked.

'I dunno.' Viv looked thoughtful for a moment. 'Pride, I s'pose. I didn't like the way that old cow in the test centre looked down her nose at me. She acted like she didn't think I was good enough to get into her precious nursing school. I just wanted to prove her wrong. And look where it's got me, eh?' She took another drag on her cigarette and grinned at them through the curling smoke. 'Never mind. I daresay they'll realise their mistake soon enough.'

She stubbed out her cigarette and finished her unpacking. Although it was hard to see what she had actually put away, as every surface seemed to be littered with her make-up, photographs and movie magazines.

Winnie noticed a glamorous Celia Wells on the cover of *Picturegoer*, and wondered if Beth had seen it too. If she had, she didn't comment on it.

And then it was time to try on their uniforms.

'Oh dear, how am I ever going to catch the eye of a handsome young doctor wearing this monstrosity?' Viv said, holding up the dress with a look of distaste.

'Why do you need to, if you've got a boyfriend?' Winnie asked, slipping off her jumper and skirt.

'It never hurts to keep your options open, does it? That's what my mum always says. Although my Roy and I are practically engaged. Look,' she pulled off her tight black jumper and showed them the ring that hung on a chain around her neck.

'Why don't you wear it on your finger?' Beth asked.

'We've got to keep it a secret. Granny Trent would have a fit if she found out. She thinks Roy's trouble. But that's why I like him. The bad boys are always more fun, ain't they?'

'I couldn't say,' Winnie muttered.

From out in the hall one of the other girls called out, 'How are we supposed to turn this bit of cardboard into a cap? Does anyone know?'

Winnie wriggled into her dress. The striped fabric was surprisingly heavy, and itched against her skin.

'Anyway,' Viv went on, 'I've got it all planned out. As soon as I'm kicked out of this place, I'm going to get my old job back at the sweet factory, and Roy and I are going to get married.'

'Can't you just leave, if you don't want to be here?' Beth asked.

'I told you, my gran won't let me! She says she won't let me live under her roof. And she means it, too. She's a hard old cow. She'd see me on the streets, I know she would.'

'What does that matter, if you're going to get married?'

'It's complicated,' Viv muttered. 'Anyway, I don't—' she looked over her shoulder at Winnie and stopped. 'Oh lord, what's happened to you?'

'I don't know.' Winnie looked down at herself. Her dress finished around the middle of her thigh, exposing her knees and a good few inches above. 'I think the sewing room must have made a mistake with my measurements.'

'I'll say they have! Here, maybe we could swap?' Viv suggested. 'I wouldn't mind showing a bit more leg, that's for sure.'

She stared down at herself in despair. Her shapely figure was nowhere to be seen, swamped by yards of voluminous fabric.

'Me neither,' Beth said. She was a petite blonde, and the uniform hung off her slight frame, almost skimming the floor.

'Look at us,' Viv said. 'We look like the bloody orphans in the storm!'

They looked at each other and suddenly they all started laughing helplessly.

The door flew open and Miss Beck swept in. 'What's going on in here? Why are you three making so much—' She stared at Winnie. 'Good heavens, girl, what have you done to your uniform?'

'I ain't done anything,' Winnie protested.

'Look,' Viv snatched up the label and showed it to Miss Beck. 'They've put her down as five foot one.'

'They must have written it down wrong,' Winnie said. 'I'm five foot ten.'

'Hmm.' The Home Sister sent her a narrow look, as if she didn't quite believe that Winnie had not taken a pair of scissors to it herself. 'Yes, well, you'd better take it off and go to the sewing room straight away. 'You can't let Matron see you like that.' She turned to Viv. 'And you,' she said. 'If I catch you smoking, you'll be straight on report!'

'Who said I was the one smoking?' Viv protested.

Miss Beck sent her a narrow-eyed glare. 'I can smell a cigarette from a mile off,' she said. 'And I know your type.'

Chapter Seventeen

One by one, the girls began to emerge from their rooms wearing their uniforms and looking self-conscious. Beth was glad to see most of them had made a complete mess of their caps, just like her.

The only one who seemed to have got it right was Camilla. She looked every inch the cool, competent nurse, in a uniform that fit so perfectly it might have been tailored especially for her. Her cap had obviously been folded perfectly the first time, judging by the lack of creases in its crisp fabric.

'Look at us! We look like a bunch of nuns!' Viv exclaimed, which seemed to shock Phil and Bernie. 'I just hope my Roy never gets to see me like this. He'll run a mile!'

'Is that your boyfriend?' asked Frances. 'The boy on the motorcycle?'

'Is he really a Teddy Boy?' Phil asked, fascinated. 'I've heard about them but I've never seen one in real life before.'

'My father says they're a disgrace to society,' Camilla sniffed.

'Is he in a gang?' Bernie asked, looking slightly anxious.

'Put it this way, no one would ever mess with him. Nor with me, either. Not while he's around.' Viv shot Camilla a dirty look.

'Girls?' Miss Coulter called up the stairs. 'Come down when you're ready.'

They hurried down to the hall, where the Home Sister was waiting for them.

'Right, let's have a look at you . . .' Miss Coulter checked them all over, her expression growing darker. 'Yes, well, I can see you've all had trouble with your caps.' She gestured to Maya. 'Here, let me show you how it's done. The trick is not to have to keep refolding it. Otherwise it very quickly loses its shape and goes limp, and then you won't be able to do anything with it.'

She folded the fabric deftly as she spoke, before placing the finished cap on Maya's head and finishing it with a hair-grip on each side. 'There. That's better.' She stepped back to admire her handiwork. 'Don't worry, you'll get the hang of it soon enough,' she reassured them. 'You'll soon be able to make them in your sleep.'

Just at that moment the front door opened and Winnie hurried in, a bundle tucked under her arm.

'And where have you been?' Miss Coulter asked, her brows rising.

'I had to get a new uniform, Sister. The sewing room got my measurements wrong.'

'I see. Go and get it on quickly, girl. Matron will be here any minute.'

Winnie reappeared again shortly before Miss Coulter summoned them into the common room. This was a large room with a bay window overlooking the front lawn and the drive. Shelves lined the walls, filled with books, games and a few jigsaw puzzles. There was a record player and a wireless on the sideboard, and several battered-looking armchairs and sofas that had clearly seen years of use. A fire crackled cheerfully in the grate.

'Well, this all looks like fun,' Viv commented dryly, looking around her.

Miss Beck and Miss Coulter stood on either side of the fireplace, flanking Helen McKay. She seemed less terrifying than she had during the interview. But Beth was still nervous as she took a seat on the sofa, wedged in between Maya and Susan, the very quiet girl, who so far still hadn't uttered a word.

Miss Cheetham was in the room, too, dressed in a stylish skirt suit. There was an unnerving steeliness in her grey eyes as she surveyed the room.

'Settle down, girls, we don't have all day!' Miss Beck snapped. Camilla took an exercise book out of her bag and sat with her pen poised.

'Look at her. Teacher's pet!' Beth heard Viv whisper at the other end of the row.

'Thank you, Miss Beck.' Helen McKay turned to face them. Had she ever looked like a shapeless sack in her uniform? Beth wondered. It was hard to believe. Her black dress looked so elegant on her tall, slender frame.

'Welcome to the Florence Nightingale Hospital,' she began. 'And may I thank you all for coming. I know some of you have travelled halfway across the world to train with us,' she glanced at the three Commonwealth girls who had banded together in one corner. 'You have all had different upbringings and different experiences. But what you all have in common is that you have all chosen to come here to embark on your Preliminary Training, which in due course will hopefully lead to three years of training for your State Registration.' She turned to the blonde in the suit. 'To which end, I would like to introduce Miss Cheetham, the Head of our Nursing School. Some of you will have already met her at your interview. She will be responsible for supervising your training during PTS.'

Miss Cheetham gave them all an assessing look, as if she could see into their souls. Beth quickly dropped her gaze to her shoes.

'I won't pretend the next three years will be easy,' Helen McKay went on. 'As you already know, our standards of nursing are very high, which is probably the reason you chose to train here.' She allowed herself a small smile. 'We demand a great deal of our students, and you will be severely tested, and no doubt pushed to the limits of your endurance. Certainly not all of you will make it to the end of the course.'

Beth looked around. The Irish girls were looking rather pale and even Camilla had stopped scribbling in her exercise book.

Mrs McKay must have noticed their dismay because she smiled and went on, 'I don't wish to frighten you. We are well aware that you are young, and you're not perfect. I have been in your shoes myself. There were many times when I sat up late into the night in one of these very rooms and wondered if I would ever be good enough, or know everything I needed to know.' Her smile grew wistful for a moment. 'But I can assure you that with perseverance and diligence you will get through. I have every confidence in all of you, otherwise I would not have selected you for this course.' Her gaze swept around them all, taking in every one of them. 'You will be daunted and overwhelmed at times, and I daresay if you're anything like I was, there will be times when you wonder if you made the right choice to become a nurse.'

Once again, her gaze swept the room, and Beth wondered if she had imagined it lingering on her a moment longer than the others. 'But I want you to know that if you have any problems, my door is open between eight and nine every morning if you wish to discuss anything with me. I am not just here to administer discipline, I promise you.'

There was a ripple of polite but decidedly nervous laughter, and then Mrs McKay stepped back and Miss Beck announced that they should all line up so that Matron could carry out her inspection.

Beth quaked as she took her place in the line between Winnie and the Irish girls. But thankfully the inspection was not too harsh. Apart from pointing out the odd missing collar stud or hair not tucked properly under a cap, and telling Viv to wipe off her red lipstick, Matron was very forgiving. At the end of her inspection, she gave them all a kind smile and praised them for their efforts.

'No doubt Miss Coulter and Miss Beck have already made you aware of the rules here,' she said. 'I expect you to follow them to the letter. They are there for your own safety as well as the smooth running of the hospital and training school.' She paused and once again her dark gaze swept down the line. 'I do not expect to see you sent to my office too often,' she warned, her severe tone belied by the twinkle in her brown eyes.

And then she left, followed by the other women. It wasn't until the door closed behind her that all the girls finally relaxed and let out the breath they had all been holding in.

'Well, I certainly don't intend to stick to their rules,' Viv announced. 'No curfew is going to keep me in, I know that!'

'Matron seems nice, though,' Frances commented.

'You wait until you put a foot wrong,' Camilla predicted. 'Then you'll see another side to her!'

'She's a lot nicer than the Reverend Mother at St Anthony's where we did our pre-training,' Bernie said. 'She was a vicious old cow, wasn't she, Phil? Remember how she told us we were going to Hell because we decided to come over and train in London?'

'You'll be led astray,' Phil mimicked a croaky Irish accent. 'You'll stop going to Mass and end up marrying a Protestant in a register office.'

'That's if Jack the Ripper or the white slavers don't get us first!' Bernie said, and they both laughed.

Maya, Lou and Frances looked nervously at each other. 'Is it really so dangerous?' Maya asked, wide-eyed.

'It is according to the Reverend Mother,' Bernie said. 'She warned us about the terrible slum conditions, and the opium dens, and the killer smog. Mind, I don't know how she knows so much about it. I don't think she's ever been as far as Dublin!'

'It's all right,' Winnie said. 'I come from round here, and I've never seen an opium den, let alone Jack the Ripper.' She looked round at the others. 'Tell you what. Since we've got the rest of the afternoon free, why don't I show you around? I could take you up to Columbia Road market, do some shopping.'

'I don't think we're meant to be going out,' Camilla said.

'What else are we going to do?' Peggy asked. 'Hang around here playing Snakes and Ladders? I don't know about the rest of you, but I could do with some fresh air.'

'I would like to have a look,' Maya ventured, and Frances and Lou nodded in agreement.

'We'll come too,' Bernie said. 'Won't we, Phil?'

'Oh yes,' Phil said. 'You never know, I might find a black-hearted Protestant to corrupt me.'

'Well, I'm not going.' Camilla's voice rose above their laughter.

'You can count me out too,' Viv said. 'I've already made other plans. I'm going up to Soho with my Roy.'

'Soho?' The Irish girls' eyes widened. They couldn't have looked more shocked if Viv had announced she was spending the evening in Sodom and Gomorrah.

'The Heaven and Hell café on Old Compton Street. You can come if you like?'

Phil and Bernie looked at each other. This was just what their Reverend Mother had warned them about, Beth could tell from their stricken faces.

'Don't forget you've got to be back before lights out at ten,' Winnie reminded her.

Viv laughed. 'I told you, no curfew is going to keep me in!'

Chapter Eighteen

Helen was deep in thought as she walked away from the nurses' home. It amazed her how young the girls seemed, little more than children. And to think, some of them had travelled halfway around the world to be there. No wonder they looked so terrified. But she trusted that they would all rally round each other soon enough. It happened in every set. They always began by keeping their distance and sizing each other up nervously, but by the end of the twelve weeks they would all be firm friends.

Although she could already pick out one or two who would be visiting her office regularly for one reason or another. These were the ones she would really have to keep her eye on. Like that redheaded girl, Vivien Trent. She was a lively one for sure. Helen had taken a real chance on her, and she hoped she would not live to regret it.

There had been a storm the previous evening, with winds howling all night long. Now, thankfully, all was calm, but the winds had left a trail of destruction, with bare branches torn from trees and shattered roof tiles on the ground. It was the Buildings and Maintenance Department's job to make sure the hospital and its grounds were kept in good order, but it was the middle of the afternoon and all the debris was still there, so Helen decided to pay a visit to the Buildings Manager.

He would not thank her for her interference, of course. But if a patient or one of her nurses were to trip on a branch or be struck by a falling tile, then it would soon become her concern.

So rather than entering the main building by the double doors, Helen left the drive and picked her way across the front lawn, being careful to step over any debris herself.

She was so busy watching the ground under her feet, she didn't notice someone hurtling around the corner towards her until they had collided, knocking her sideways.

'Oh! Pardon, Madame.'

Helen looked up and found herself staring into the tearful face of a young woman. She was no more than eighteen, her slender frame huddled in a coat several sizes too big for her, a red silk scarf loosely tied at her throat. Her delicate face, framed by a cap of short fair hair, was blotchy and swollen from crying, her large brown eyes red-rimmed.

'Are you all right?' Helen said, but the girl was already gone, hurrying away down the path.

Helen watched her for a moment and thought about going after her, then gave up the idea. Whatever was wrong with the girl, she obviously wanted to be alone.

Helen skirted the building on the far side, where the maintenance huts were, as well as the door leading down to the boiler room. Steam belched from a battered metal chimney above the door.

She was just about to enter the Building Manager's office

when she noticed a familiar figure hunched on the step leading to the boiler room.

'William?'

He looked up and for a moment she caught a glimpse of his troubled expression. The next moment he was all smiles again.

'Hello, Sis. What are you doing here? Don't tell me one of your new students has done a bunk already?'

'They were all present and correct the last time I saw them. Did you see a woman here just now?'

'What woman?'

'Small, blonde, in floods of tears. You must have seen her?'

William shrugged. 'I didn't notice anyone.'

'How strange. I could have sworn she came from here.'

'You must be mistaken. Unless she was a ghost?' He pulled a horrified face and waggled his fingers in a spooky way.

'Don't be ridiculous!' Helen shook him off. 'I suppose I must have been mistaken,' she admitted. 'I can't say I was really watching where I was going. It was a bit odd, though. I wonder who she was?'

'Are you sure she wasn't one of your lot, got herself lost?'

'I told you, they're all accounted for.' She turned her gaze back in the direction she had seen the young woman. 'I hope she's all right. She did seem very upset.'

'Well, I've been sitting here for the past ten minutes and I haven't seen anyone.'

She turned her attention back to her brother. 'What are you doing out here, anyway?'

'Oh, you know me. I always used to like sneaking behind the boiler house for a cigarette.'

Helen laughed. 'You're the Chief Surgical Consultant now, don't forget. Surely you don't have to sneak anywhere?'

'Old habits die hard.' He looked rueful. 'Actually, I needed a few minutes by myself. I've just lost a patient.'

'Oh, I'm sorry to hear that. Who was it? I don't recall any of the sisters mentioning it when I did my ward rounds this morning.'

'He was a new admission, came in a couple of hours ago. Peritonitis. There wasn't much chance of saving him, but I did my best.'

'I'm sure you did.' She put her hand on his shoulder.

'You'd think I'd be used to it after all these years, wouldn't you?'

'I don't think you ever get used to it.' Helen sat down on the step beside him. He offered her his cigarette but she shook her head.

They sat in silence for a moment. There was something troubling Helen, something that had been bothering her since Christmas. But she was not sure how to put it into words.

'Will, can I ask you something?' she said.

'As long as it's not to borrow money!'

'That private patient – the one you rushed up to London to see at Christmas?'

He frowned. 'What about her?'

'Who is she?'

119

'Mrs Oliver. Ovarian cancer. Very sad case,' he shook his head. 'I had her transferred to a nursing home on Christmas Eve. She asked me to go with her, which is why I was late home.' He looked at Helen. 'Why? What about her?'

'Nothing. I just didn't think we had any private patients on the female wards, that's all.'

'Checking up on me?' His brows rose.

'Of course not. I was just curious.'

'Well, as it happens, this particular lady wasn't at the Nightingale. She was at Bart's.'

'So why weren't the doctors there attending to her?'

'They were, but I was asked to consult. I do have something of a reputation, you know,' he grinned.

He dropped his cigarette and ground it out with his heel. 'Anyway, I'd better get back. Are you coming?'

'In a minute.'

'I'll see you on the ward, I daresay. Sorry I couldn't help you with your phantom girl.'

Helen watched him sauntering away, his hands in his pockets. His tuneless whistle carried on the air after he had turned the corner.

It all made sense now. Surgeons at the Nightingale were occasionally asked to consult on cases at other hospitals. And as her brother had ruefully reminded her, he was one of the most eminent gynaecologists and obstetricians in London.

If only she had stopped to think about it, she would have realised how utterly ridiculous she was being to even think—

And then another thought suddenly struck her.

Your phantom girl.

That was what William had called her. A phantom girl. He had even made a joke about her being one of Helen's students.

And yet Helen did not recall mentioning that she was young. On the contrary, she had referred to her as a woman, not a girl.

The last notes of her brother's whistling faded away.

Oh William, she thought. *What are you playing at now?*

Chapter Nineteen

Viv caught the bus up west, and went straight to Old Compton Street.

Crowds of people thronged the pavements, spilling out from the numerous cafés and brash, colourful espresso bars that lined the street. Even in the late afternoon, there were all kinds on the Soho streets – working girls plying their trade on the corners, scruffy, Gauloise-smoking bohemians and West Indian immigrants.

And, of course, there were the Teddy Boys.

Most of the cafés did not like them, but they had no choice but to let them in. They would only make trouble if they didn't, and besides, they had plenty of money to spend.

Viv checked through every window of the brightly lit cafés, with their Formica-topped bars, metal stools and lively music vying with the wheezing, burbling sounds of the giant Gaggia coffee machines. But she already knew where she would find everyone. Most of the teenagers liked to gather around the 2i's Coffee Bar, hoping to see some up-and-coming stars, or better still, get spotted themselves. But next door at number 57 was Roy's favourite hang-out, the Heaven and Hell.

Sure enough, as Viv approached she spotted a couple kissing passionately on the pavement outside.

'You want to be careful, Bobby Jackson,' Viv grinned. 'You'll get yourself a bad name!'

Her friend Bobby pulled away from her boyfriend's embrace.

'In Soho?' she grinned. 'You must be joking. Have you seen what goes on upstairs?'

She nodded towards the window above, where they all knew a French woman called Suzy entertained a stream of customers behind her gauzy net curtains. She was rarely seen herself, although her maid was frequently spotted coming in and out.

'Is Roy upstairs or down?' Viv asked.

'You know Roy. He's gone straight to Hell!' Pete, Bobby's boyfriend, grinned. He was Roy's best friend, tall and lanky with a quiff of sandy hair. Viv often wondered what Bobby saw in him. She was small and so pretty, with her big brown eyes and curly black hair, she could have had any boy in the gang.

'You coming in?' Viv asked Bobby.

'In a minute.' Her friend went back to kissing Pete. *There's no accounting for taste*, Viv thought. She gave a little shrug and made her way into the café.

The Heaven and Hell was a curious place. On the ground floor it was decorated with ethereal white walls, and sunflower lights with cherubs' faces. But downstairs it was a different story. You entered through a giant devil's mouth into a black painted cellar with mock flames shooting from the walls. It was lit by the glowing red eyes of devil masks.

Not surprisingly, this was where all the Teds liked to congregate.

There was a queue down the staircase to get in, but the doorman at the foot of the stairs spotted Viv and ushered her straight down. She could hear the tide of resentful mutterings following her as she sashayed down the stairs ahead of them.

Tough, she thought, turning to give them a friendly little wave. It was just one of the perks of being Roy Carter's girlfriend.

Roy was by the jukebox with his friends, the centre of all the attention as usual. They made a formidable huddle in their drape jackets, slim Jim ties and thick-soled shoes, and everyone was giving them a wide berth. Except for a couple of Teddy Girls, who were hanging around on the edge of the group. One in particular, a bleached blonde in a skin-tight pencil skirt, was leaning against Roy, her arm resting on his shoulder.

Viv took a deep breath, walked over and firmly eased herself between them.

'Hello, love.'

As he turned round, she cupped his face in her hands and kissed him passionately, her tongue insinuating into his mouth. He tasted of stale beer and cigarettes, but at least it had the desired effect. His friends began to jeer, while the blonde looked on with an expression of sick jealousy.

'Oh, it's you,' Sandra Ellis said when Viv came up for air at last. 'I thought you'd be all locked up in your nurses' home by now?'

You wish, Viv thought. 'It's a hospital, not bloody Holloway!' she retorted, sending her a dirty look.

'All the same, you shouldn't be here.'

'Says who?' Viv turned to Roy. 'Would you rather I wasn't here?'

'Not me!' he grinned, slipping his arm around her waist. 'You couldn't stay away, could you, sweetheart?'

'More like she's checking up on you,' Sandra muttered.

Viv turned to her. 'Now why should I do that? I don't see any competition.'

Sandra pulled a sour face and drifted off to join a couple of the other boys. Viv stared after her. She had some nerve! Viv had only been gone a couple of hours and Sandra Ellis was already trying to make her move. But Viv knew she shouldn't be too surprised. Sandra had been sniffing around Roy for ages, flirting and batting her eyelashes.

Well, just let her try. Viv was more than a match for any girl.

'Did you see the way she was hanging all over you?' she said to Roy.

'Can't say I noticed.' Roy pulled her close, nuzzling her neck. Viv flinched as he nipped the soft skin between his teeth.

You might one day.

She remembered what her mother had said in her last letter. *You want to watch your Roy, Viv. You know what men are like. Out of sight, out of mind.*

She pulled away from his embrace. 'Yes, and it had better stay that way, too,' she warned, tapping his chest playfully. 'Because if you start looking at the likes of Sandra Ellis, I might find myself a good-looking medical student!'

'As if I'm bothered about them chinless wonders!' Roy gave her a lazily arrogant smile.

Viv was sitting at a table sipping a coffee a few minutes later when Bobby came down the stairs. She saw Viv and made her way over to her.

'Everything all right?' she asked.

'Not really.'

'What's up?' Bobby lit up a cigarette. 'Let me guess – you caught Sandra on the prowl?' she sighed. 'I warned you about her, didn't I?'

'That sneaky cow! I don't trust her as far as I could throw her.' Viv glared over to where Sandra was hovering on the edge of the group, her greedy gaze still fixed on Roy. 'You've got to keep an eye on her for me, all right?'

'You know I will,' Bobby promised, passing her the cigarette.

'Hopefully I'll be back soon.' Viv took a puff and handed it back. 'The sooner I get out of that nurses' home, the better.'

Bobby frowned. 'I don't understand why you want to leave. Why don't you stay and give it a chance?'

'I don't belong there,' Viv shook her head. 'You should see those other girls. They ain't our sort.'

Even Winnie, a working-class girl like herself, didn't seem like any fun.

'You passed the test to get in, didn't you? That means you're every bit as good as they are.'

Viv laughed. 'Listen to you! Anyone would think you didn't want me to come back.'

'I can't understand it, that's all. You've been given the chance to better yourself. Why would you throw it all away? Nursing's got to be better than packing peppermint creams for the rest of your life.'

'Now you sound just like Granny Trent!' Viv said. 'Anyway, I won't be a factory girl for the rest of my life. Just until me and Roy get married.'

'And you reckon that's going to happen?'

'Don't you?'

Bobby glanced past her towards the jukebox where Roy stood. 'If anyone's going to tame him, I s'pose it would be you,' she said.

Viv felt for the ring on its chain around her neck. It was only a cheap one from Woolworth's, and it had come at a price.

If you're going to let a boy have his way with you, make sure you've got a ring first, was her mother's sage advice. *Don't give it away for nothing*.

It was more than a ring. It was her talisman, her hope for the future.

She looked at Roy as he pumped coins into the jukebox. She tried not to show it, but he was her whole world. Her hopes, her dreams, her whole future was wrapped up in him.

She just prayed he would not let her down.

Chapter Twenty

The Preliminary Training School was housed in a large out-building to the rear of the main hospital block.

It was a cold, draughty place, about the size of a normal hospital ward. But half the space was given over to a class-room where, on a frosty January morning, Beth and the other eleven students sat shivering in rows of wooden desks facing the raised dais.

Miss Cheetham stood on the dais, flanked by a solemn-looking younger woman with thick spectacles, and a burly man in a white coat.

A yellowing skeleton dangled disconcertingly from a frame just behind her. Beth half expected him to raise a bony hand and place it on the Sister Tutor's shoulder.

'Welcome to your first day of Preliminary Training,' Miss Cheetham greeted them, her cool gaze moving along each row in turn. 'Matron has already given you the warm words, so I'm not going to waste my time repeating them. What I am going to say is that this is where the hard work really begins.'

Beth looked along the row and was glad to see everyone looked as terrified as she felt. Except for Camilla, who was making notes with a great big smirk on her face, and Viv, who was stifling a yawn in the back row. The two Irish girls were staring at the colourful anatomical schemata of the major organs of the body displayed on the walls. The one of the male reproductive system seemed to have particularly caught their attention.

'As you already know, I am in charge of the Nightingale's nursing school, and I will also be overseeing your Clinical Practice teaching for the next twelve weeks. So I am the one you need to impress if you wish to continue your training at this hospital.'

Miss Cheetham's smile grew steelier. 'I will be assisted by Miss James here, along with other visiting sisters from time to time. Mr Allenby will be taking you for lectures on anatomy, physiology, chemistry, first aid and nutrition.'

'Is he a nurse?' Beth heard Bernie whisper beside her.

'Surely not?' Phil replied. 'I didn't know men could be nurses, did you?'

'Shh!' Camilla hissed. 'Some of us are trying to listen.'

'This is where you will be spending most of your time over the next twelve weeks,' Miss Cheetham went on. 'The mornings will be spent learning practical skills, and the afternoons will be given over to lectures. At the end of the twelve weeks of Preliminary Training you will face a practical and written test to determine whether you are suitable to continue training. If you pass, you will be returning to this school for lectures and study periods every week while also working on the wards. You will then take your State Preliminaries at fifteen months, before progressing to your State Finals at the end of the three years of training. Are there any questions so far?'

No one dared to put up their hand. Even the ever

confident Camilla seemed cowed into silence by the daunting task ahead of them.

'Now some of you may consider you're at some advantage since you've already done some training . . .' Miss Cheetham's gaze fell on the Irish girls. 'But I can tell you now, your experience counts for nothing. As far as I'm concerned, you are all starting from scratch and learning the proper way of doing things. And we will begin by learning how to make a bed. Come with me.'

She led the way from the classroom into the adjoining practical area, which was laid out like a small ward, with half a dozen beds separated by lockers. At the far end of the room was a tall cupboard, left open to reveal neat piles of fresh linen, bowls and various instruments.

A kitchen led off one side, as well as a couple of glass cubicles.

'That's where you do your fever training,' Phil said knowledgeably. 'We learned all about barrier nursing at St Anthony's. Didn't we, Bernie?'

'You heard what Miss Cheetham said. Your experience counts for nothing here,' Camilla reminded them. 'You've got to learn the proper way of doing things.'

'I'd like to see Miss Cheetham telling the Reverend Mother she wasn't doing it right!' Bernie muttered. 'She'd eat her alive!'

'Now watch very carefully,' Miss Cheetham instructed. 'Miss James and I will show you what to do, then I expect you to copy us exactly.'

It was like watching a ballet. Miss Cheetham and Miss James faced each other from either side of the bed but they seemed to move as one, deftly working together to strip off the sheets and blankets one at a time, folding them into three and then draping them over the two chairs Miss Cheetham had placed at the foot of the bed.

'Notice we do not shake the sheets too much, to avoid spreading germs,' Miss Cheetham said. Then they worked together once again to make up the bed. Beth could only stare in awe at the tightly drawn sheets, crisply folded corners and precisely turned down cover. She was still struggling to master the folds on her cap.

'Now it's your turn. Get into pairs and find a bed.'

The two Irish girls immediately paired off, as did Frances and Lou, and Alice and Peggy. Maya ended up with Silent Susan. Winnie caught Beth's eye and looked as if she was about to approach her, but Camilla got there first.

'I'll partner up with you,' she told Beth, sidling next to her. Beth caught the look of disappointment on Winnie's face as she was left with Viv.

Making the bed proved to be a lot more difficult than it had first appeared. Everyone took ages, and most of them made a mess of it, except for the Irish girls.

'A good first effort,' Miss James told them, but Miss Cheetham cut her short.

'It's an absolutely monstrosity,' she declared. 'Take it all off and do it again.'

'That'll show them,' Camilla muttered with a smile of pure malice. 'Thinking they know it all.'

They're not the only ones, Beth thought. She had known Camilla for less than a day, but she had already made up her mind that they would never be friends.

It took them three attempts to get their bed made. Camilla managed to do her side perfectly every time, but Beth kept getting it wrong.

And her partner's growing frustration didn't help matters.

'Honestly!' Camilla sighed, loud enough for the rest of the class to hear. 'You tuck the lower part of the flap in first, then turn the rest downwards. It isn't that hard, surely?'

'Leave her be,' Winnie said.

'I'm only trying to help,' Camilla protested.

'You're making her more flustered by keeping on her.'

Beth shot Winnie a quick, embarrassed look. It was kind of her to stick up for her, but she was already drawing enough attention to herself with her hopeless efforts.

It was a relief to finally escape to the dining room for lunch. As they gathered round the table and tucked into corned beef hash, they all laughed and compared notes about their morning's work.

'Ours looked like it had already been slept in!' Alice and Peggy said.

'What hope is there for us if we can't even make a bed?' Maya said.

'Speak for yourself.' Camilla glared at Beth. At least she probably wouldn't insist on being her partner again, which was something.

Then the conversation turned to their tutors. They all agreed that Miss James seemed very sweet but nervous, and that Miss Cheetham probably bullied her terribly. Camilla, of course, wouldn't hear a word said against the Nursing Tutor, and insisted that Miss James probably needed to buck up her ideas.

But it was Mr Allenby who intrigued them the most.

'I still don't understand how a man like him came to be a nurse,' Bernie said.

'It would never have been allowed at St Anthony's,' Phil agreed.

'If you ask me, him and Miss Cheetham are up to something.'

Everyone turned to look at Viv. She sat at the far end of the table, spearing peas on to her fork with an air of nonchalance.

'What do you mean?' Frances asked.

Viv sent her an old-fashioned look. 'What do you think I mean?'

'You think they're courting?' Peggy said.

'If that's what you want to call it.' Viv speared another pea and put it into her mouth.

'No!' Alice said. 'What makes you say that?'

'Just a feeling,' Viv shrugged. 'I've got a nose for that sort of thing.'

Beth looked at her. She did seem to have a very knowing air about her. And from what she had told Beth and Winnie the previous night, she wasn't lacking in experience where men were concerned.

'Well, I think it's nonsense,' Camilla declared. 'Miss Cheetham is far too professional.'

'Suit yourself,' Viv said. 'But you see if I ain't right. Like I said, I've got a nose for that sort of thing.'

Given what Viv had said, they were all intrigued to get back to the classroom that afternoon to get a better look at Mr Allenby.

'Good afternoon,' he greeted them as he entered the room, a stack of books under his arm. He was a tall, heavy-set man of around forty, with short sandy hair and a face that looked as if it had been carved out of granite. 'For our first anatomy lecture we are going to cover the osseous system, which is the basic framework of the body. And for that, I'll need the assistance of my colleague Algernon . . .'

He indicated the skeleton dangling limply to his right. A few of the girls giggled dutifully, but Mr Allenby did not crack a smile.

'As you'll notice, the framework of the body is made up of bone. But what is bone, and how does it form?'

Pencils started scratching all around the room as the girls frantically began to take notes. Beth took notes too, but it was a struggle to keep up with Mr Allenby as he talked about cells and blood vessels, mineral matter, collagen and calcium. He described the anatomy of the bone, how it was made up of a hard outer compact tissue, with spongy tissue inside, and how red and white blood cells were manufactured in the central core of bone marrow.

Beth scribbled frantically, but the words seemed to lose any meaning for her as fast as she wrote them down.

She wondered if Viv was right about him and Miss Cheetham. They would make a good couple, she thought, with her made of steel and him made of stone. Even his deep, slow voice sounded like honey poured over gravel.

She studied his craggy profile. His face was interesting rather than handsome, with his long, slightly hooked nose, the surprisingly sensual curve of his mouth, and green eyes fringed by golden lashes.

Without thinking, Beth began to sketch it, committing his features to paper, her pencil taking on a life of its own. As she drew, the world slowed down around her, becoming a frozen tableau in front of her eyes. The girls stopped scribbling, their pencils still poised, and Mr Allenby stood rigid in mid-sentence, his finger pointing towards the skeleton. The only movement was the figure that passed swiftly across the back of the dais, there one minute and then gone the next.

Alison . . .

And then, as quickly as everything stopped, it started up again, like a movie coming back to life. But the picture had changed, as if Beth had somehow jolted forwards in time.

'Is everything all right?' Mr Allenby stood right in front of her, staring down at her with a frown of concern.

'Yes, sir.' Beth looked around at the concerned faces that surrounded her.

So it had happened again. Another lapse, an absence. A moment when the world froze in front of her eyes, just for a few seconds.

She'd had them since she was a child. But they had been happening more and more since Alison died.

'You dropped your pencil. We thought you'd fallen asleep.'

He bent to pick up the pencil for her. As he placed it on her desk, his gaze fell on the drawing Beth had done in the margin of her notes.

His brows lowered and Beth froze, fearing his reaction. But he simply murmured, 'It's a good likeness, Miss Bradshaw.'

Their eyes met for a moment and he gave her the smallest of smiles before he moved back to the dais to continue his lecture. All around her Beth heard the other girls tittering, and did not dare to look up or meet anyone's eye for the rest of the lecture.

Chapter Twenty-One

February 1957

Preliminary Training School
Week 3

> *Dear Walter*
>
> *Thank you for your letter. Sorry I haven't replied sooner, but I've been so busy, I've hardly had a minute to myself this past fortnight.*
>
> *I hope you haven't managed to blow yourself up since I last heard from you? Honestly, who in their right mind would give you a gun? At least we don't have those here, which is just as well because I can think of a few people I'd happily shoot. Including a certain room-mate of mine . . .*

Winnie looked up from her writing to glare across at the empty bed on the other side of the room. Needless to say, Viv was out on the town again. It was the third time that week, and she was never back before lights out. Winnie had grown used to waking up to the sound of her room-mate stumbling about in the darkness.

Beth was sitting up in her own bed, her textbooks and notes spread out on the quilt. She was the complete opposite of Viv; every night straight after supper she would retreat to their room to study. Much good it did the poor girl.

Winnie sighed and went back to her writing.

Can you believe, nearly three weeks have gone by and I'm still here? Talk about a miracle! I don't think Mum's recovered from the shock yet. Although knowing her, I daresay she's thinking there's still plenty of time for me to blot my copybook.

I expect our training must seem a bit tame compared to yours. I mean, learning to wash out a bedpan hardly compares to learning how to chuck a grenade, does it? Although you'd never believe how complicated nursing is. Not just all the chemistry and the anatomy and that sort of stuff, although that's hard enough to take in. No, it's the ordinary things, like mopping a floor or dusting a cupboard. I thought I knew how to clean, but there's so much to the simplest task here. Everything takes such a lot of explaining.

I don't want to sound big-headed, but Miss James reckons I'm the best bed maker in the set. She said my corners were the neatest she had ever seen. I reckon it was all those years spent watching Mum do it!

Have you heard from Mum? I'm sure she must have sent you endless food parcels by now. You know how she worries that you're not eating enough.

I've been home a couple of times. I'm lucky we live so close by – a lot of the other girls haven't managed to see their families at all, although we're all getting this weekend off, so many of them are going home then. But I think every

time I walk through the door, Mum expects to see me with
my suitcase in my hand!

Winnie felt a twinge of sadness as she wrote the words. Part of her had hoped that nursing might have brought them closer. But if anything it had driven them even further apart. Dora barely showed any interest in her training.

What are the other boys like at your camp? We're all still getting on well in my set, bar the odd one or two. We all spend most of our evenings together in the common room, listening to music or playing cards or just chatting. We've been out a couple of times to the local café, but since we're not allowed out past 10 o'clock while we're in PTS, there's hardly any point in going up west. Unless your name happens to be Viv Trent, and then the rules don't apply, apparently . . .

'What are the three types of membrane that line the cavities and the hollow organs?' Beth interrupted her thoughts. 'I can't seem to find them in my notes.'

'Serous membrane, mucous membrane and synovial membrane,' Winnie replied without hesitation.

Beth looked at her admiringly. 'How do you remember all these names so easily?'

'I dunno,' Winnie shrugged. 'They just seem to go into my head and stay there.'

'I wish they stayed in mine,' Beth sighed. She looked so forlorn, Winnie felt sorry for her.

139

'You'll get there in the end, I'm sure,' she said, turning back to her letter.

But no sooner had she put pen to paper than the Home Sister's cheery Scottish voice rang out from the landing below.

'Lights out in five minutes, girls!'

Miss Coulter wants us all tucked up in our beds, so I'll finish now. But I've still got so much to tell you about, including our fascinating day out at the sewage works! Yes, I know what you're thinking. But apparently knowing all about where clean water comes from is a vital part of being a nurse. The same with the milk processing plant. Honestly, what I don't know about the pasteurisation process really isn't even worth knowing!

Anyway, write back when you can and let me know all your news. I hope they're feeding you properly? Although if you're anything like you are at home, I expect the cooks are working overtime just to keep up with you!

Seriously, Wal, I hope you're doing all right? You will tell me if you aren't, won't you? I think about you all the time and wonder how you're getting on, even if I don't write that often. Look after yourself, won't you? And try not to shoot anyone!

Love,

Your Sister, Win x

'Lights out, girls. Sleep well,' the Home Sister's voice sang out again. Winnie quickly set aside her pen and paper, switched off her bedside lamp and slid down under the covers. Beth set aside her books and did the same.

They lay in the darkness, listening to Miss Coulter's footsteps crossing the landing below them.

'I wonder what time she'll roll in tonight?' Winnie said into the darkness.

Beth sighed. 'God knows.'

'She must have the luck of the devil not to have been caught yet. If it had been you or me sneaking out every night, I'll bet we would have been sent to Matron by now.'

'Hmm.' Beth sounded as if she was already half asleep. But when Winnie turned over, she could hear her roommate softly whispering to herself, over and over,

'Serous membrane, mucous membrane and synovial membrane. Serous, mucous, synovial. Serous—'

The knock on the door made them both sit bolt upright.

'Yes?' Winnie's voice sounded loud in the darkness.

'It's Miss Coulter. May I come in?'

Before Winnie could reply, the door opened and the Home Sister stood there, her bulky body silhouetted against the light from the hall below.

'Where is Trent?' she demanded.

Winnie's heart raced in her chest. 'I – I don't . . .'

'I'm here, Sister.'

As Winnie grasped for words, Viv suddenly appeared in the doorway behind Miss Coulter, wrapped in a dressing gown.

The Home Sister swung round to face her. 'Where have you been?' she demanded.

'Just brushing my teeth, Sister. Why? Was there something you wanted?' Viv asked sweetly.

Miss Coulter looked her up and down, seemingly lost for words.

'Hurry up,' she snapped finally. 'You should have been in bed five minutes ago.'

'Yes, Sister. Sorry, Sister.' Viv smiled back at her, as if butter wouldn't melt.

It wasn't until the door had closed and they had heard the Home Sister's creaking tread going back down the stairs that Viv collapsed on her bed laughing.

'Blimey, that was close!' she giggled. 'Did you see her face? She really thought she'd caught me out that time!'

'How did you manage it?' Beth's voice came out of the darkness.

'I left my dressing gown hidden in the airing cupboard. Then I sneaked into the bathroom and put it on over my clothes, see?' She switched on the light and then pulled off her dressing gown to reveal a bold red dress underneath. 'Mind, I've had to hide my stilettos in the bathroom cupboard. I hope no one finds them before the morning!'

Seeing her laughing made Winnie's temper rise. 'Never mind that!' she turned on Viv. 'You do realise you could have got Beth and me in trouble?'

'Yes, but I didn't, did I?' Viv sat down on the edge of her bed and started peeling off her stockings.

'That ain't the point. The point is you're being selfish.'

'Oh, keep your barnet on,' Viv snapped back. 'It was only a bit of fun. You should try it sometime,' she added, stifling a yawn with the back of her hand.

'We're not all here for a laugh!'

'You're telling me,' Viv muttered, collapsing back on her bed.

'If you don't start sticking to the rules, I'm going to ask the Home Sister if she can move you to another room,' Winnie said. 'I don't see why we should have to put up with – are you listening to me?'

'I think she's asleep,' Beth whispered.

Winnie glared at Viv as she lay on her back snoring softly, still in her dress with a stocking draped from one hand.

With any luck she would be out on her ear before long, and good riddance to her.

Chapter Twenty-Two

Her mother was not at home when Beth returned to their house in Kensington for her weekend visit.

'I expect her rehearsals went on longer than she expected,' Grace said. 'You know what actors are like. And the director is working them all very hard. She didn't come home until nearly midnight last week.'

'Are you sure she isn't just avoiding me?' Beth helped herself to a morsel of cheese from the piece Grace was grating.

'No! How could you think that? She's so looking forward to seeing you.'

She kept her head down as she said it. Beth knew Grace didn't believe the words coming out of her mouth any more than she did.

She went to pick up another piece of cheese, but Grace slapped her hand away. 'There won't be any left for lunch,' she said.

'Why are you making it, anyway?' It was unusual to find Grace in the kitchen.

'It's Mrs Parry's day off, so you've got the pleasure of my cooking.'

'God help us,' Beth muttered.

'Do you mind? It just so happens I learned Cordon Bleu cookery at school.'

Beth wasn't surprised. There was very little Grace Wooley couldn't do. She was thirty-two years old, elegant and efficient, with a lively, attractive face and a swathe of brown hair. Her father was a diplomat and she had spent most of the war at a finishing school in Switzerland, before giving it all up to join the Wrens when she was eighteen. She had been engaged twice, was fluent in five languages, and she had been working as Celia Wells's assistant for the past ten years.

Although 'assistant' was hardly the right word for her. She did everything for the family, from running the house to organising her mother's diary. She had also taken care of Beth and her sister since they were children. She was like a mother, a big sister and a confidante all rolled into one.

'So what are we having?' Beth asked.

'Cauliflower cheese.'

Beth laughed. 'You're putting Escoffier to shame!'

'I'll have you know *chou-fleur au gratin* is a great delicacy in the dining rooms of Paris.'

Beth smiled. Grace was always so funny, she was guaranteed to cheer her up, even on her darkest days.

'Come on, then,' Grace urged her as she rinsed the cauliflower under the tap. 'Tell me what you've been up to these past three weeks. I want to know everything!'

'Well . . .' Beth hesitated. She had always confided in Grace, and she desperately needed someone to talk to about everything that was going on.

She was feeling utterly drained. The first three weeks of training had been exhausting for her. There had been so much to learn, so much to take in.

She had never imagined it would be so difficult. She just couldn't seem to grasp things the way everyone else did. Even Viv, who had no interest in nursing, seemed to be managing better than her.

But she knew Grace already had doubts about her decision to become a nurse, so she did not want to speak up.

Instead she said,

'It's hard work, but it's so much fun, honestly.'

'And what about your room-mates?'

'Oh, they're lovely. But they argue constantly, unfortunately. Viv's very untidy and always breaking the rules, and it drives Winnie to distraction.'

'I'm sure it does. We had a girl like that in the Wrens. The rest of us were always getting into trouble over her slovenliness. It only takes one bad apple to ruin the whole barrel.'

'Viv's not a bad apple,' Beth defended her. 'She just doesn't take it very seriously, that's all. She's rather fun, actually.'

'Well, I hope you're not having too much fun?' Grace regarded her severely. 'I've noticed those shadows under your eyes. You'd better not be burning the candle at both ends, young lady?'

If only you knew, Beth thought. Most of the time she was poring over her textbooks into the early hours, trying to keep up.

Moppet, their cat, strutted into the kitchen. Beth called out to her but she took one look and turned away.

'Take no notice of her,' Grace said. 'She's so aloof.'

'She was always more Alison's cat than mine.' Beth watched as Moppet headed for the windowsill with a disdainful swish of her tail, dismissing her for the disappointment that she was.

'She misses her,' Grace said quietly.

So do I, Beth thought.

Alison would not be struggling with her nursing studies, she was sure of that. She would never fall behind, or break thermometers. She would know how to execute a perfect hospital corner or name the various parts of the digestive system, because that sort of thing came so easily to her.

She had only been training at the Nightingale for six months before she died. But she was already top of her class. Unlike Beth, who struggled at the bottom.

'What about your training?' Grace interrupted her thoughts. 'What have you learned?'

Beth thought about it for a moment. 'I can apply a divergent figure of eight bandage,' she said at last. 'At least I think I can,' she added uncertainly. The last time she'd tried it hadn't exactly been a triumph.

'Really?' Grace looked up from the pan she was stirring. 'And why would anyone need one of those?'

'You use it to bind a flexing joint, like an elbow or knee.'

Grace put down her spoon and turned off the gas. 'Go on, then,' she said.

'What?'

'Show me how it's done.'

'But I'm not very good—'

'You just said you knew how to do it?'

'Yes, but—'

But Grace was already sitting down at the kitchen table, her arm held out expectantly.

'Now, shall I moan and groan in pain, to make it a bit more authentic?' she asked.

'Definitely not. You'll put me off.'

'You're probably right. I'd best leave the acting to your mother.'

Beth looked around the room, trying to think. 'I need a dressing . . .'

'There are bandages in the first aid box. On top of the dresser?' Grace nodded towards it. 'I'd fetch it myself, but I have a sprained elbow,' she said, her expression piteous.

Beth shook her head as she went to fetch the box. 'This is silly,' she complained.

'Nonsense, it's good practice for you.'

Beth fetched the bandage and tried to remember everything she had been taught in class.

Start with an oblique turn below the joint, then take a turn round the joint so that the point lies in the middle of the bandage . . .

'It's not easy, is it?' Grace said, as Beth fumbled the bandage for the third time.

'No,' Beth muttered. She could feel her face flaming with embarrassment.

'I daresay this is a lot easier on a dummy?'

'Not really. I pulled its arm off last week.'

They caught each other's eye and they both burst out laughing. It was hard to see the funny side at the nursing school with Miss Cheetham breathing down her neck, but now Beth could see how absurd it all was.

'Goodness, what's going on here?'

Her mother stood in the doorway. Beth immediately stopped laughing, but Grace carried on chuckling to herself.

'Beth has been practising her dressings,' she explained, holding up her arm with the tangle of bandages hanging from it.

'I see. It all looks very – instructive.' Even from across the room, Beth could see the forced edge to her mother's smile.

It was the radiant smile that lit up billboards and had made her famous. Celia Wells may have lost some of her starlet prettiness, but even in her forties she was still a bewitching beauty, with soft waves of platinum blonde hair framing her perfect oval face and luminous green eyes. Beauty magazines devoted pages and pages advising women how to achieve her flawless skin, exquisite cheekbones and enviable slender curves.

'Darling!' Celia turned to her daughter and held out her arms. 'Welcome home. We've missed you so much, haven't we, Grace? The house hasn't seemed the same without you.'

'I've missed you too, Mother.' Beth went dutifully to hug her, and was enveloped in a wafting cloud of Chanel.

'Let me look at you.' Celia held her at arm's length. 'You're looking very well.'

Am I? Beth shot Grace a sideways glance. If the housekeeper had noticed the hollows in her cheeks and the shadows under her eyes, then why couldn't her mother see them?

Perhaps it was because Celia Wells only ever saw what she wanted to see.

'I must finish getting lunch ready,' Grace got to her feet, disentangling herself from the bandages.

'I'll help—' Beth offered, but the housekeeper shook her head.

'Go and be with your mother,' she said. 'It's why you came home, isn't it?' she added in a low voice.

Was it? Beth always told herself she missed her mother. But when they were together, it only brought it home to her how very distant they were.

They went into the sitting room, which overlooked the sunny garden.

'I'm sorry I wasn't here when you arrived,' her mother apologised as she led the way into the room. 'Rehearsals were an utter nightmare.'

'Grace said you'd been working very hard,' Beth said.

'Oh darling, I can't tell you!' her mother raised her eyes heavenwards. 'It's a shambles. Johnny can barely remember his lines, the director is on the verge of a nervous breakdown, and we open on Tuesday.' She gave a delicate little shudder. 'I'm honestly beginning to wonder why I ever thought it was a good idea to go back to the stage. Thank God it's only a short run.'

She beamed at Beth. 'Listen to me, talking about myself! What about you? How is your training going? Are you having fun?'

She leaned forward, eager to listen, her face bright. Anyone watching her would have sworn she was interested.

'I'm having a wonderful time.' Her mother wasn't the only one who could put on an act.

'How marvellous. Tell me all about it.'

Beth gave her the same carefully edited version she had given Grace. She told her about the other girls in her set, and how much she was learning, and how fascinating it all was.

But she knew it didn't really matter what she said,

because her mother was not listening to her. She gazed towards the French windows, her thoughts elsewhere.

Beth knew exactly where her mind had drifted.

'I keep thinking about how much Alison used to enjoy it,' she said, and had the perverse pleasure of seeing her mother wince at the name.

'Yes,' she said faintly.

'I feel so much closer to her now I'm there,' Beth went on. 'When I'm in the classroom, listening to a lecture, or just walking around the hospital. Sometimes it almost feels as if she's with me . . .'

She didn't tell her mother how often she thought she had seen Alison's face at a window, or glimpsed her in the crowded dining room. Was that part of grief? She would have liked to ask her mother, but Celia could barely bring herself to talk about Alison. The pain of her loss was like a huge gulf between them.

Celia opened her mouth, and for a moment Beth thought she might be about to say something about Alison. But the next moment her brilliant smile was back in place.

'I've brought you a gift,' she said.

She hurried to fetch a carefully wrapped small package from the bureau drawer and handed it to her.

'What is it?' Beth asked.

'Open it and see!'

She could sense her mother's excitement as she carefully untied the ribbon. Inside was a small blue velvet box containing a silver locket engraved with a delicate filigree.

'Isn't it just perfect?' Her mother breathed. 'I saw it and thought of you straight away.'

'It's beautiful.'

How very like her, Beth thought. Her mother was for-ever trying to buy her way out of difficult situations. Beth would never forget the sad face of the pony her mother had presented her with days after Alison's funeral. The poor, forlorn little creature had remained alone and unloved until her mother finally gave up and had it sold.

Beth opened the locket, but it was empty inside.

'I didn't put a photograph inside, because I wasn't sure what you'd like,' her mother said. 'I thought it might be a nice little keepsake—'

Of what? Beth wanted to ask. *Of how little you actually care about me?*

'We're not allowed to wear jewellery at the hospital,' she said bluntly.

'Well, perhaps you could just keep it with you?'

'I'd better not.' Beth put the box down on the small table between them. 'It's so valuable, I wouldn't want it to get lost or stolen.'

'Oh.' Her mother looked crestfallen. But before she could speak, Grace's voice drifted up from the kitchen, summoning them to lunch.

The rest of the visit was very strained, and it was almost a relief when Grace drove her back to the Nightingale.

'She was only trying to be kind,' Grace said, when Beth told her about the locket.

'By giving me a trinket?'

'It's just the way she shows her love . . .'

'She could just try talking to me!' Pent-up emotion made Beth snap.

152

'What have you been doing all afternoon?'

'Making polite conversation, like strangers. It's what we always do these days.'

Grace looked sideways at her. 'You could try talking to her. It takes two, you know.'

'What's the point? She'd never listen. She can hardly bring herself to look at me.'

'That's not true. She loves you.'

'She pretends to love me. She's playing a part, saying all the right lines and hitting her marks just like a good actress should. But she's never shown me any real love or affection, not since Alison died.'

'She's still grieving,' Grace said. 'She lost her daughter—'

'But I'm still here!' Beth cried, bitterness choking her. 'I need her, but she's just cut herself off from me. Sometimes I think—'

'What?'

'That she wishes it was me who'd died instead of Alison.'

'No!' Grace stared at her. 'You mustn't say that. You mustn't ever even think that.'

'But it's true. Alison was always her favourite. And if it wasn't for me, she wouldn't even be dead.'

'Beth, stop! It was an accident, that's all. Your mother doesn't blame you for what happened.'

Beth fell silent, her eyes fixed on the road ahead. Perhaps Grace was right, she thought. Perhaps her mother didn't blame her. But perhaps she didn't need to, because Beth blamed herself enough.

Chapter Twenty-Three

Granny Trent lived in the middle of a tumbledown terrace in Clapton with an outside privy and cracks in the walls where a doodlebug had fallen at the far end of the street twelve years earlier. The corporation had declared it structurally unsound and offered to rehouse her, but Granny Trent was too stubborn to move anywhere decent.

'I was born in this house and I'll die in it too,' she always said.

'We could all die in it if that roof caves in,' Viv would always reply.

Viv returned home just before lunch on Saturday morning to find her grandmother sitting at the kitchen table, soaking her feet in a bowl of steaming water and Epsom salts. *Music While You Work* was blaring out from the wireless on the sideboard.

'Oh, it's you,' Granny Trent greeted her unenthusiastically. 'I was beginning to think you'd forgotten where you lived.'

'How could I ever forget this palace?' Viv muttered, looking around her.

'It's been nearly three weeks since I've seen you. They must have been keeping you busy at that hospital?'

Viv turned away from her grandmother's keen gaze. 'Yes, well, you were the one who wanted me to go.'

'At least it's keeping you out of trouble.'

Viv ignored the twinge of guilt she felt. She looked down at her grandmother's bare, gnarled feet splashing in the water. 'I'm glad to see some things never change,' she commented dryly.

'I'm entitled to give my feet a rest. I've been cleaning offices since five o'clock this morning.' Granny Trent took her feet out of the water and carefully placed them on the towel she had laid out beside the bowl. 'Well, don't just stand there,' she said. 'Make yourself useful and put the kettle on.'

Viv went to fill the kettle at the sink while her grandmother dried her feet and then bent down stiffly to roll on her wrinkled stockings.

'Are you sure you weren't just making yourself beautiful for your fancy man?' Viv teased, her voice rising over the sound of the running water.

'Fancy man, indeed!' her grandmother tutted. 'I leave all that nonsense to you and your mother. Talking of which, a letter arrived for you.'

She nodded to the mantelpiece, where a red and blue airmail envelope was wedged behind the clock.

Viv plucked the flimsy envelope from the mantelpiece. She immediately recognised the flowery handwriting. 'When did this come?'

'A couple of days ago.' Granny Trent groaned as she bent to pull on her battered old slippers.

'I gave Mum my address at the nurses' home.'

'You know your mother. She never listens to anything unless it's about herself.'

Viv sat down at the kitchen table and tore open the envelope.

'I s'pose I'd better finish making that tea, since you've got better things to do now,' her grandmother said sourly.

Viv ignored her. She turned down the volume on the wireless and started to read the letter.

'Well?' Granny Trent asked as she filled the teapot. 'What does she have to say for herself this time?'

'Shh, I'm still trying to read it.' Viv skimmed through the contents. 'She sends her love,' she said.

'Does she now? There's a first time for everything, I suppose,' Granny Trent sniffed. 'Anything else?'

'She says it's snowing in Idaho.' Viv went through the letter, picking out bits she considered suitable for her grandmother's ears. 'She and Harold have both had colds.'

'Is that it?'

'That's it.'

Before she knew what was happening, her grandmother had swiped the letter out of her hands.

'Give that back!' Viv protested, but Granny Trent was already reading it out loud.

'I hope the old cow is treating you all right,' she quoted. 'Oh yes, that sounds very loving, don't it?'

'I didn't want you to read it,' Viv muttered.

'Oh, I ain't bothered,' Granny Trent said. 'It's nothing I ain't heard from her a hundred times.' She looked back at the letter in her hands. 'But if she's that worried I'm ill-treating you, how come she don't come home and make sure you're all right?'

'It's difficult for her, you know that,' Viv said. 'She can't afford to come all this way. And Harold doesn't like her to be away from him and little Bradley . . .'

'But it's all right for her to be away from her daughter?'

Viv was silent. Granny Trent was just trying to provoke her, and she refused to rise to it.

Her grandmother wanted her to hate her mother as much as she did. God knows, she had tried hard enough to poison her mind against her. But Viv had long since stopped being angry with Pauline Trent.

It hadn't been easy at first, but as she grew older she had understood it all better. Her mother had no choice. She had fallen in love and married a GI, but the US army rules would not allow her to bring Viv with her when she emigrated to America in 1946.

And so she had done the only sensible thing, and left her seven-year-old daughter with her grandmother.

'Just give me a few weeks to get settled,' she had said. 'And then I'll send for you, and we'll all be together.'

And yes, it had hurt when those weeks turned into months and then years. And it had hurt even more when Viv discovered that her mother had given birth to a son with her new husband.

Viv could not help feeling a twinge of resentment when she saw photographs of Pauline with her new family, posing outside their large, beautiful house. Especially when she was stuck with Granny Trent, eking out their coal and sticking cardboard over the cracked windows to keep out the draughts.

And God knows Granny Trent did her best to fan the flames of her resentment. She never stopped reminding Viv how her mother had abandoned her, left her behind without a second thought.

But Viv knew it wasn't her mother's fault. As Pauline had explained, it was Granny Trent she had been running from, not Viv.

And after living with her grandmother for so many years, Viv understood why, too.

They sipped their tea in silence. The only sound was the creaking of her grandmother's chair and the ponderous tick of the clock on the mantelpiece.

'Well?' Viv said. 'Ain't you even going to ask me how I'm getting on?'

'You're still there, so that must count for something.'

'Yeah, well, it won't be long before I end up out on my ear, I reckon.'

'More fool you if you do. And don't think you're coming back here, either,' her grandmother said. 'You know where I stand, my girl. There's no place for you under this roof if you walk out.'

'I didn't say I was going to walk out, did I?'

'Get yourself sacked, then. I know your little tricks,' Granny Trent wagged a bony finger at her. 'Your mother was just the same. Always worming her way round things, trying to find an easy way out. But I was always wise to her. And I'm wise to you, too. I might be old, but I ain't daft.'

'I never said you were.'

'No, but you think it. You've been given a good chance to make something of your life, and if you've got any sense you'll take it. Stop wasting your time and buckle down. You'll thank me for it later on.'

'Yeah, yeah, I've heard it all before,' Viv said. Honestly, was it any surprise her mother had fled the country, after putting up with Granny Trent's nagging for so many years?

It was almost a relief to be at the nurses' home. True, there were a lot of rules. But Viv didn't follow them anyway, so they didn't matter too much to her. And there were warm rooms and indoor toilets and a bathtub you didn't have to fill with boiling kettles, so it wasn't all bad.

'Go on, then,' Granny Trent said. 'Tell me how you're getting on.'

'It's all right, I s'pose,' Viv shrugged.

'Made any friends?'

'Hardly!' her lip curled. 'They ain't my type.'

'You mean they don't go round fighting and robbing and causing trouble?'

Viv ignored her and drank her tea. Her eyes strayed to the clock. She had promised she would meet her friends at six, and it was gone five now.

'Have you learned anything?' her grandmother wanted to know.

'This and that.' Viv didn't want to admit how much she had taken to the training. Not so much the lectures, which reminded her too much of school. But she quite enjoyed the practical side of things. The days certainly passed a lot quicker than they had when she was on the production line at Clarnico's.

But that didn't mean she wanted to stay. Far from it. She was keen to be back with her friends, and with Roy. Especially when she couldn't stop worrying what he was up to while she wasn't around.

But at least she had stopped pining and counting the days until she could escape, which was something.

'Well, I'm glad you're settling in all right,' Granny Trent said. She leaned forward to set down her cup and let out a hiss of pain.

'What's up with you?' Viv asked.

'Just a bit of muscle strain. I told you, I've been on my feet since five this morning.'

'You shouldn't work so hard.'

'Oh, and how else am I going to pay the rent and keep a roof over my head?'

'I used to help you until you made me give up a perfectly good job,' Viv reminded her.

'Yes, well, I'm sure you can keep me in fine style when you're one of them ward sisters, or whatever they call them . . .' Granny Trent winced again.

'Are you sure you're all right?' Viv said.

'Of course I'm all right. I just told you, didn't I?'

'Is there anything I can do?'

'What's this?' Her grandmother's eyes glinted. 'You've been at that hospital three weeks and you already reckon you're Florence Nightingale?'

'I was thinking of taking you to see a doctor.'

'I don't need a doctor, thank you very much. Now stop making such a fuss.'

Her grandmother was never one for a fuss. Viv still vaguely remembered when the doodlebug landed at the end of the street on a wet June night in 1944, taking their back door and half their scullery with it. She recalled how Granny Trent had dug them both out of the rubble, left

Viv with a neighbour in the next street and then gone off to do her office cleaning job with her hair and skin caked in dust.

'What are you smiling about?' her grandmother's sharp tone quickly brought Viv back to reality.

Granny Trent might be a hero in her own way, but Viv could never let herself forget that she was also the woman who had not wanted her to be born. Viv's mother had told her how Granny Trent had tried to talk her into having a back-street abortion. Then, when Pauline refused, she had packed her off to an unmarried mothers' home, with strict instructions never to return with her baby.

'But as soon as I held you in my arms, I knew I could never give you up,' Pauline had told Viv. 'So I took you home with me and fought to keep you, even though she threatened to throw us both out on the streets. Honest to God, that woman's a wicked old cow.'

It was knowing that Granny Trent resented her very existence that fuelled the fire of Viv's dislike whenever she felt herself softening towards her grandmother.

Viv left her grandmother sipping her tea and went up to her bedroom to change her clothes. When she returned, Granny Trent was peeling potatoes at the sink.

She looked Viv up and down, taking in her dress and high heels. 'And where are you off to?' she asked.

'I said I'd meet Bobby and some of the others at the Savoy Café.'

'But you've only just got back.'

'I know, but it's my only day off and I want to make the most of it.'

Her grandmother's toothless mouth tightened. 'I suppose he'll be there?' she said.

'If you mean Roy, then I hope so.'

'You know what I think about him, Vivien.'

'Yes, Gran.' Viv leaned in to the mirror over the mantelpiece and teased a curl with her finger.

'But I suppose there's no point in trying to warn you, is there?' Granny Trent sighed. 'What time will you be home?'

'I don't know. But don't bother to wait up, anyway.'

'You mean you won't be home for your tea? Vivien Trent, I'm talking to—'

But Viv had already slipped out of the back door.

Lil Trent stood at the window and watched her granddaughter skipping out of the back gate. She looked as if she couldn't wait to get away.

Just like her mother, Lil thought bitterly.

She looked down at the half-peeled potato in her hand. She had been down to the market on her way back from work that morning and bought some lamb chops specially because she knew they were Viv's favourite. Now she felt utterly foolish for caring so much. She should have known better.

But she had tried so hard to make it different this time. She had no intention of allowing Viv to go off the rails and become wayward like her mother.

She dropped the potato back into the sink and dried her hands on her apron. As she turned away, she noticed her daughter's letter on the kitchen table. Full of nonsense as usual, she thought. Empty words and empty promises, that was all that ever came out of Pauline's mouth.

She might be her own flesh and blood, but Lil could have cheerfully strangled her daughter for some of the things she'd done. All those times she had let poor little Viv down, it just wasn't fair.

And yet the girl went on trusting her and believing in her. It hurt Lil to see how eagerly she had fallen on that letter, as if it was the only thing in the world that mattered to her.

She would have liked to put her right on a few things, but she did not want to break the girl's heart any more.

Besides, Viv would never believe her. Pauline had poisoned her mind so much, she held nothing but resentment in her heart for her grandmother now.

But that wouldn't stop her trying. Lil set the letter back down on the table. She might have made some terrible mistakes with her daughter, but she would not make them with Viv.

She would see her granddaughter have a better life if it was the last thing she did.

Chapter Twenty-Four

February 1957

The first thing Helen heard as she entered the Female Surgical ward was the sound of a woman crying.

Miss Warren, the ward sister, seemed very distracted when she met her at the doors, as well she might. Like every other sister, she liked to present a well-ordered ward when Matron did her rounds, and someone having hysterics did not give the right impression.

But she did her best to ignore it as she greeted Helen, her voice almost lost under the sound of the woman's wailing.

'Who's that?' Helen asked.

'Jarvis, bed three. Wertheim's hysterectomy.' Miss Warren was not a woman to waste words. She spoke in short, terse sentences, as if she was quoting from a telegram. 'Sorry,' she added. 'Can't shut her up.'

Helen looked down the ward at the curtains drawn around the bed at the far end. The howls sounded like a wounded animal's.

'Is she in pain?'

'No more than expected.'

'When did she have the operation?'

'Yesterday.'

'And she's been crying ever since?'

'Yes.' The ward sister looked faintly disgusted.

'How old is she?'

'Twenty-five.'

'Married?' Miss Warren nodded. 'Any children?'

'No.' Miss Warren winced as the howling grew louder. She turned to the staff nurse standing behind her and said, 'Do something, Nurse. Can't hear myself think.'

'I'll go and see her,' Helen said.

The ward sister looked put out. 'Can't understand it,' she muttered. 'Doesn't know how lucky she is.'

'A radical hysterectomy at twenty-five years old? I daresay lucky is the last thing she's feeling at the moment,' Helen murmured.

Mrs Jarvis was lying on her back, sobbing. Her face was so swollen and red from crying, her features looked as if they were melting. Her sheets were pulled back to reveal the dressing on her lower abdomen, laced with various drainage tubes.

'Hello, Mrs Jarvis.' Helen took the notes from the hook where they hung at the foot of the bed and consulted them briefly. 'How are you feeling today?'

'How do you think?'

The woman's eyes followed Helen balefully as she sat down at the side of the bed.

'I think I'd be counting myself very fortunate, after what you've been through,' Helen said calmly. 'The cancer was quite advanced. You were very lucky the surgeon was able to save you.'

'Yes, well, I wish he hadn't bothered.' The young woman's voice was thick with tears. 'I'd rather be dead than the way I am now.'

'Please, Mrs Jarvis, you mustn't think like that. You've got your whole life ahead of you . . .' Helen went to reach for her hand, but Mrs Jarvis snatched it away.

'And what good is that?' She turned wretched eyes to meet Helen's. 'All I ever wanted was to be a mum, and you've taken that away from me. What reason have I got to live?'

'You've got your husband, and your family—'

'For how long? Barry wanted kids even more than me. We've only been married six months. How long do you think he's going to stick with me when he finds out I can't give him what he wants?'

Her words stung in a way Helen did not expect, like salt touching a hidden wound.

'If he loves you he'll understand, surely?' Even as she said them, she realised how hollow her words sounded.

The woman gave a bitter laugh. 'You've got no idea, have you? What would you know about it? You can't understand how I feel!'

She subsided into sobbing again, her body convulsing, as if her grief was coming from somewhere deep within her. Helen did her best to comfort her, but it was like trying to stem an all-engulfing tide. In the end she left the poor woman still sobbing and slipped away.

She was surprised to see her brother William on the other side of the curtains.

'I heard you talking to her and I didn't like to interrupt,' he said. 'How is she?'

'Devastated,' Helen replied. 'Much as you might expect when your whole life has been shattered.'

'I had to do it,' William looked distraught. 'I had no choice. The disease had already taken hold—'

'I know.' She laid her hand on his arm. 'Hopefully she'll calm down soon. But she needs time to come to terms with everything.'

'Time heals all wounds, eh?'

Not all of them, Helen thought. She knew deep down Elaine Jarvis would never come to terms with her loss. Her external scars might heal, but the ones she carried inside her never would.

Time would never heal, but it might dull the pain and grief she was feeling.

'I heard what you told her, about her husband loving her even if she couldn't have children. That was good advice,' he said.

Helen slid her gaze away so she wouldn't have to meet his eye. She knew what he was trying to say to her, but she would not listen.

'I only said it to make her feel better,' she said dismissively. 'I don't know what the future holds for them. For all I know she could be right. He might abandon her.'

'If she doesn't leave him first?'

She sent him a sharp look.

'I'd best get on with my rounds,' she said.

She went to move past him, but he reached out and way-laid her. 'Helen—'

'Miss Warren is waiting for me.' She gently but firmly disentangled herself and walked away.

Chapter Twenty-Five

Preliminary Training School
Week 5

'Now, who would like to tell me the five main functions of the liver?'

Mr Allenby looked around the classroom. Beth kept her head down, her gaze fixed on her scrawled notes, and prayed that he would not pick her.

'Anyone? Miss Bradshaw?'

Beth's heart sank. She took a deep breath and searched her brain for the information.

'Um . . . the manufacture of bile?' she ventured.

'Very good. And what does bile do?'

'It helps in the digestion of . . .' she glanced down at her notes, desperately trying to find the answer scribbled somewhere. 'The digestion of . . .'

'Fats,' Winnie whispered beside her.

'Fats,' Beth repeated.

'Very good, Miss Bradshaw. Now, I wonder if you can tell me the four other functions, preferably without Miss Riley's help?'

Blushing furiously, Beth managed to drag the removal of urea and the storage of glucose from her memory, but she could not for the life of her remember in what form it was stored.

She stumbled and mumbled through several awkward seconds before finally Mr Allenby took pity on her.

'Can anyone help Miss Bradshaw?' he asked, looking up and down the rows. Naturally, Camilla's hand shot up so fast she nearly lifted out of her seat.

'Miss Simpson?'

'Glycogen, sir.'

Glycogen. Of course. Beth cursed herself silently. Why hadn't she remembered that word? She'd only revised it the previous night.

'Very good. Now perhaps you'd like to tell us the other functions of the liver?'

Camilla smirked, as if she would like nothing better.

'It makes some of the protective substances that the blood carries to fight bacteria. And it produces heparin, which prevents blood from clotting inside the body,' she said, with a quick smug look at Beth.

'Quite right, Miss Simpson. A very concise and accurate answer, as always.'

Beth risked a glance up and caught Viv's eye across the classroom. The sympathetic smile she sent her made her feel even more mortified.

She could hardly wait for the lecture to end. But as they all filed out of the classroom, Mr Allenby said,

'Miss Bradshaw, can I speak to you for a moment?'

Beth sat back down in her place until all the other girls had left. As soon as the door had closed, she blurted out,

'I'm sorry, sir. I did study it last night, but—'

'Calm down, my dear, I'm not going to reprimand you.' Mr Allenby held up his hand to silence her. He moved to sit on the bench beside her. 'But I have noticed you're struggling with a number of subjects?'

Colour flooded her face. 'I – I . . .'

'Don't look so worried, I'm not going to report you to Matron.' He smiled. 'I'd like to help you, that's all.'

'Help me?'

'Would you be interested in some private tuition? I thought perhaps we could meet here on a Saturday afternoon, and I could help you with any subjects you might be struggling with? Of course, I know that Saturday afternoons are supposed to be your free time, so you're not under any obligation to—'

'I'd love to,' Beth said. 'If you're sure you wouldn't mind?'

'Of course not,' Mr Allenby smiled. 'That's what I'm here for, to get you all through PTS, by hook or by crook!'

'Thank you, sir.' Beth stared at him, overwhelmed. It was like the answer to a prayer.

Mr Allenby waved away her thanks. 'Not at all. As I said, it's my job.' He looked at her. 'You could be a very able student, Miss Bradshaw, if you had a bit more confidence in yourself.'

Chapter Twenty-Six

'Here you go, Mrs Jones. All nice and clean for you. I'll bet that feels better, don't it?'

Mrs Jones stared back at Viv, not a hint of appreciation in her glassy eyes. But Viv carried on undaunted.

'Now, let's turn you over and have a look at your back. That's it, gently does it . . .' She rolled the dummy carefully over on to her side. 'Ooh, that looks a bit red. Does it hurt, love? Let's get some methylated spirit on it, shall we? We don't want any nasty pressure sores, do we?'

Listen to me, chatting to a dummy! Viv thought as she applied the spirit in the sweeping circular movements that Miss James had demonstrated. But it helped pass the time.

'Right, you're all done. Let's see if we can find a nice clean nightie for you to wear . . .'

Bobby would probably die laughing if she could see her now, with her sleeves rolled up and a cap on her head, wrestling a dummy into a nightgown. But strangely, Mrs Jones had taken on a life of her own. Viv could almost imagine her as a helpless old dear with heart trouble.

She was so absorbed in her task she forgot anyone was watching her until she heard Miss James say,

'Very good, Trent.'

She looked round to see a ring of faces staring back at her.

'It's always nice to chat to the patient and let them know what you're doing,' Miss James went on. 'It's usually only something that comes with experience, so well done.'

'Ta, miss – I mean, Sister.'

Viv blinked at Miss James, caught off guard by the unexpected praise.

She was a decent sort, she thought. Better than Miss Cheetham, at any rate. At least Miss James tried to find a good word to say to everyone, no matter how hopeless they were.

Although looking at her now, Viv longed to get her hands on her and do something about those owlish specs of hers, maybe get rid of those monstrous brows, too. She was only about thirty but she looked twice her age. A perm and a bit of make-up would soon sort her out . . .

'The rest of you would do well to follow Trent's example,' the Junior Tutor told the rest of the group. 'You could learn a lot from her.'

From me? Viv could scarcely believe her ears. She was usually held up as a bad example, certainly never a good one.

She looked round at the other girls. They were all smiling, looking so pleased for her – except for that little cat Camilla, of course – who never liked being outshone. Just for a fleeting moment, Viv felt like one of them, like she really belonged . . .

She pushed the idea away. Those sorts of thoughts had been creeping in far too much lately, and she couldn't allow them.

It was Saturday, which meant they had a free afternoon. As they all made their way to the dining room, Viv could hear the other girls whispering among themselves.

'Making plans for this afternoon?' she teased them. 'What's it going to be today, girls? More studying? Or don't tell me you've found another jigsaw to do?'

'Actually, we're going to a matinee at the pictures,' Peggy said to her. 'They're showing the new Paul Newman film at the Regal.'

'I love Paul Newman,' Phil sighed. 'Those blue eyes . . .'

'You can come with us, if you like?' Bernie offered.

For a moment, Viv was almost tempted. She loved Paul Newman too, and she rarely got to watch a movie all the way through. Whenever Roy took her to the pictures, he was always more interested in wrestling in the back row than watching the screen. But before she could reply, Winnie said,

'No point in asking her. She's bound to have other plans.'

Viv glared at her room-mate. 'As a matter of fact, I have,' she said.

'Seeing your boyfriend again?'

There was something about the way she said it that got Viv's back up.

'At least I've got a boyfriend,' she snapped back.

'And I s'pose you're going to roll in at midnight at usual?'

'Depends if I'm having a good time, don't it? You never know, it might be even later.'

Winnie scowled. 'As long as you don't expect me to cover for you.'

'As if I'd ever expect you to do me any favours!'

'Then let's keep it that way, shall we?'

'Fine by me,' Viv said, and walked off before Winnie could have the last word.

Chapter Twenty-Seven

At first Beth thought Mr Allenby must have forgotten about their lesson. The classroom was in darkness when she crept in, her books tucked under her arm. It was a dull, rainy afternoon, and no light came through the windows.

She was about to turn and leave when a voice said,

'I wasn't sure you'd come.'

Beth turned round. Mr Allenby was sitting at the far end of the row, on one of the benches, smoking a cigarette.

'Why not?' she asked, genuinely puzzled.

'I overheard your friends discussing a trip to the cinema this morning. I thought you might prefer to go with them.'

'I promised I'd be here.' Beth set her books down on the nearest desk. 'I'd never let you down, especially as you've been kind enough to offer to help me.'

'I'm glad.' Mr Allenby stubbed out his cigarette and stood up, uncurling his tall, burly body from behind the desk. In his shirt and corduroy trousers, he seemed less intimidating than when he stood on the dais in his white coat.

'Shall we get started?' He switched on the lights, then put down his papers and sat down at the desk beside her. Her dismay must have shown on her face because he said,

'I didn't think there was any point in standing up in front of you. But if that's what you'd prefer . . . ?'

'No, no,' Beth replied quickly, feeling foolish. 'Please, sit wherever you like.' She shuffled along to make room for him.

'Thank you.' He settled himself next to her and set out his papers and books. 'Is there anything you'd particularly like to study?' he asked.

'Whatever you like. I'm awful at everything!' Beth replied ruefully.

It was meant to be a joke, but Mr Allenby's eyes were serious as he turned to look at her. His eyes were not quite grey and not quite green, she noticed.

'If I'm going to help you, I want you to stop saying those things about yourself,' he said. 'You're a lot brighter than you give yourself credit for, Beth.'

'I don't know about that . . .' Beth felt herself blushing.

'Then I'll prove it to you. And don't look so worried,' he said. 'It's just you and me here, and I want to help you.' He consulted his notes. 'Now, if you've no objections, I suggest we tackle the digestive system first . . .'

Mr Allenby was kindness itself as he patiently explained the various organs, and how they all worked together. Beth was almost mesmerised, listening to his deep voice. But for once, his words seemed to sink in.

Finally, after an hour, he said, 'Right, I think that's enough for today. We don't want to overload you, do we?'

'Yes. I mean, no.' Beth blinked at him. She had been transfixed, staring at his profile and wondering if she could commit it to paper later. At least she hadn't sketched it on her notes this time! 'Thank you for your time, sir. It's been a great help.'

'I'd be very happy to continue, if you'd like?'

Beth stared at him, unable to believe her luck. 'Would you? Oh yes, please. That would be wonderful.'

'Good. Now before we go, do you have any more questions for me?'

'How did you become a nurse?' Beth blurted out without thinking.

Mr Allenby smiled, his green-grey eyes crinkling. 'I mean about the digestive system.'

'Oh! Oh, I'm sorry.' Beth was mortified.

'It's quite all right. I'm flattered that you'd be interested. If you want to know, I was with the Royal Army Medical Corps in the war. When it all ended I decided I didn't want to go back to my old profession, so I finished my formal nursing training and here I am.'

'And what were you doing before?' Beth asked.

He sent her a sideways look. 'Would you believe, I was an apprentice undertaker.'

'An undertaker?'

'Ironic, isn't it? I suppose you could say I'm trying to do myself out of business now!' He turned to her. 'What about you? What made you want to become a nurse?'

A picture of Alison immediately came into Beth's mind, but she stayed silent. This was her moment, and for once she didn't want to share it with her sister.

'My father was a doctor,' she said.

'Was?'

'He was killed during the war. A bomb hit the field hospital where he was working.'

'I'm sorry.' Mr Allenby looked grave. 'You must have been a baby then?'

'I never knew him.'

'So it's just you and your mother?'

Once again, a picture of Alison came into her mind. 'Yes,' she said.

'And you decided to become a nurse because of your father?'

Beth hesitated for a moment. 'That's not the only reason—' she started to say, but then she was interrupted by a voice from behind her.

'What's going on here?'

They looked round to where Miss Cheetham stood in the doorway. She was staring at them, steely-eyed.

'I was passing by and I thought I saw a light on.' She looked from one to the other. 'Well? Would someone like to explain what you're doing here?'

Beth was too stricken to speak, but Mr Allenby said calmly, 'I'm helping Miss Bradshaw with some extra tuition.'

'Extra tuition?' Miss Cheetham's eyes narrowed.

'Mr Allenby saw I was struggling, so he offered to help,' Beth found her voice at last. 'He's been very kind,' she added.

'I'm sure he has.' Miss Cheetham shot him a glance. 'Well, class is over for today,' she said briskly. 'And there will be no more private lessons. Is that understood?'

'Yes, Sister.'

Beth looked at Mr Allenby. His face was impassive, but a muscle flickered in his jaw.

'Now, go back to the nurses' home,' Miss Cheetham dismissed her.

Beth could hear their raised voices before the door was even closed.

'What were you thinking?' Miss Cheetham was shrieking. 'You know very well that students are not allowed to be alone with a man. Do you realise the kind of trouble you could have been in if Matron had found out?'

'I was only trying to help the girl, Chris . . .'

And then the door slammed shut behind her, and Beth did not hear any more.

'He offered you private lessons?' Winnie asked.

The other girls had returned home from the cinema in the middle of the evening. The matinee had finished at teatime, but they had gone off to a café to get something to eat afterwards.

As soon as she saw Beth, Winnie had noticed that she seemed very agitated. But it wasn't until they were getting ready for bed that she heard the full story. It was the first she'd heard of Mr Allenby's offer.

'He was just being nice,' Beth said. 'He was trying to help me, because he could see I was struggling.'

'What did Miss Cheetham say to him?'

'She dismissed me, so I didn't get a chance to find out. But I heard her shouting at him as I walked away. Poor Mr Allenby, what if I've got him into trouble?'

'You did nothing wrong. He was the one who broke the rules, not you.'

'But it's all my fault. If only I wasn't so stupid . . .' She bit her lip. 'I wonder if I should go to Matron and explain . . .'

'No,' Winnie said quickly. 'Definitely not. Just stay out of it, that's my advice.' She looked at Beth's troubled face. 'Just go to bed and try to forget about it,' she said. 'I'm sure it will have all blown over by the morning.'

'I hope you're right. I'd hate to think of him getting the sack because of me. Especially when he's been so nice.'

Winnie sent her a searching look. Poor Beth looked genuinely upset.

'You like him, don't you?' she said.

'Of course I like him. He's been so kind to me.'

'I don't mean that way.'

Beth stared at her for a moment, then a blush flooded her face. 'Of course not! He's a teacher, I don't think of him in that way.'

But Winnie was still left wondering as they settled down to sleep. She could tell from her room-mate's steady breathing in the darkness that she was not sleeping. Winnie hoped she wasn't worrying too much about Mr Allenby. She certainly hoped she wouldn't do anything rash like going to Matron. In her experience, it was never wise to speak up . . .

Anyway, for once it wasn't her problem, she told herself as she snuggled deeper under her quilt, drowsiness already claiming her.

It didn't feel as if she had been asleep for more than five minutes when a booming voice snapped her awake.

'Get up!'

Winnie opened her eyes to see Miss Beck standing over her bed. Beth was already sitting up, rubbing her eyes.

Winnie's heart shot into her mouth, certain there must be a fire or something. 'What is it?' she said, throwing back the bedclothes. 'What's wrong?'

'Don't try to come the innocent with me!' Miss Beck glared at her. 'Tell me the truth, girl. Where is Trent?'

Chapter Twenty-Eight

It was nearly midnight when Viv crept up the drive towards the nurses' home, cursing the soft crunch of gravel under her feet. As well as making too much noise, it played hell with her stilettos.

She was in a foul mood. She had been so excited to spend the day with Roy, but it had all gone wrong.

First of all, he'd stood her up. Viv had waited ages for him to meet her at the Savoy Café as they'd arranged, but he didn't come. Finally, she had tracked him down to the backstreet garage where he worked as a mechanic. He was in the workshop with his mates, laughing and joking together as they tinkered with his motorbike.

'Oh, hello. I forgot you were coming,' he had greeted her coolly, much to the amusement of his sniggering friends.

Viv had been mortified, but she forced herself to hide her feelings behind a bright smile.

'Well, I'm here now,' she had announced. 'So where are you taking me?'

'Nowhere. I'm working on my bike.'

'Can't you do it some other time?'

'I want to do it now.' Roy had glared at her, his teeth gritted.

'You can hang about with us if you want?' his best friend

Pete had offered quickly. 'We wouldn't mind, would we, boys? Give us something nice to look at anyway, instead of your boyfriend's ugly mug!'

The others had all leered appreciatively. All except Roy, who had glowered at Viv and then gone back to his work without speaking.

She'd had nothing better to do, so she spent the afternoon hanging around the workshop, making cups of tea for the boys and listening to their juvenile jokes.

Once upon a time she would have laughed along with them, but she suddenly seemed to find their talk cruel and pathetic.

She even started to wish she'd gone to the pictures with the others. They might have had a laugh. And even if they didn't, an afternoon in a warm cinema, eating chocolate and ogling Paul Newman, would have been better than hanging around a cold and dirty workshop.

It was gone seven o'clock before the bike was repaired and Roy's friends finally left and she had him to herself.

'Now can we go dancing?' she pleaded.

''Course we can, sweetheart. Anything you like.' Roy smiled lazily as he pulled her into his arms. 'But we've got plenty of time, ain't we?'

Viv recognised the gleam in his eyes and her heart sank. 'Do we have to?' she sighed. 'You'll mess my hair up.'

'Never mind your hair . . .'

Roy had guided her backwards, pushing her until she felt the edge of the heavy wooden workbench pressing into her back.

'Careful,' Viv had said. 'You'll get my skirt all filthy.'

'Better take it off, then.'

'Roy, no.'

His eyes grew cold and narrow. 'What's wrong with you?'

'Nothing, I just don't feel like it, that's all. Can't we do something else?'

'Like what?' There was a nasty edge to his voice.

'I dunno. Talk, or something?'

'Talk?' his lip curled. 'What do I want to waste time talking to you for? Especially when we could be having a bit of fun . . .'

Viv had not protested any more. She hadn't wanted to put Roy in a bad mood. And besides, she knew from past experience that he would get what he wanted in the end. Even if he had to get rough with her to get it.

And so she had submitted to him, squeezing her eyes closed as the hard, oil-stained brick floor scraped her back and the cold air goose-pimpled her bare thighs above her stocking tops.

He loves me, she told herself over and over again. *That's why he wants me so much.* And she had to give in to him, had to be the girl he wanted her to be, if she wanted him to go on loving her.

At least he'd taken her dancing afterwards, which was something. But all the fun had gone out of the evening by then. And even though she had stayed out late, Viv found herself looking forward to getting back to the sanctuary of the nurses' home.

She pulled off her shoes, hitched up her skirt and

clambered in through the kitchen window. She had noticed the latch was broken on her first day, and no one had got around to fixing it yet, thank goodness.

'Ow!' She cursed as she felt her stocking snag on a nail. That was the third pair she'd ruined climbing in and out of this window. She would have to find a new way of sneaking in soon, it was costing her too much money.

She squeezed through the window and on to the draining board, then slithered to the ground. But no sooner had her stockinged feet touched the cold linoleum floor than she heard a sound in the darkness and realised she wasn't alone.

She stiffened, listening. Then, just as she was daring to breathe again, a voice said,

'Well, well, here she is at last.'

Suddenly the light flicked on and there was Miss Beck, arms folded across her chest, eyes full of fury.

'There you are, Trent,' she said, tight-lipped. 'We've been waiting for you . . .'

Chapter Twenty-Nine

They all stood together in Matron's office on the Monday morning.

Viv stared straight ahead, but she could feel Beth and Winnie on either side of her. She couldn't bring herself to look at either of them, especially not Winnie. But she could almost feel the waves of animosity coming off her.

This is it, she thought. After four weeks of trying, she was finally going to be dismissed.

But now it came down to it, she was shocked at how much she didn't want it to happen.

'Well,' Matron said, her gaze moving between them, one by one. 'What do you have to say for yourselves?'

Viv took a deep breath. 'Please, Matron, it was nothing to do with Winnie and Beth,' she said.

'They should have reported you if you hadn't returned by ten o'clock. For your own safety, if nothing else. Anything could have happened to you.'

'They knew I'd be all right. I always—' She realised what she'd said and pressed her lips together.

Matron's brows rose. 'So it's happened before?'

Beside her, Winnie gave a heavy sigh.

'I'm the one who should be punished, not them,' Viv insisted.

'Thank you for your advice, Miss Trent. But I'll decide who gets punished, not you. You've already overstepped the mark, so please don't do it again.'

Once again, her dark gaze went from one to the other. The silence stretched, becoming unbearable.

Viv's palms began to sweat, and she rubbed them surreptitiously on the folds of her uniform. Why was she so worried? This was what she wanted, after all.

'Riley and Bradshaw,' Matron spoke at last. 'Miss Beck has told me she is satisfied you were not entirely complicit in this scheme. As Trent has pointed out,' she flicked Viv a quick glance, 'I can hardly hold you responsible for your room-mate's antics. However,' she went on, 'if it happens again you are to inform me at once. Is that clear?'

'Yes, Matron,' they both murmured, and Viv caught the dirty sideways look Winnie gave her.

'And as for you, Trent,' Matron looked at her. 'Under normal circumstances, I would have suspended you from training. But I fear that you might never return, and that would be a loss for everyone concerned. Miss James speaks very highly of you, and tells me you have great potential. I would hate to see that go to waste. But the fact remains that you broke the rules, and you must be punished for it. So for the next two weeks, you will spend every evening assisting Miss Beck in the Infirmary.'

'No!' Viv gasped. But Matron did not seem to hear her as she continued,

'Not only will the experience prove instructional, but

hopefully it will also keep you out of trouble. And during that time you will also sleep in the ground-floor room beside Miss Coulter's, so she can keep a close eye on you.'

Winnie shifted beside her. Viv did not have to look to know she was trying not to smile at that.

'I'll have Miss Coulter prepare your room, and you can move your belongings straight after this afternoon's lectures. Then, after supper, you should report to the Infirmary.'

'Yes, Matron.'

They went back to their room in silence. Viv felt the weight of Winnie's disapproval on her shoulders as they climbed the stairs. She knew she needed to apologise, but she couldn't find the words.

Besides, she was too preoccupied with Roy to think about anyone else. What was going to happen when she wasn't there to keep an eye on him?

'Shall I help you pack up your things?' Beth asked.

'Let her do it herself,' Winnie snapped, before Viv could reply. 'It will do her good to tidy up after herself for once!'

Viv looked around at her belongings scattered around the room. She'd never noticed before but they did seem to be everywhere.

'Look, I'm sorry, all right?' she blurted out. 'I didn't mean to get you two involved.'

'Yes, but you did, didn't you?' Winnie clapped back. 'We might have been dismissed.'

'It wouldn't have come to that. Matron knew you weren't really to blame—'

'You really think you know it all, don't you? You were even trying to tell Matron what was what.'

'I was trying to get you two out of trouble!'

'We don't need your help! We just need you to leave us alone.'

'Yes, well, I'm going, ain't I?' Viv mumbled.

'You're only moving downstairs. You could have been out on your ear. I bet you're disappointed you ain't, eh?'

Viv was silent. She truly didn't know what to think.

Matron's words kept going around in her head. *You have great potential.* No one had ever praised her like that before. Certainly none of the teachers at school had ever had time for her. And even her own grandmother constantly told her she would never amount to anything.

'You've never taken it seriously, have you?' Winnie was still going on at her. 'This is all a big game to you. But some of us want to be here. Some of us want to learn, and you're just getting in everyone's way!'

'Winnie—' Beth started to say, but Viv cut her off.

'Yes, well, you won't have to put up with me for much longer, will you?' she snapped.

'Thank God! Maybe now we can actually enjoy our time here, without worrying about what you're doing and whether we'll get into trouble for it!'

'I won't be sorry to see the back of you, either! You're about as much fun as a bad case of tonsillitis!'

She stormed off, slamming the door behind her. As she headed down the stairs, Viv heard Beth saying,

'You didn't have to be so hard on her, you know.'

'She deserved it,' she heard Winnie mutter.

'I feel sorry for her.'

'Why? If you ask me she got off lightly. She should have

been dismissed. But I daresay it won't be long before that happens,' Winnie went on. 'You mark my words. It won't be long before she gets too cocky again. And then she really will be out on her ear. And good riddance, too!'

Chapter Thirty

'No, no, no, Bradshaw. It's supposed to be a single mastoid dressing, not an Easter bonnet!'

Winnie paused, still holding the end of the bandage she was wrapping around Maya's head, and looked across the practice room to where Beth stood helplessly.

'I – I'm sorry, Miss Cheetham,' she stammered.

'You've made the first fixing turn far too tight. It needs to be firm, but not so much that it cuts off the blood supply. And then you bring it round here, beneath the occiput, and up over the ear – you see?'

'Yes, Miss Cheetham.'

'Girls, look at this.' The Sister Tutor turned and addressed the rest of the room. 'As usual, Bradshaw has given us a very good example of how *not* to apply a dressing.'

Camilla tittered at the joke. Everyone else stared in sympathy at Beth, who had turned bright red.

'Poor thing,' Maya whispered. 'She looks as if she might cry.'

Don't, Winnie willed her silently. *Don't give that cow the satisfaction.*

She had met bullies like Christina Cheetham before, and she knew how much they thrived on seeing their victims crumble.

Thankfully, the Sister Tutor moved on, and everyone let out a sigh of relief.

Beth started to unwind the dressing from Lou's head, a sadly resigned expression on her face. She looked utterly defeated. She tried again, but she still didn't seem to be getting it right.

'Look at her,' Camilla said from the seat beside her. 'She's utterly hopeless. That dressing will fall off within five minutes – ow!' she yelped in protest.

'Oh, sorry,' Viv said. 'Did I do it too tight? Don't want it to fall off within five minutes, do we?'

Winnie caught her reflection in the mirror. Viv wore a butter wouldn't melt expression, but the glint in her eye told a different story.

Winnie went back to her bandaging, trying not to smile. She still hadn't forgiven Viv for getting them into so much trouble that morning.

'Now, what's going on here?' Miss Cheetham came over to examine their handiwork. 'Acceptable, I suppose.' She turned Maya's head this way and that. 'And you too, Trent,' she looked over at Viv and Camilla. 'Quite satisfactory.'

'Don't go overboard, will you?' Viv muttered, as the Sister Tutor strutted away. Once again, Winnie found it hard not to smile. She dearly wanted to be angry with Viv, but she couldn't seem to keep it up for long.

When they'd all finished their dressings, it was time to swap round.

'Not you, Bradshaw,' Miss Cheetham called out, as Beth took her place in the chair. 'You'll have to do it again since you made such a mess of it last time.'

Once again, Winnie saw the girl's face redden.

'She's just picking on her now,' Viv muttered, taking her seat. 'And you make sure you're careful,' she warned Camilla. 'If you mess up my hair I'll have something to say about it.'

Winnie looked around the classroom. The Irish girls were in fits of giggles, as usual. But all Miss Cheetham's attention was focused on Beth. She stood over her, criticising every move she made. The poor girl's hands were shaking so much she could scarcely hold the bandage, let alone apply it to Lou's head.

'Look at her,' Camilla sneered. 'Utterly hopeless.'

'Leave her alone,' Winnie snapped. 'It's bad enough that Miss Cheetham keeps picking on her, without you joining in.'

'We're supposed to be helping each other,' Camilla said loftily.

'There's a difference between helping her and making her feel like a fool.'

'But she *is* a fool,' Camilla said, loud enough for Beth to hear.

'And you're a cow,' Viv muttered. Winnie was about to nod in agreement when she remembered they weren't speaking to each other.

After the class, they headed off to lunch in the dining room. Beth trailed along by herself at the back of the group, looking thoroughly downcast.

'I don't know why she was picking on you like that,' Phil said. 'You were no worse than anyone else in the class. Bernie made a real mess of her dressing and Miss Cheetham didn't say a word.'

'Thanks a lot!' Bernie retorted.

'She's just trying to show us the right way of doing things,' Camilla said. 'It's hardly her fault if *she* can't do it, is it?' She sent Beth a scathing glance over her shoulder.

'I know why she's picking on her,' Viv muttered, so only Winnie could hear.

Winnie glared at her. 'And why's that, then?'

'She's jealous.'

'Jealous?'

'I told you, she's got a thing going with Mr Allenby. She probably still hasn't forgiven him for giving Beth those private lessons.'

'Rubbish,' Winnie dismissed.

'Suit yourself,' Viv shrugged. 'But you see if I ain't right.'

She sauntered off. Winnie watched her sashaying ahead, her hips swaying. How anyone could look manage to sexy in their dowdy uniform was beyond her.

She fell back in the group until Beth caught up with her.

'Don't look so glum,' she said. 'You know, you will get the hang of it in the end.'

'I hope so.' Beth smiled, but she didn't look too sure.

''Course you will. You just need a bit more practice.' Winnie thought about it for a moment. 'Tell you what, why don't we have a go tonight? We could borrow some dressings from the Infirmary and I could help you.'

'Are you sure? I'd be really grateful.'

'It's no trouble,' she said. 'I could so with some extra practice myself.'

'But you're so good at everything.'

'I dunno about that . . .' Winnie felt herself blushing. 'Anyway, I'd like to help you.'

'Thank you, I'd really appreciate it.' Beth sighed. 'Honestly, I really think I must be getting worse, not better. I know Miss Cheetham always picks on me, but she's never usually this bad!'

She's jealous. You see if I ain't right.

Winnie thought about Viv's words, but she did not reply.

Chapter Thirty-One

After the gruelling morning of Clinical Practice she'd had, Beth wasn't looking forward to that afternoon's lectures.

And another reason she wasn't looking forward to them was the thought of having to face Mr Allenby again.

She hadn't seen him since two days earlier, when Miss Cheetham had found them together on that Saturday afternoon. Beth still felt hot with mortification when she thought about the scene. Even though she knew it wasn't her fault, she hated the idea that he had got into trouble trying to help her.

Mr Allenby was standing on the dais when they walked in. Beth didn't meet his eye as she took her seat at the back of the classroom, next to Winnie. She kept her head down during the class, scratching away furiously at her notes, and prayed that he would not call on her. But for once Mr Allenby barely looked her way.

It wasn't until the afternoon's lecture ended and they were leaving the classroom that he called her name.

'Stay behind for a moment, Miss Bradshaw,' he said.

Beth glanced at Winnie and saw her shake her head slightly. But how could she refuse? Beth stopped by the door and dutifully waited until everyone had gone.

She would have stayed by the door, but Mr Allenby gestured her towards him.

'Don't worry, I won't bite,' he said. His kind smile crinkled his eyes. 'I just wanted to apologise for what happened on Saturday. Miss Cheetham should not have acted as she did. I'm your tutor and I was only helping you. You do understand that, don't you?'

Beth nodded mutely.

'But I could see how worried you looked when you came into the classroom this afternoon, and I'd hate you to feel you'd done anything wrong. I don't like to think of you being upset, Beth.'

'Thank you.'

He hesitated for a moment, then he said, 'Well, I suppose this is the end of our private lessons?'

'Yes, sir.'

'It's a shame, I must say. I meant what I said, Miss Bradshaw. You could be a very able student if you had more confidence in yourself.'

That's not what Miss Cheetham says. Beth thought of the Sister Tutor picking on her in the classroom. It was hard to have confidence in the face of such scalding ridicule.

'Are you all right, my dear?' Mr Allenby was looking at her in concern. 'Is there something you want to tell me?'

Beth opened her mouth then closed it again. She'd already put the poor man in a difficult position once; she didn't want to cause an even bigger rift between him and Miss Cheetham.

'No, sir,' she said quietly.

'Are you quite sure?' His hands rested on her shoulders, his eyes searching hers. His touch was so firm, so reassuring, Beth almost wanted to throw herself into his arms. She could trust him, she was sure of it.

'Yes, sir.' She glanced uneasily over her shoulder, terrified Miss Cheetham might appear again at any moment and catch them. 'May I go, sir?'

'Of course.' He released her, his arms dropping to his sides. 'Go and join your friends. I'm sure they'll be wondering where you are.'

No sooner had she turned to leave than he called after her, 'Beth?'

She turned. 'Yes, sir?'

'I understand how hard all this is for you. If you ever need someone to talk to, I'm always here. You know that, don't you?'

'Yes, sir. Thank you, sir.'

'I feel wretched about it,' Beth told Winnie when they were back in their room after supper that evening. 'He was being so nice, and I just turned him down flat.'

'You did the right thing,' Winnie told her.

'Did I? It doesn't feel like it. I feel as if I've let him down.'

'Look, we've already had one telling-off from Matron. You don't need another. Anyway, let's get on with practising this capeline dressing, shall we?' Winnie went on. 'I've been down to the Infirmary and borrowed a double-headed roller bandage so we don't have to pin anything.' She held it up for Beth to see.

'Did you see Viv while you were down there?' Beth asked.

'I did. Miss Beck had her scrubbing the bathrooms. And thoroughly miserable she looked about it, too!' Winnie laughed.

'Poor Viv,' Beth sighed, looking around. 'The room seems very quiet without her, doesn't it?'

'It's a lot tidier, that's for sure,' Winnie said sourly.

She was right, Beth thought. But she missed Viv's belongings strewn all over the place and her make-up littering the bedside table. She even missed the dirty coffee cups she sometimes left under her bed.

They made a start on the dressing. Winnie sat down in the chair while Beth stood behind her. She checked the middle of her forehead and started the bandage just above her eyebrows. She carefully unfolded both bandages at once, taking them around the head just above the ears. But as she came to cross them at the nape of the neck, her hands crossed and she lost her grip.

'Are you sure you've got the vertical bandage in your right hand and the horizontal one in your left?' Winnie asked.

'No, I haven't.' Beth felt instantly miserable. How could she have made such a simple mistake?

'Try again,' Winnie encouraged.

And so she did. But with each attempt, she only seemed to get worse. The more she tried, the more she ended up all fingers and thumbs.

'It's no good,' Beth sighed wretchedly, after the bandages had got horribly twisted for the fourth time.

'Try again,' Winnie said.

'What's the point? I'm not improving. I'm getting worse, if anything. I'm wasting my time and yours.'

'I ain't got anything better to do, have you?'

Beth thought of her sketchbook under the bed. She had

lasted two weeks before she had taken it out of her suitcase and started filling its pages. Landscapes, portraits, close studies of leaves, and flowers, and faces. Beth drew anything that came into her mind.

And Alison. Always Alison.

It was like an addiction to her. The more she told herself she shouldn't, the more Beth craved to feel her pencil flowing across the blank page.

It was the only thing that made her feel good. While her days were filled with mishaps, badly made beds and broken thermometers, and her evenings were spent staring at the pages of her textbooks and trying to cram facts into her unwilling brain, Beth knew that once the lights were out she could sketch by torchlight and know this was a world in which she felt safe. Within the pages of her sketchbook, she knew what she was doing.

'Beth?'

She looked up sharply to see Winnie staring at her in the mirror.

'Are you all right? You were miles away.'

'I'm fine.'

Beth gathered her scattered thoughts and started again on the dressing, forcing her brain to go through the motions.

Apply the centre of the bandage to the middle of the forehead just above the level of the eyebrows. Unfold both bandages simultaneously, carrying them round the head at low level but above the ears, until they reach the nape of the neck. Cross the ends.

Carry the vertical bandage forwards over the head to the middle of the forehead and lock it by bringing the horizontal bandage around to the front . . .

Beth's palms started to sweat.

'Go on,' Winnie urged. 'You're doing really well.'

Continue by passing the vertical bandage backwards and forwards, each time a little to the left and right alternately, leaving a third of the previous turn uncovered. Complete by passing the horizontal bandage twice around the head and end in the front . . .

'You did it!' Winnie cried. Beth looked in the mirror. The capeline dressing wasn't perfect, but at least it was recognisable. And it hadn't unravelled in her hands, either.

'So I did,' she murmured, scarcely able to believe her eyes.

And then she caught a flash of movement in the mirror behind her. A fleeting glimpse of a fair-haired girl, staring at her from the doorway, a look of resentment on her face . . .

'Beth?'

Winnie's voice brought her back to the present. 'I'm sorry,' Beth said. 'What were you saying?'

'I said you should take a picture, show it to Miss Cheetham. She won't believe you did it.'

'No.' She looked back in the mirror, but the girl had gone.

'Are you all right? You look like you've seen a ghost,' Winnie said.

'I did,' Beth murmured.

'What?' Winnie twisted in her seat to stare at her.

Beth froze. The words had come out before she'd had time to think about them.

She looked at Winnie. She was so kind, and Beth had come to trust her. But did she dare share the burden of what had happened two years earlier, or would Winnie turn away from her like her own mother had?

Chapter Thirty-Two

'I saw my sister,' she said.

Winnie felt a shiver run through her, but she tried not to let it show. 'Your sister?' she repeated quietly.

'She was standing over there, by the doorway. She's gone now,' she added, as Winnie glanced over her shoulder. 'She never stays for long.'

'You've seen her before?'

'Oh yes, I see her quite often.' Beth spoke matter-of-factly. 'Usually in lectures, or the practice room. She watches me.'

Winnie was silent for a moment, trying to take it in.

'I suppose you think I'm strange?' Beth sent her a guarded look.

'No, not at all. My Nanna Winnie used to see ghosts all the time. She said they were very comforting.' Although she still wasn't sure she would like to see one for herself.

'I don't think Alison wants to comfort me,' Beth said quietly. 'I think she resents me being here.'

'Why?'

'Because she knows she should be here, not me.'

Winnie frowned. 'But surely she'd be proud of you for what you're doing? You're training to be a nurse in her memory, aren't you?'

'You don't understand. I'm the reason my sister isn't here.'

'How do you work that out?'

'Because I killed her.'

Winnie was very shocked, but she forced herself to stay calm. 'What happened?' she asked.

Beth was silent for a long time as she started to unwind the bandage from Winnie's head. And then, after a while, her story began to unwind with it.

'We were renting a cottage in Cornwall,' she said. 'Mother had just finished shooting a film in Hollywood. She'd been away for ages, and so she decided to take Alison and me away on holiday.

'The cottage was right by the sea and there was a little boat in the shed. I so wanted to try it out. I kept nagging Alison to come with me, but she always said no.' Beth's hands were working mindlessly, unwinding the dressing, as if they'd taken on a life of their own. 'But on this particular day I decided I was going to take the boat out to visit a cove down the coast. Of course, Alison said no. She said the tide was too strong, she didn't want to risk it. We argued about it for a long time, and in the end I told her if she didn't come with me I was going to take the boat out by myself—'

'And so she came with you?' Winnie guessed.

Beth nodded. 'She had no choice. She couldn't let me go alone, she knew Mother would never allow it.' She spoke in a flat, mechanical voice. 'I was supposed to be rowing, but we were still arguing. The sea was rougher than it looked, and almost immediately Alison wanted to turn back. But I refused. I knew if we went back I'd never get her to come out with me again. I should have turned back,' she said quietly.

'It was only a small boat, and even I was a bit frightened when we started rocking about. But I didn't want to admit I was wrong.'

She wound the dressing around her hands, over and over again, as if she wasn't even aware of what she was doing.

'I don't know what happened next.' She looked confused, remembering. 'I can't have been paying attention. But then I heard Alison shouting at me, and when I turned to look at her all I saw was this huge wave, coming towards us. The next minute the boat had turned over and we were both in the water.'

Winnie held her breath, waiting.

'I'm not a strong swimmer, and the tide started pulling me under, away from the boat,' Beth went on. 'Alison had to swim out to reach me and pull me back. We managed to get the boat the right way up and she helped me back in. I thought Alison would get in after me. But when I looked round there was no sign of her. She'd just disappeared under the waves . . .'

Winnie stared at her. Beth's face was a mask of misery, her eyes wide and lost.

'I'm sorry,' Winnie whispered. The words hardly seemed enough, but she didn't know what else to say. She couldn't imagine what it must be like to lose someone so close to you.

A sudden, horrible vision of Walter on a foreign battlefield came into her mind, and she pushed it away, shutting her mind to it.

'I didn't want to go home without her,' Beth's voice sounded quiet and faraway. 'I couldn't. I stayed in that boat, drifting further and further out to sea, just staring at the water and calling out her name. I kept thinking any minute she'd suddenly come spluttering to the surface . . . I was still looking when a fishing boat found me and brought me home. They found Alison's body two days later, when the tide brought it in to a cove down the shoreline.'

'Thank God you were safe, at least.'

She knew straight away it was the wrong thing to say. Beth sent her a strange, cold look.

'Don't you understand?' she said. 'My sister is dead because of me. It should be me who drowned, not her. She never wanted to go out on that wretched boat in the first place.'

'You can't think like that—'

'Can't I? It's what everyone thinks. My own mother—' she stopped, her voice choking on the words.

'What?'

'Nothing. It doesn't matter.' Beth looked away from her. 'Anyway, that's why I decided to be a nurse. If Alison couldn't do it, then I thought I'd do it for her.'

Winnie looked at the dressing, wound tightly around Beth's hands.

'Even if your heart's not in it?' she said.

'That doesn't matter,' Beth said. 'Whatever I have to give up for Alison, it can't compare with what she gave up for me.'

The poor girl looked so wretched, Winnie could only imagine how heavily guilt must weigh on her.

'Surely she wouldn't have wanted you to be unhappy?' she ventured.

'Why shouldn't I be unhappy?' Beth turned on her, anger flaring in her eyes. 'I don't deserve to be here, living this life. It's my sister's life. I know it and Alison knows it, too. That's why she's here, watching me. She wants me to know she hasn't forgotten. She wants me to know that it should be her here, and that I should be the one who's dead!'

Beth's words were still on Winnie's mind later as she got ready for bed.

She felt desperately sorry for her. The poor girl was clearly finding it all a terrible strain, and nothing came naturally to her.

Winnie looked across at Beth. She was sitting up in bed, frowning over her textbooks as usual. Perhaps she needed to suffer to assuage her terrible guilt?

'Lights out, girls.'

Miss Coulter's voice rang out from the landing downstairs. Winnie switched off her light, wished Beth goodnight and they both settled down for the night.

'You won't tell anyone, will you?' Beth's voice came out of the darkness.

'Of course not,' Winnie replied. 'It'll be our secret.'

'Thank you.'

Winnie lay awake, staring at the ceiling, kept awake by thoughts of Beth. After a few minutes she heard the other girl's bedclothes rustle as she fumbled about in the dark under her bed.

Winnie knew exactly what Beth was looking for. She had often watched her illuminated by dim torchlight, with her sketchbook on her knees, her hand flying across the paper with a certainty she never seemed to show in class. She had never disturbed her because it was the only time she ever saw her truly happy.

It was just another of Beth's secrets that she kept close to her heart.

Chapter Thirty-Three

Preliminary Training School
Week 6

'How's that girl of yours getting on at the hospital?'

Dora smiled as she placed the thermometer between Mrs Roper's lips.

'She's doing all right, thanks for asking.' She crossed her fingers in the folds of her apron as she said it. Winnie was halfway through the course and doing very well by all accounts.

'She came top in her anatomy test last week.' Dora took the thermometer out of Mrs Roper's mouth and held it up to check the reading. 'And her tutor reckons she's got all the makings of an excellent nurse.'

'You shouldn't sound so surprised about it,' Mrs Roper said. 'She sounds like a chip off the old block.'

'Maybe she is.'

The thought surprised and pleased Dora. She didn't like to count her chickens too soon, but she was beginning to feel cautiously optimistic that nursing might work out for Winnie, after all.

She checked the old lady's pulse, and was dismayed to feel it skittering under her fingers.

'Your heartbeat's a bit lively,' she said, making a note of it on her chart. 'Are you sure you've been resting like I told you to?'

'Of course,' Mrs Roper said, but her eyes did not meet Dora's as she said it.

'Mrs R?'

'Oh, all right. I might have gone downstairs to make myself a cup of tea a couple of times. But it does no harm, does it? I could do with the exercise.'

'Not in your condition, you couldn't.' Dora shook her head. 'You've had a bad bout of rheumatic fever that's left your heart weak. That last thing you want to do is strain it by gadding all over the house.'

'Going downstairs to put the kettle on is hardly gadding!' the old lady protested. 'Besides, what else was I meant to do? I was parched.'

'Ask your son.'

'Gordon's at work all day.'

'Then knock on the wall for your neighbour.'

'I told you, Gordon's funny about people coming into the house when he's not here.'

'Then get him to make you a thermos flask before he goes in the morning!' Dora replied, exasperated. 'But whatever you do, you ain't to get out of this bed. Do you understand?'

'Yes, Nurse.' Mrs Roper sent her a cheeky sidelong look.

'And don't think you can get round me by calling me nurse,' Dora said, smiling in spite of herself. 'I'm still cross with you.'

'Sorry, Nurse.'

'I worry about you, that's all. Now, how are your joints today? Still giving you some pain, are they?'

'A bit.'

'Let's have a look. I'll give you a massage and rub in some wintergreen. That should help.'

'Thank you, love. You're a real godsend.'

As she rolled up the sleeve of Mrs Roper's flannel nightgown to get to her shoulder, Dora noticed a couple of dark blemishes on the thin, papery skin of her upper arm.

'How did you get these bruises?' she asked.

'Would you believe I bumped myself, while I was making that cup of tea? I turned round too quick and walked right into the corner of the dresser, silly old fool that I am!'

Dora looked carefully at the old lady. 'Are you sure that's what happened? They look more like finger-marks to me.'

'Finger-marks, indeed! Now how would I have done something like that?'

How indeed, Dora thought.

She didn't push it any further, not wanting to aggravate poor Mrs Roper in her weakened state. Instead they had a cup of tea together and chatted about this and that, and Dora kept her eye on the clock all the while, waiting for five o'clock to come round.

She carried their cups down to the kitchen and took her time washing and rinsing them until, sure enough, she heard the rattle of keys in the front door.

She finished washing up and went out into the hall, wiping her hands on her apron.

'Hello, Mr Roper.'

He jumped at the sound of her voice. He was a little runt

of a man, small and wiry with a narrow face. Suspicious eyes scowled at her from behind his spectacles.

'Oh, it's you,' he grunted. 'I thought you'd be gone by now?'

'I stopped to have a chat with your mother. She was feeling a bit lonely.'

He took off his hat, revealing a shiny scalp plastered with sparse strands of greasy hair. 'I'd have thought you'd have better things to do than gossip with old women?'

Dora held on to her temper with the utmost effort. 'It's part of my job, Mr Roper.' She watched him shrug off his overcoat and hang it on the stand. He wore a suit and tie. Mrs Roper had told her he had an office job, as a clerk of some kind. 'Don't you want to know how she's getting on?' she asked.

'I don't have to ask, I live with her.'

'Then you probably know she's been up and about?'

'I can't do anything about that, can I? I have to go out to work every day. Besides, it'll do her good.'

Gordon Roper pushed past her and went into the kitchen. He stood at the sink, staring down at the two cups she had left on the draining board.

Dora followed him. 'And how do you work that out?' she asked.

'It's what they say, isn't it? Exercise is good for you.'

'Not if you've got an infected endocardium as a result of rheumatic fever.'

'I've heard that Eileen Fowler on the radio when I'm getting ready for work in the morning. She's doing all right on it.'

Dora stared at him. 'Funny,' she said. 'I ain't seen your name on the register down at the GP practice.'

'Eh? What are you talking about?'

'Well, you must be a doctor, surely? To have all that medical knowledge at your fingertips.'

His face reddened. 'I don't need medical knowledge,' he muttered. 'It's just common sense.'

'Common sense that could kill your mother.'

He turned on her. 'I don't like your tone.'

'And I don't like you knocking your frail old mother about.'

He looked away. 'I don't know what you're talking about.'

'I've seen the bruises on her arms. What happened? Was she getting on your nerves? Did she ask you to make her a cup of tea, or fill a hot water bottle for her?' She shook her head in disgust. 'She's your mother, Mr Roper. After everything she's done for you, you think it's all right to get rough with her?'

Gordon Roper's face twitched, and for a moment Dora wondered if he was going to throw a punch at her. *Just let him try*, she thought. He'd soon find she was more of a match for him than a frail old lady.

'Get out,' he hissed.

'Don't worry, I'm going.' Dora snatched up her medical bag. 'But I'll be back, Mr Roper. And I'll be keeping a very close eye on you in future!'

Chapter Thirty-Four

Preliminary Training School
Week 7

On a dull, wet afternoon in late February, Helen caught the train down to Billinghurst for her niece Lottie's eleventh birthday party.

She knew David would be there, as he was Lottie's godfather, and she was fully prepared for seeing him. Coming face to face with him at Christmas had unsettled her only because it had been so unexpected, she told herself. But this time around she would be ready.

All the way down on the train she had imagined meeting him at Billinghurst, pictured herself greeting him cordially. There was no reason why they shouldn't be friendly, she thought. They had been together for so many years; they had always been good friends as well as a married couple. Just because she had chosen to leave, it didn't mean she hated him.

If only she did, she thought, as she watched the countryside passing the train window. This would all be a lot easier if she had no feelings left for him.

But even though she had prepared herself for their meeting, she was completely caught off guard by the sight of him sheltering under a black umbrella on the gate when she got off the train at the halt.

Her startled reaction must have shown on her face because David shrugged and said, 'I know. I'm probably the last person you want to see. But William's away and Millie's caught up in birthday party preparations, so . . .' He shrugged expressively. 'It was either me, or walk all the way to Billinghurst in the rain.'

'I don't mind at all,' Helen recovered herself quickly. 'I'm grateful to you for coming to pick me up.'

'Couldn't leave you to get soaked, could I?'

He held the umbrella over her as she got into the passenger seat of his battered old Morris Minor. The worn leather seats and faint smell of soap and Lysol immediately brought the memories rushing back.

David shook the rain off his umbrella and took off his coat. As he threw them in the back, Helen noticed his old leather medical bag.

'Are you on call?' she asked.

David shook his head as he started up the engine. 'Not officially. But Mrs Joyner up at Willow Farm got into a bit of trouble with her latest delivery, so I went up there to see what I could do.'

'What sort of trouble?' Helen asked, immediately interested.

'Breech birth. I told her she should go to hospital, but after six children I suppose she thought she knew best.'

'Were you able to help?'

He nodded. 'We got him out in the end. A big one, too.

Nine pounds three ounces. Quite an effort for the poor woman.'

'You did well to deliver a breech that size.'

He shrugged it off. 'The midwife and Mrs Joyner did most of the hard work. I just turned up at the end and—'

'—took the credit?' Helen finished his sentence without thinking, then realised what she had done and closed her mouth like a trap. It was something he always said, that midwives did all the hard work while all he did was turn up for a celebratory sherry.

David smiled, but said nothing.

They drove in silence for a minute or two, while she composed herself.

'Did you say William was away?' she asked finally, when she could trust herself to speak again.

David nodded. 'He went up to London this morning on some errand or other.'

'What kind of errand?'

'How should I know?' He looked sideways at her. 'You look worried. Why?'

Trust David to notice, she thought. He had always been very good at reading her.

'I'm not,' she said. 'I just think it's a shame he's missing Lottie's birthday.'

'He won't,' David said. 'He'll be back in time for the party, I'm sure. He'd never disappoint his daughter.'

'I daresay you're right,' Helen said. But her thoughts were elsewhere. She had only visited Billinghurst twice in the last eight months, and both times William had had to go up to London unexpectedly. How many more times did he visit when she wasn't there? she wondered.

As they rolled up the drive towards the house, Millie was waiting on the steps to greet them.

'Look at her. She doesn't exactly look overburdened with domestic duties, does she?' David spoke Helen's exact thoughts aloud.

'No, she doesn't.'

David turned to face her, mock dismay written all over his face. 'You don't think her sending me to pick you up was some kind of clumsy ruse, do you? Designed to engineer some kind of reconciliation?'

Helen caught the glint in his eyes and couldn't help smiling. 'Heaven forbid,' she said. 'My sister-in-law would never be that transparent, surely?'

She was still smiling as she got out of the car. And when she saw Millie's face light up, she knew she and David had been right in their suspicions.

'Hello, you two.' She greeted them brightly. 'You look very happy together.'

'It's all an act,' David said dryly. 'We haven't stopped arguing since we got in the car.'

'Take no notice of him,' Helen said, seeing the dismay on Millie's face. 'He's having you on.'

'Oh. Oh well, at least you're speaking, anyway,' Millie said in an undertone as they entered the house. 'You seemed so friendly as you got out of the car, I wasn't sure what to think. It was almost like old times.'

Yes, it was, Helen thought. She was shocked at how

quickly she had fallen back into that easy banter she and David used to have.

'There's no reason why we shouldn't be friendly,' she said, a bit more sharply than she had intended.

'There's no reason why you shouldn't still be married, as far as I can see,' Millie replied shortly. 'All right, all right, I'll mind my own business,' she added, holding up her hands before Helen had a chance to respond.

'There's a first time for everything.'

Helen sent a quick look over her shoulder at David. But Lottie and Tim had run out of the house to greet him, and he was too absorbed in them to be listening.

Her sister-in-law might not be the subtlest of matchmakers, but she knew how to throw a party. And big-hearted as she was, she had invited all the children in the village to celebrate. The grand house was soon ringing with the sound of laughter as the children ran around the miles of passageways and played hide and seek and sardines among the vast rooms.

'Aren't you worried they might break a priceless antique?' Helen asked, but Millie just laughed and said,

'Lord, no! It's our home, not a museum. And houses are meant to be lived in, don't you think?'

Helen smiled at her. That was Millie all over, happy to share her good fortune with everyone. In spite of her faults, she was honestly the most lovable creature Helen had ever known.

She suddenly thought of her brother. She only hoped William appreciated how lucky he was to have her.

It wasn't just the local children who were invited. Their

mothers gathered in the ballroom, chatting amongst themselves and enjoying the tea and cakes that Millie had provided.

Helen joined them for a while, but she felt very out of place. The room fell silent when she walked in, and even women she had known and been friendly with for years scowled at her. She could feel their hostile eyes on her as she helped herself to a cup of tea from the long table.

Undaunted, she tried to make friendly conversation with a couple of them. She had nursed Betty Carrick's daughter through a bout of scarlet fever, and Jean Moreton's husband when he'd injured his foot at work. But when she tried to speak to them, they cold-shouldered her as if she was a stranger.

In the end she gave up. But as she walked away, she heard Betty whisper to her friend,

'Hark at her! Talk about brazen.'

'I know,' Jean agreed. 'I don't even know how she's got the front to show her face, after what she did to poor Dr David!'

Helen retreated to the library. On her way, she met her brother William in the hall. He had just come in and was shaking the rain off his dark hair.

'Awful day, isn't it?' he greeted Helen. 'Millie was hoping the children might play in the grounds, but I suppose the little monsters are all trapped inside?' He grimaced at the sound of feet thundering overhead.

'Where have you been?' Helen asked, ignoring his remark.

He frowned. 'I had to go to London.'

'Why?'

'I had to go to Garrard's to pick up a bracelet for Lottie.

I was supposed to collect it two days ago, but Millie asked me to get it engraved and like an idiot I forgot, so I had to go back this morning.' His frown deepened. 'Why do you ask?'

'I just wondered where you were, that's all.'

'Here, you can have a look if you don't believe me.' He reached into his pocket and pulled out a leather box.

'I do believe you—'

'No, have a look.' He opened the box. Inside was a delicate silver bangle, engraved with the words, 'To Lottie with love'.

'It's beautiful,' Helen said. 'Lottie will love it.'

'Now do you believe me?' There was an edge to William's voice.

'Of course. Why shouldn't I?'

Their eyes met and held. Usually, Helen could read her brother like a book, but this time his gaze was dark and unfathomable.

'I'm glad to hear it.' William snapped the box shut and slipped it back into his pocket. 'Now, are you coming back to the party?'

As if a light had switched on, suddenly he was back to his old self and all smiles again.

Helen shook her head. 'I thought I might sit in the library for a while.'

'Good idea,' William said. 'Children's parties are not for the faint-hearted.'

As if to prove his point, there was an ominous thud from overhead. 'Oh God,' William said, 'I'd better go and make sure one of the little devils isn't trapped under a suit of armour, or something.' He looked at Helen. 'I'll see you later, all right?'

'Actually—' Helen started to say, but William was already running up the sweeping staircase, his long legs taking the stairs two at a time.

Helen sat on the window seat in the library with her cup of tea and gazed out on to the rose garden. Even on a rainy February afternoon it looked beautiful.

She was still sitting there when the door flew open and David called out,

'Come out! You're not supposed to be in here, you know—' He saw Helen and stopped dead. 'Oh, sorry. I was playing hide and seek with the children.'

'And you found me instead?' Helen smiled.

'At least I've found someone. I've been searching the house for ages. I think those children are having me on.' He looked rueful. He had taken off his jacket and tie and rolled up his shirtsleeves, so he was clearly taking the game seriously. 'Do you mind if I join you?'

'Please.' Helen shifted along the window seat to make room for him. She could hardly say no, she thought.

'Why do I get the impression you didn't want to be found?' David said, as he sat down beside her.

'Is it that obvious?'

'Children's parties are an acquired taste, I suppose. Unless you're a child, of course.'

Not for you, Helen thought. David had always been wonderful with children. She had watched him earlier, on his hands and knees with a toddler on his back. He adored them, and they adored him in return.

He would have made a wonderful father, she thought with a pang.

221

'It isn't the children I'm avoiding,' she said. She looked down into her cup. 'I get the impression I'm *persona non grata* with their mothers.'

'Why?'

'You.' She looked at him. 'I don't think they've quite forgiven me for leaving.'

'Oh.' His expression darkened. 'I suppose they're just struggling to understand what happened. As am I,' he added in an undertone.

'David, don't,' Helen sighed. 'I explained everything to you—'

'Yes, and I still don't understand it! All that nonsense about wanting me to be happy—'

'I do want you to be happy.'

'But I was happy with you!' He turned back to face her. 'And I'm miserable now, so what good has it all done?'

The anguish in his dark eyes went straight to her heart.

'You will be happy one day,' Helen said quietly. 'You'll see, it'll be for the best. I can't give you what you want—'

'I want you.'

She couldn't look at him. One glance into those eyes and she knew she would be lost.

'I want you,' David repeated quietly. 'I don't care about all the rest. Honestly, Helen, I'm trying to understand why you'd do this. Why you'd throw away ten years of happy marriage—'

'Were they really happy?' Helen threw back at him.

'They were for me.' He frowned. 'Were you unhappy, Helen?'

Images flashed up in her mind, like a film at top speed

running through her brain. Her wedding day, clinging to his arm and feeling like the luckiest girl in the world. Moving into Lowgill House, so full of hopes and plans and dreams. All the laughter and happy memories they had made there . . .

And then it had all started to unravel. One tragic event had cast a dark shadow over the rest of their marriage and brought them to this point, sitting here like strangers, talking about the unthinkable.

'I think we should discuss the divorce,' she said.

'Go on, then.' David's voice was flat.

Helen hesitated. She had expected him to argue, but he suddenly seemed resigned.

'I'm not quite sure how we should go about it . . .' she ventured.

'Aren't you? I assumed you would have instructed your solicitor by now, since you seem so keen to end this marriage.' He turned to face her. 'I'll tell you what I know, shall I? You need grounds for divorce, Helen. Separation, adultery, cruelty or insanity.' He counted them out on his fingers. 'Now, I think we can agree that neither of us has been particularly cruel to the other during the course of our marriage?'

'No.'

'And even though I question what you're doing, I wouldn't go as far as to say you were insane—'

'Thank you,' Helen said tightly.

'What about adultery?'

She looked at him sharply. 'Are you serious? I've never been unfaithful to you. I—'

I love you. The words had been about to slip out.

'Neither have I. And before you suggest it, I don't intend to get involved with a sordid fling to provide you with grounds for a divorce. Although you might consider it, since you seem so desperate to get rid of me?' He sent her a sideways look. 'I understand you can pay for someone to oblige? Unless you already have someone in mind?'

'Don't.' Helen looked away.

'Which leaves us with separation.' David counted the last point on his fingers. 'We would have to spend two years apart before we could apply for a divorce on those grounds.'

'Two years?' Helen blurted out.

David's brows rose. 'Goodness, you really are keen to be rid of me, aren't you?'

'I just want us both to be able to get on with our lives, that's all,' she murmured.

'Of course.' He stood up. 'Well, I suppose I'd best leave you alone. The sooner we get started on this separation, the better.' There was a bitter edge to his voice. 'Wouldn't want anyone catching sight of us and getting the wrong idea, would we?'

As he left the room, Helen called after him, 'David?'

He turned to face her.

'It doesn't have to be like this,' Helen pleaded. 'We can still remain friends, surely?'

He sent her any icy look. 'I don't want to be friends, Helen,' he replied coldly. 'I want you to be my wife. And if I can't have that, then I'd sooner have nothing at all.'

224

Chapter Thirty-Five

Preliminary Training School
Week 8

'How did you sterilise this syringe?' Miss Beck asked.

'I drew it through with carbolic acid, then alcohol and sterile water. Just like you showed me.'

'Why didn't you boil it?'

She was looking severe, but after two weeks, Viv knew when she was being tested.

'Because it would have ruined the washer.'

'And what proportion of carbolic acid did you use?'

'One to twenty parts water.'

'Hmm,' Miss Beck sniffed. 'I suppose it's nice to know you've listened to something I've said, at least.'

Viv smiled to herself. It might have seemed like scant praise, but for Miss Beck it was fulsome indeed. The elderly sister scarcely ever bestowed a smile or a compliment.

'Show me how you would fill a syringe for a hypodermic injection using one of these tablets,' she said.

'Yes, Sister.' Viv could feel the Infirmary Sister's critical gaze on her as she dissolved the tablet in the correct amount of hot sterile water, then drew up the solution into the syringe. She sensed Miss Beck was waiting to pounce, but she was confident she knew what she was doing.

Miss Beck knew it too, which was why she had been giving her extra responsibilities.

It hadn't been easy at first. Viv had bitterly resented her time in the Infirmary, having to report there straight after supper every evening. While the other girls were relaxing and enjoying themselves, Viv was washing floors and scrubbing toilets and on her hands and knees cleaning bed castors with an old toothbrush. All she could think about was Roy and how much she was missing him, and what he might be getting up to when she wasn't there.

Every night she would return to her new room and fall into bed exhausted. She had even begun to have some sympathy for her grandmother. If she found all that sweeping and scrubbing so tiring, no wonder Granny Trent was always in such a bad mood after cleaning offices all day.

But after the first week, things had begun to change. The work was still hard, but Miss Beck gradually began to provide some instruction too. Viv was allowed to help looking after the patients who came into the Infirmary. Under Miss Beck's watchful eye, she dressed injured hands and sprained joints, treated scalds and burns and even helped to nurse some of the girls who were laid up in bed.

Gradually, all the clinical practice training began to make sense. Viv suddenly understood why it was so important to keep everything clean to prevent the spread of infection, and the difference a well-made bed made to the comfort of a patient.

'It's your last day, isn't it?' Miss Beck said, as Viv was sweeping the ward just before lunch.

'That's right, Sister.'

'You don't have to come back after lunch, since it's a Sunday.'

'Oh, but I don't mind—'

'Nonsense, enjoy your day off. You've earned it.' The Infirmary Sister gave the smallest of smiles. 'I daresay you'll be wanting to spend some time with your friends?'

'Yes, Sister.' Viv looked around her. She was loath to admit it, even to herself, but she had even started to enjoy her work in the Infirmary.

'You may be going back to your old room, but I hope you won't be going back to your old ways?' Miss Beck eyed her severely. 'You have the makings of a good nurse, if only you would apply yourself.'

'Thank you, Sister.'

'I'm serious, Trent. You should know I don't say anything I don't mean. I can see you have an excellent future ahead of you, as long as you don't choose to throw it away. You're a born nurse, even if you won't allow yourself to accept it.'

Viv stared at her, lost for words. She was so used to hearing a reprimand, the Infirmary Sister's words caught her completely off guard.

She was still thinking about them as she returned to the attic room, her arms full of her belongings.

Winnie and Beth looked up as she entered. As usual, they both had their heads in their books.

'Hello, you two,' Viv greeted them brightly. 'Have you missed me?'

'Like a hole in the head,' Winnie muttered, but she was smiling when she said it.

'Take no notice of her,' Beth said. 'It's been very quiet without you.'

'I'll bet.' Viv crossed the room and dumped her belongings on to her bed. 'There's never a dull moment with me around.'

'More's the pity,' Winnie said.

'I'll bet you're glad not to have Miss Beck breathing down your neck any more?' Beth said.

'Actually, she ain't a bad old stick, once you get to know her.'

Viv saw the look of surprise that passed between Winnie and Beth.

She unpacked her belongings, being careful to keep to her side of the room. She could feel Winnie watching her as she went on studying with Beth.

'What are the three types of injection?' Winnie asked.

'Hypodermic, intramuscular and intravenous,' Beth replied promptly.

'What type of syringe would you use for a hypodermic injection?'

Beth thought for a moment. 'One or two cc graduated in minims.'

'And where would you usually inject?'

'That's easy. The arm.'

'Right, let's look for something more difficult . . .' Winnie flipped over the pages. 'What can you tell me about the different coloured labels for insulin?'

'Let me think . . .' Beth screwed up her nose. 'The bottle

containing twenty units has a buff label, the bottle containing forty units has a green – no, blue – label. The bottle containing eighty units is the one with the green label.'

'Don't forget about the pink label for protamine zinc insulin, and the orange one for globin zinc insulin,' Viv put in. 'I had a lot of chance to read up when I was confined to my cell with Miss Coulter keeping guard,' she shrugged, seeing Winnie's look of surprise.

'I daresay you'll be making up for lost time now?' Winnie said. 'Going out all night, I expect?'

You may be going back to your room, but I hope you're not going back to your old ways? Miss Beck's stern voice came into her mind. *You're a born nurse, even if you won't allow yourself to accept it.*

'Actually, I don't have any plans,' she said.

Winnie was surprised. 'I thought you'd be rushing straight out to see your boyfriend?'

'I'm meeting him later.' She looked at them. 'Are you going to the dining room? I'll walk with you.'

Winnie and Beth exchanged an awkward glance. 'Actually, we're going out,' Beth said. 'Winnie's mum's invited me round for Sunday dinner.'

'That's nice.' Viv swallowed down her disappointment. She had been looking forward to catching up with her room-mates. She was surprised at how much she had missed them. Alone in her little room at night, she had longed to chat with them. She had even missed Winnie's constant nagging.

'You're welcome to join us,' Winnie offered. Viv shook her head.

'Oh no, it's all right. I ain't been invited.'

'I'm inviting you now.'

She and Winnie looked at each other. They were both tough East End girls, but Viv recognised an olive branch when she saw it.

'In that case, I'd love to come,' she said.

Chapter Thirty-Six

Winnie's family turned out to be a riot.

Viv didn't expect them to be so much fun, especially knowing what a sourpuss Winnie could be. But even her room-mate seemed different and more relaxed when she was with her lively collection of relatives.

After being stuck with just Granny Trent all her life, Viv had often wondered what it would be like to have a big family. And she was not disappointed. Being with the Rileys was like being thrown into the middle of a continuous party, with laughter and chaos and everyone talking at once.

And in the centre of it was Winnie's mother, Dora. She was standing by the stove in the kitchen when they arrived, enveloped in a fug of steam and holding a pan of roast potatoes aloft while shouting to three children who were heading out of the back door.

'Yes, all right, you can go and play,' she called out. 'But watch your cousins, and mind you don't go further than the corner. Your dinner will be ready in a minute, and I don't want to go all over Bethnal Green looking for you.'

She didn't seem at all put out that there would be an extra guest at the table, either.

'It's no trouble at all,' she told Viv, brushing back a faded red curl that stuck to her perspiring cheek. 'Any friend of

Winnie's is welcome here. If you can find somewhere to sit, that is!' She looked ruefully around her.

Viv took to her immediately. Dora was definitely the matriarch of the family, the centre around which everyone else revolved. But she was kind and down to earth with it, a real salt of the earth East Ender with no airs or graces. She spoke to everyone in the same rough and ready way, but Viv saw the love in her eyes whenever she looked at Winnie and she envied them.

And to think Winnie always frowned when she talked about her mother, and made out they had little time for each other. Viv would have loved to be in her position.

She took to Winnie's aunts, too. Especially Aunt Bea, the youngest. She reminded Viv of her own mother, so lively and glamorous. Especially when she turned to Viv and said,

'Vivien, eh? Like Vivien Leigh, the actress? I love her, don't you? Such a star.'

'Beth's mum is in the movies, too,' Winnie said. 'You know – Celia Wells?'

'Never!' Auntie Bea let out a squeal that made Winnie's grandmother jump beside her. 'You mean to tell me your mum is famous? Blimey, Dor, you've got royalty come to dinner!'

'As long as there's enough meat and Yorkshire puddings to go round,' Dora shrugged.

They ate all squashed around the little table, packed in so tightly their elbows clashed whenever they tried to lift their knives and forks. But still no one seemed to mind the chaos.

Viv glanced at Beth, sitting across the table from her. She was talking to Auntie Bea, trying to answer her endless questions about Hollywood and which famous actors she had met, but Viv could see the hint of panic in her eyes. She clearly wasn't used to noisy East End family gatherings, either.

It might have seemed like a nightmare to Beth, but Viv was in her element. This was exactly the kind of family she had always dreamed of having.

Across the table from her sat Winnie's father Nick. He was in his forties, but still very attractive, tall and hard-muscled with his daughter's dark curls and brilliant blue eyes.

Dora sat beside Viv, and asked about her family. She seemed very interested when Viv told her how her father had been killed at Dunkirk before she was born, and how her mother had struggled to bring her up. She didn't mention that he'd died before he had a chance to marry her, or that Granny Trent had tried to give her up for adoption.

She was especially interested when Viv told her how her mother had fallen in love with a GI and ended up going off to make a new life for herself in America.

'She wanted to take me too, but it was against the rules,' she explained. 'So I had to stay here with my gran.'

'It must have broken her heart,' Dora said. 'I know it would break mine to be apart from my children.'

The light faded from her eyes when she said it, as if even the thought was too much to bear.

For a moment Viv thought about her mother's letters, and the photographs she often sent. She didn't look very heartbroken. If anything, she looked as if she was having the time of her life.

But appearances could be deceptive, and Viv was sure Pauline Trent must have learned to put on a brave face after so many years.

'So how did you two meet?' She changed the subject deftly, looking from Dora to Nick and back again.

They glanced at each other. 'We grew up together,' Dora said. 'Nick and his family lived next door to us in Griffin Street, just the other side of Victoria Park. It's not there now,' she added. 'Hitler saw to that.'

'And good riddance to it,' Auntie Bea muttered. 'Nasty fleapit of a place.'

'It was a roof over our heads when we needed it,' Dora said firmly. Viv noticed the look she shot her sister down the length of the table.

'He was a right tearaway,' Nanna Rose chimed in. She was a gentle soul, very graceful with delicate bones and a hint of the beauty she must have once had. She couldn't have been more different from Viv's own bulldog of a grandmother. 'Everyone was frightened to death of him.'

'Except me,' Dora muttered.

'Take on anyone, he would,' Nanna Rose continued. 'He was always looking for a fight.'

'I certainly got one when I married your daughter, Rose!' Nick laughed.

'Oi!' Dora glared at him. But Viv saw the laughter in their eyes as they looked at each other. They were so in love, it shone out of them.

She thought about Roy. He was a right tearaway too. Surely if Dora could tame Nick Riley, then she could do the same?

She smiled to herself, imagining them sitting around a table like this twenty years from now, surrounded by their own family. It was all she had ever wanted, a home and a family of her own, and someone to love her.

That was the thought on her mind when she climbed the stairs to Barrie's dance hall later that evening, teetering on her high heels.

She left her coat with the cloakroom girl and handed over her one shilling and sixpence for her ticket. The dance floor was already heaving, with couples jiving to the sound of the rock and roll band. Around the edge of the floor, some girls sat modestly sipping their drinks and trying to feign indifference to the young men in suits who circled around them.

They all turned to look at Viv as she walked in. She could feel their admiring glances and the jealous gazes of some of the girls. She was looking her best, with her lips painted crimson, auburn hair held off her face with a mother of pearl comb. She was wearing a new white dress, tightly cinched with a shiny black plastic belt to show off her wasp waist and the curves of her hips and bosom.

She was out to show her man what he had been missing. She was sure the likes of Sandra Ellis would have been making the most of her absence in the last two weeks, but Viv had already made up her mind that whoever Roy might have been flirting with wouldn't stand a chance now she was back.

'Well, well, look what the cat's dragged in.'

Viv stifled a sigh. Of course, the first person she saw had

to be Sandra. The other girl looked her up and down with an insulting sneer. 'You're dressed to kill, ain't you? What's the occasion?'

'I don't need an occasion to look nice.' Viv muttered, looking over the heads of the dancers, still searching for Roy.

'If you're looking for your boyfriend, he ain't here.'

Viv swung round to face her. 'What?'

'He's gone up to Notting Hill with some of the other boys. He heard there was going to be trouble.'

She knew immediately the sort of trouble Sandra meant. Notting Hill was a cheap, run-down area, which made it popular with immigrant families. The Teddy Boys often went over there to stir things up with the young West Indian men.

'But I was supposed to be meeting him here tonight.' Bitter disappointment rose in her throat.

'I suppose he must have forgot. You have been away a while, after all.' Sandra inspected her shiny red nails. 'And you know what they say. Out of sight, out of mind.'

Viv glared at her. It was all she could do not to grab her and swing her round by her blonde bouffant.

'I'm surprised you ain't gone after him,' she said, pulling her dignity together. 'It ain't like you to miss the chance to chase after my boyfriend.'

'Do me a favour, I ain't that pathetic!' Sandra's mouth curled. 'Not like some,' she added under her breath.

'And what's that supposed to mean?'

'You work it out.'

Viv turned to her. 'Have you got something you want to say, Sandra Ellis? Only if you have, you'd best come out with it.'

Their eyes met for a moment. 'Like I said, you work it out,' she said.

Viv sighed. 'I ain't staying here to listen to your nonsense.'

'You've bought your ticket, you might as well stay and get your money's worth.' Sandra looked around. 'I'm sure you can find someone to flirt with while Roy's away. I know he has,' she added with a sly smile.

Viv stared at her. Whatever happened, she wouldn't give Sandra Ellis the satisfaction of seeing her rattled. She was just trying to make trouble, Viv was certain of it. Roy had probably turned Sandra down and she was angry and bitter about it, so she was trying to make trouble.

But as she went to leave, Sandra suddenly said,

'I ain't your enemy, y'know.'

'Really?' Viv sneered. 'You could have fooled me.'

'I mean, I ain't the one you want to watch out for.'

'I ain't seen anyone else chasing after my boyfriend.'

'No,' Sandra said quietly. 'And they're the ones you should be worried about.'

Chapter Thirty-Seven

'A complaint? What do you mean, a complaint?'

Dora stared across the desk at the supervisor. She could scarcely believe what she was hearing.

It was a Monday evening, and she had just returned to the surgery after her last call when Mrs Hearst called her into her office and told her the news.

Eileen Hearst was not the most warm-hearted of women, and she was a stickler for rules and regulations, but even she seemed sympathetic about it.

'I can see you're shocked,' she said. 'I hardly knew what to make of it myself when I heard about it. But one of your patients has written to complain about your behaviour.'

'Can I see the letter?'

'I'm sorry, that's not allowed.' Eileen turned the envelope around in her hands.

'Then how can I defend myself, if I'm not even allowed to know what I'm supposed to have done?'

The supervisor hesitated a moment. 'Apparently you threatened this particular patient's son.'

Realisation began to dawn. 'Is this Mrs Roper we're talking about?'

Eileen Hearst looked up sharply. 'So you remember the incident?'

'I do,' Dora said. 'But I'd be very surprised if Mrs Roper sent that letter. The poor old dear can barely hold a pen.'

'The letter did come from her son,' Eileen Hearst admitted reluctantly. 'But he said he wrote it with his mother's blessing.'

'I doubt it!' Dora muttered.

'He says she's been very distressed by the whole incident.'

'Oh, she's in distress, all right. But only from the way he treats her.'

'Is that why you threatened him?'

'I didn't threaten him. I just told him I had my eye on him.'

'He says you accused him of trying to kill his own mother. Is that right?'

'I don't remember. I was very angry at the time, and I just saw red.' Dora watched the supervisor scribble a note on the piece of paper in front of her. 'I'd noticed bruises on Mrs Roper's arms and I thought he might be getting rough with her.'

'Did you ask Mrs Roper about them?'

'Of course I did.'

'And?'

'She said she'd knocked against a cupboard. But they looked more like finger marks to me,' she said quickly,

Mrs Hearst's eyes narrowed. 'But you have no proof that Mr Roper caused these bruises?'

'No, but—'

'And his mother says she did it herself?'

'Yes, but only because she's too frightened to speak up. She won't hear a word against him.'

'Or it might be because he's done nothing wrong?' Mrs Hearst made another note on the paper in front of her.

Dora stared at the supervisor's implacable expression. Eileen Hearst might have been a good district nurse in her day, but she had been stuck behind a desk for too many years, wrapped up in all her rotas and paperwork. She had forgotten what it was like to meet these families on her rounds day after day, to get involved with them and their lives. District nurses developed an instinct for when things weren't right, and Dora's alarm bells were ringing all over the place.

'You don't know them like I do,' she insisted. 'Gordon Roper is a nasty piece of work. He's got no time for his mother. If you ask me, he's just waiting for her to die so he can inherit the house.'

Mrs Hearst's brows rose. 'If you go round making accusations like that, I'm not surprised the poor man doesn't want you in his house.'

'Poor man indeed!' Dora scoffed. 'He neglects her. He won't even bring the poor old soul a cup of tea or a hot water bottle. And he won't let her have any company, either. She never sees a soul from one day to the next. He won't even allow the neighbours to pop in and see if she's all right.'

'Perhaps he doesn't get on with them? The man has a right to his privacy, Dora.'

'Does he have the right to set about his mother, too?'

The supervisor's cheeks turned red, and Dora knew she

had gone too far. But she was too upset and angry to hold back.

'So what happens now?' she asked. 'Will I be suspended?'

'No, of course not. You're one of our best nurses, we'd be lost without you. But it might be best if one of the others visits this Mrs Roper from now on.'

'Who?'

'Cath Garvey.'

'Cath Garvey won't give Mrs Roper the time she needs. She's always in too much of a rush.'

'Nurse Garvey is very efficient.'

Too efficient, Dora thought. She was forever watching the clock and giving patients scant treatment. She could never imagine her sitting down for a chat and a cuppa. 'Couldn't you send someone with a bit more experience? How about Jean Franklin?'

Mrs Hearst's lips tightened. 'It's hardly up to you to decide which nurse gets assigned where. Unless you think you can do my job better than me?'

Dora pressed her lips together to stop herself blurting out another impetuous comment. She had already come close to losing her job. She didn't need to give Eileen Hearst any more reason to get rid of her.

Chapter Thirty-Eight

The first signs of spring were appearing. Trees in acid-green leaf, crocuses and daffodils nosing from the ground. The dull, relentless rain of February had given way to fresh, sunny days, and the sun had some warmth to it at last.

It was on a day just like this, exactly two years earlier, that Beth Bradshaw had begged her sister to take the boat out.

She relived every agonising minute of it now as she stood before Alison's grave. The way she had pleaded with her, nagging and cajoling and arguing until Alison had finally given in. Why hadn't she just taken no for an answer? They could have gone for a walk, or played draughts or read a book, and Alison would still be here.

But no, she had to have her way. And her precious sister had paid the price for Beth's stubbornness.

At least Beth was paying a price too. She might not have lost her life, but the one she was living made her utterly miserable. She hoped that might be enough.

She wished she could remember what had happened that day. She recalled getting into the boat and pushing off from the shore. She was rowing, she remembered that. But the swell of the tide soon became too much for her, and her arms began to ache as she fought against it. The sea that had looked so inviting from the beach, with the sun sparkling off its rippling surface, seemed dark and hostile as it rolled and swelled underneath them.

She remembered the panic in Alison's voice as she told her to row back to shore. And finally Beth had the good sense to agree with her. She was trying to turn the boat round, her aching arms straining against the heaving tide, when suddenly—

Nothing. No matter how hard she tried, the memory wouldn't come. It was as if her mind was a book with pages torn from it. The next thing she knew she was in the water, being carried helplessly away, and Alison was swimming towards her, telling her to hold on, that she was coming to get her . . .

She looked down and realised she was gripping her posy of spring flowers so tightly she was crushing the tender stalks in her fist. She bent down and placed them on her sister's grave. The bright purples and yellows looked incongruously cheerful against the white of the marble headstone.

Alison Eleanor Bradshaw
1937–1955
Beloved daughter and sister
Always in our hearts and thoughts

The painful irony of the words was not lost on her.

There were two more bunches of flowers on the grave, one of spring flowers like hers and another tasteful bouquet of white roses. One was from Grace, the other from Beth's mother. Both cards were written in the housekeeper's flowing handwriting.

Always in our hearts and thoughts.

Alison might be in Beth's, but she was not in their mother's. That epitaph might as well have read, *Out of sight, out of mind*.

But even so, Beth dutifully headed to the house in Kensington rather than going straight back to the nurses' home. She still held on to a shred of hope that her mother's brittle shell might finally crack and that she would share the sorrow Beth knew she must feel inside.

It was all she wanted, to be able to talk about Alison and share their memories of her, even laugh together about her. And perhaps Beth might even be able to share the heavy burden of guilt she felt. Then she might not feel so utterly alone.

But the moment she let herself in and heard her mother singing upstairs she knew it was not to be.

'Grace? Is that you?' Her light voice drifted down the stairs. A moment later her mother came to the top of the stairs. She looked sunny in white slacks and a pale primrose-yellow top that perfectly complemented her blonde hair. 'Oh, hello.' She smiled broadly when she saw Beth. 'I thought Grace might have taken pity on me and changed her mind about taking the weekend off. It's such a nuisance that she's decided to visit her family now, when we're supposed to be flying to New York on Monday.'

Beth stared at her. Only her mother could be so self-absorbed.

'I daresay she wants to see them before she leaves,' she said. 'Especially with her father being ill.'

'Yes, I know. Poor man.' Celia Wells arranged her features into a suitably sympathetic mask. 'But it's only a bout of flu. I'm sure he'll get better. And meanwhile I have no idea where she keeps my passport . . .'

'Top drawer of the bureau,' Beth said. 'I'll get it for you.'

'Thank you, darling.' Her mother smiled gratefully. 'Honestly, this trip couldn't have come at a worse time. I don't know why I ever agreed to it. The last thing I need to be doing is packing today of all days.'

Beth's heart lifted as she went to the bureau drawer. Perhaps she hadn't forgotten, after all?

'I mean, it's the last night of the play tonight,' Celia went on in her light, trilling voice. 'I'm utterly exhausted, and I really should rest before I take on more work. But we're transferring to Broadway in a week, so—' She shrugged her slim shoulders helplessly. 'Anyway, I suppose I should make the most of it, shouldn't I? I'm getting a bit long in the tooth now – I daresay it won't be long before I'm making way for some little starlet. Better make hay while the sun shines!'

Her bright laugh went through Beth like a blade. Her mother had never stopped working. The day after Alison's funeral, she had flown to California to film a romantic comedy with Gregory Peck.

'Here's your passport,' she said. As she went to close the drawer, a small leather jewellery box caught her eye. She immediately recognised the locket her mother had tried to give her a few weeks earlier.

'Ah, I see you've found my little surprise,' her mother smiled archly. 'I wanted to give it to you before I left. Go on, have a look.'

Mystified, Beth opened the box. Sure enough, there was the locket inside, nestling on its bed of pale satin.

'Open it,' her mother urged. 'I know how disappointed you were that I hadn't put a picture inside for you. It's one of my favourites. We were in Scotland, do you remember? It rained every day except the very last—'

Beth stared down at the open locket in her hand. Two tiny faces stared back at her, herself and her mother, both laughing at the camera, their faces alight with happiness.

'Where's Alison?' she asked. 'She was with us when this photograph was taken, but you've cut her out.'

Her mother's smile faltered. 'I wasn't sure you'd want—'

'To remember my own sister?' Beth finished for her harshly. 'No, Mother, it's you who wants to forget her, not me!' She turned on her mother, all her pent-up anger finally erupting out of her. 'Have you forgotten what day it is?'

'Of course I haven't forgotten,' her mother said quietly. 'How could I?'

'But you haven't once mentioned her name since I arrived. All you've talked about is yourself, and your wretched play and your trip to New York. You haven't even visited her grave,' she said bitterly.

'I prefer to remember her in my own way.'

'You mean you prefer not to remember her at all!'

'Beth, please,' her mother pleaded. 'Let's not talk about this—'

'Why? Why can't we talk about her? You never say her

name. There isn't a single photograph of her around the house. It's as if she never existed—'

'Has it ever occurred to you that it might be too painful for me to remember?' Her mother's smile was suddenly gone, replaced by a raw emotion Beth had not seen before. 'Yes, you're right, I don't talk about her, because the truth is I can't bear it. Just because I can't look at her photograph doesn't mean I don't remember every single detail of her face, the way she smiled, the smell of her hair. And I don't need to visit her grave to know I've lost her. Believe me, there is not a day goes by when I don't think, "What if—"' She stopped herself abruptly.

'What?' Beth prompted.

'It doesn't matter.'

'No, tell me. I want to know.'

Her mother's gaze met hers. 'I said it doesn't matter,' she repeated in a quiet, firm voice.

Chapter Thirty-Nine

It was past six o'clock and darkness was gathering when Beth's mother drove her back to the Nightingale.

The rest of the visit had been strained, to say the least. After they'd spoken, Celia had gone upstairs to pack. When she'd finally emerged half an hour later, her brittle smile was back in place and she was behaving in her usual bright and breezy fashion.

'I'm leaving for America in a couple of days, and we won't see each for at least a month,' she had said. 'Let's just enjoy our time together while we can, shall we?'

Beth agreed. She didn't want to push the matter, either. She'd already had a frightening glimpse into her mother's heart and she wasn't sure she could cope with any more.

It doesn't matter, she had said. But Beth knew it mattered very much. Her mother had spoken volumes without ever saying a word.

She knew now what she had always suspected – that her mother blamed her for Alison's death. She might not want to say it outright, but it was there. Beth could feel it in her silence, the bitterness that she had been holding back, the reason she had put up such a wall between them.

No wonder Beth felt as if her mother had been putting on an act with her for all these years. Even for an actress as accomplished as Celia Wells, it must have been a terrible strain for her to feign affection for a daughter she resented so deeply.

Beth had always felt guilty that she had survived the accident. It had been her idea to take the boat out, and she should have been the one who died, not her sister. And now she knew her mother felt the same.

Celia stopped the car outside the hospital gates.

'Don't you want to drive up to the nurses' home?' Beth asked. 'It would be nice for you to see where I'm staying. And I'm sure my friends would all like to meet you—'

But her mother was already shaking her head. 'I'd love to, darling, but I must get to the theatre. I don't want to miss curtain up on my last performance!'

Beth saw the reluctance underneath her smile, and understood. It was the same reason her mother had not come with her on that first day. She couldn't face seeing Beth living the life that should have been Alison's.

She got out of the car and looked back at her mother. 'Well, goodbye, then,' she said. 'I hope it goes well on Broadway.'

'If it does, it will be nothing short of a miracle!' her mother grimaced.

'Just think, by the time you come back I should have passed PTS—'

But her mother had already driven off before she'd reached the end of her sentence.

Beth walked up the drive to the nurses' home with a heavy heart. It was getting dark, and the lights were on downstairs. As she approached, she could see the other girls inside. Lou and Frances were doing an elaborate mime, acting out some medical procedure, while the other girls fell about laughing.

Then, before her eyes, the scene began to slow down until Frances and Lou were frozen in mid-gesture. The other girls were frozen too, their mouths still open in silent laughter.

The only movement was Alison. She was standing by the bookcase, watching the scene from a distance. As Beth stared, her sister turned slowly to face her and shook her head.

This is my place, she heard her sister's voice in her head, as clear as day. *You don't belong here.*

'Beth?'

She snapped awake, as if from a dream, to find Mr Allenby beside her. His arm was around her waist, as if he was holding her up.

'I was just coming round the corner, and I saw you standing here,' he said. 'Then you started swaying on your feet. I just managed to catch you before you fell. Are you all right?'

'I – I'm fine.' Beth looked back at the nurses' home. The curtains had been pulled, shutting her out. *When had that happened?* she wondered.

'You don't look it.' He released her and held her at arm's length. 'You seemed as if you were in a trance.' He frowned down at her. 'Has this happened before?'

A vision of Alison floated into her mind. 'I – I'm not sure . . .'

'Come with me.'

He took her hand and started to lead her away. Beth

looked back over her shoulder towards the nurses' home. 'I should be getting back—'

'Not until I've made sure you're all right.'

He led her around the side of the nurses' home. Beth thought he must be taking her to the Infirmary, but they walked past and headed towards the nursing school.

'You need peace and quiet to recover,' he explained, as he unlocked the door and ushered her inside and switched on the light. 'Go and lie down on one of the beds in the practice room, and I'll fetch you a glass of water.'

Beth obediently took off her shoes and propped herself up on the bed. She watched as Mr Allenby went around the room pulling the curtains. It all felt strangely unreal, as if she was watching a play.

'Here, drink this.' He handed her a glass of water. 'It'll make you feel better.'

Beth took a sip and pulled a face. It had a strangely bitter taste. She went to put it down on the locker beside the bed but Mr Allenby said,

'No, drink it all. It will do you good.'

'What's in it?'

'Just something to help you sleep.'

Beth eyed him warily over the rim of the glass but she did as she was told. She was being silly, she told herself. She had no reason not to trust Mr Allenby. He had always been so kind to her.

'That's it,' he said, when she handed him back the empty glass. 'You'll feel better when you've properly rested.'

'I'd better get back—' She started to sit up, but he gently pushed her back against the pillows.

'Peace and quiet is what you need,' he said. 'You've been overdoing it, Beth. That's why you nearly passed out earlier.'

He perched on the bed beside her, and took her hand in his to check her pulse. 'Your heartbeat's quite rapid,' he said, after a moment. 'Hopefully the medication will help relax you.'

It was already beginning to work, Beth thought. She could feel her body sinking into the mattress, as limp and heavy as a sack of damp sand. It was all she could do to keep her eyelids open.

'I am rather tired,' she said.

'I'm not surprised. I daresay you haven't been sleeping well, have you?' She shook her head. 'I thought not. I've seen those shadows under those pretty green eyes of yours.'

He was still holding her hand. Beth wanted to move it, but she couldn't seem to summon the energy.

'I've been worried about you for a while, Beth,' he said. 'I've noticed how much strain you've been putting yourself under lately, trying to keep up with the others.'

He pushed up her sleeve and began to stroke her arm, his hands moving rhythmically against the bare skin.

'A little trick I learned in the army,' he said. 'Massage helps to induce a sense of calm. You do feel calmer, don't you, Beth?'

'Mmmm.' His fingers were warm, gently caressing her bare skin. Listening to his deep, quiet voice, Beth felt herself sinking deeper and deeper into the darkness.

'Close your eyes, that's it. Sleep if you want to . . .'

The feeling of his mouth on hers startled her awake. Beth

tried to push him off but her arms were so heavy she could scarcely lift them. She jerked her head to one side but he grabbed her chin and turned her back to face him as his mouth came down on hers again, hard and demanding.

The next moment he was on top of her, pinning her to the bed. Beth squirmed and wriggled, trying to escape him, but that only seemed to excite him as he fumbled and tore at her clothes. He was grunting like an animal, his breath hot and urgent against her face. He was pressing down on her, crushing her so she could scarcely breathe.

It took every last ounce of strength she had to fight him off. She lashed out, punching and scratching, dragging her nails down the side of his face. He let out a cry of surprise and released his grip for a moment, long enough for her to squirm from under him. But before she could get free, his fingers closed around her arm, tightening like a vice until she cried out in pain.

'Leave her alone!'

Miss Cheetham's voice rang out across the room, stopping them both in their tracks. Beth turned her head to see the Sister Tutor standing in the doorway, her face a rigid mask of rage.

Chapter Forty

The next moment Mr Allenby's weight had rolled off her and Beth shifted quickly away from him. She tumbled off the bed and onto the floor, gasping for breath.

'What the hell do you think you're playing at?' Miss Cheetham's voice was taut with fury.

Once Beth had scrambled to her feet she realised that the Sister Tutor was looking at both of them, her gaze flicking from one to the other.

'It – it wasn't me,' she protested. 'He attacked me—'

But Miss Cheetham wasn't listening. 'I can hardly believe what I'm seeing,' she said. 'To think a student at this school would do such a thing—'

'But it wasn't me!' Beth cried, her voice rising. 'He brought me here. He put something in my drink, and then—'

'Stop, I don't want to hear it.' Miss Cheetham held up her hand. She turned to Mr Allenby, her mouth a tight line. 'I think it would be best if you let me deal with this.'

'Yes. Of course.' Mr Allenby couldn't meet Beth's eye as he reached for his jacket.

'Leave by the back door, so no one sees you.'

Beth heard the door close softly and then turned back to face Miss Cheetham. 'You're just letting him go?' she said. 'After what he tried to do to me?'

Miss Cheetham did not reply. She crossed to the clinical area and took a basin from the cupboard, then filled it from the sink.

Beth watched her, but none of it seemed real. It was as if she was walking through a dream, like one of the waking dreams she sometimes had. She looked around, expecting to see her sister lurking in a shadowy corner. But there was no one there.

Suddenly she was shivering uncontrollably, as if ice was flowing through her veins. She pulled a blanket from the bed and draped it around her shoulders. It smelled of Mr Allenby's animal sweat. She threw it off, bile rising in her throat. She started retching as Miss Cheetham returned with basin of water and a face cloth draped over her arm. In the other hand she held a small glass of amber liquid.

'Brandy,' she said, handing it to Beth. 'Go on, drink it. It will do you good.'

Beth did as she was told. The brandy lit a fiery trail down her throat and burned in her stomach, but it seemed to settle her.

'Now, let's have a look at you.' Miss Cheetham crouched down and tilted her head this way and that, peering at her. 'You're probably going to need some ice on the lip to stop it swelling.'

She inspected her arms. 'There are some bruises, too. But your sleeves should hide them.'

Beth stared at her in confusion. Hide them? What on earth did she mean? 'But surely I should tell Matron—'

'Tell her what? That you came in here alone with a man, and it went further than you intended?'

'But that's not what happened! You saw him, he was—'

'What I saw were two people who should not have been alone in here together. And that's exactly what I shall tell Matron, if she asks me.'

Beth stared at her in disbelief. Whatever Mr Allenby had given her had made her head foggy. The thoughts weren't joining up as they should. Otherwise why would she be hearing this? None of it made sense.

'But—'

'Look, if I were you I'd keep quiet and forget any of this happened,' Miss Cheetham said firmly. 'I'm only thinking of you, Bradshaw, believe me. You've got three weeks left of PTS, and I want you to get through it. Three weeks, that's all,' she cajoled. 'Do you really want to give up everything you've achieved for the sake of one silly mistake?'

'A silly mistake? But I didn't do anything. You saw, he was attacking me!'

'I didn't see anything,' Miss Cheetham insisted stubbornly. 'As far as I'm concerned, nothing happened. And it's best for everyone if it stays that way.'

She took a comb from her pocket and handed it to Beth. 'Now, tidy yourself up, and go back to the nurses' home. It might be wise to say you have a headache and go straight to bed. A good night's sleep will do you good in any case. And remember what I said. Not a word to anyone,' she warned. 'It will be a lot worse for you if Matron gets to hear of this, believe me.'

Winnie couldn't quite believe it. It was a Saturday night, and Viv was not going out.

True, she was painting her nails bright red so she wasn't exactly a reformed character. But at least it was a start.

Besides, as she had explained to Winnie, staying in was all part of her strategy to show her boyfriend Roy what he was missing.

'I want him to come begging,' she said, as she blew on her nails to dry them. 'He needs to know he can't just treat me like dirt and then expect me to be there whenever he wants me.'

'Why do you want to be with him at all, if he treats you like dirt?' Winnie asked.

'Because I love him.'

Winnie frowned. The more Viv tried to explain about boyfriends, the more relieved she was that she'd never had one. They sounded like a lot of hard work to her.

When Viv's nails were dry she went off to run herself a bath. Winnie got out her textbooks. They were three weeks away from the end of the course, and everyone had started to fret about the forthcoming examinations. There was no more music or laughter or playing cards in the common room. Instead everyone was furiously swotting up and testing each other.

Winnie was struggling to get to grips with the anatomy of the heart when Beth returned.

'Quick question for you. What are the three layers of the heart muscle—' She stopped, the question dying on her lips when she saw Beth standing in the doorway. 'Blimey, what's happened to you?'

'I've got a headache.'

'You don't look well.' She was shockingly pale, poor girl.

She looked limp, as if every drop of blood had been drained from her body. 'Shall I go to the Infirmary and get an aspirin for you?'

'No, thank you. I'll be all right. I just need to sleep.' She sounded dazed.

'What happened to your stockings? They're ripped to shreds.'

'I tripped and fell.'

'You look like you've gone ten rounds with Floyd Patterson!' Winnie moved to peer closer, but Beth turned her head away.

'I'm all right, honestly,' she insisted. 'I just want to go to bed.' She spoke in a strange, flat voice, as if she was already half asleep.

'If you're sure there's nothing I can do?'

Winnie watched her uneasily from behind her textbook as she undressed and put on her nightgown. Odd, she thought. Her stockings were torn, but there were no grazes on her legs where she would have fallen. And as she climbed into bed, Winnie thought she saw bruises blossoming on her thighs.

She remembered what she had seen earlier, and a cold feeling of dread crawled up her spine as a picture began to form in her mind.

No, it couldn't be.

'Beth?' she whispered.

'Yes,' Beth mumbled from beneath the bedclothes.

'Did anything happen to you tonight?' There was a long silence. 'You know you can always tell me, if anyone—'

'Nothing's happened,' Beth said flatly.

'But earlier this evening, as I was going to close the curtains, I saw—'

There was a strangled cry from under the bedclothes.

'Beth?' Winnie threw aside her textbook and jumped up. 'Beth, are you all right?'

Beth threw back the cover and struggled out of bed, her eyes wide with terror. She reached out her hands towards Winnie, her fingers flexing, grasping thin air. But no sooner had her feet touched the floor than she suddenly went rigid and fell forwards, hitting the ground with a thud.

'Beth!' Winnie screamed.

Beth lay rigid on the ground, fists clenched, her teeth gritted in a ghastly grimace. Her eyes stared vacantly up at the ceiling, but her chest was still.

'Would you believe it? Someone's nicked all the hot water. Now I've got to wait till the—' Viv stopped dead in the doorway, her towel tucked under her arm. 'Bloody hell, what's going on?'

'I don't know.' Winnie put her hand out cautiously to check Beth's neck, looking for a pulse. But before she could touch her, Beth suddenly came to life and began to twitch and jerk like a puppet.

'Christ!' Viv threw her towel down and rushed over to where Beth writhed on the floor. 'Quick, pass me that pencil!'

Winnie handed it over, and watched as Viv deftly wrapped it in her face flannel and stuck it between Beth's teeth. She held it there grimly as the girl's jaws moved convulsively, flecks of foaming spittle frothing from the corners of her mouth.

Winnie stood over them, too transfixed with terror to move.

'Don't just stand there – get help!' Viv said.

Winnie ran to the door. 'Come quick!' she yelled down the stairs. 'Beth's having a fit!'

'It's all right, Beth love,' she heard Viv saying behind her. But the girl seemed possessed, her limbs thrashing about as if they had taken on a life of their own.

Winnie's cry for help must have echoed down to the ground floor, because a moment later Miss Coulter came thundering up the stairs in her dressing gown. The other girls followed.

'What's going on?' the Home Sister asked, pushing her way past Winnie to kneel beside Viv.

'She collapsed,' Winnie said. 'I thought she'd fallen down dead, but then she started twitching—'

The other girls started to crowd into the room, but Winnie pushed them out and closed the door in their faces.

The fit only lasted a minute or so, but it felt like an eternity. Soon enough, Beth's spasms subsided and she lay limp.

'What happened?' Her eyelids fluttered open, taking in her surroundings.

'You had a seizure.' Miss Coulter sounded matter-of-fact as she unfastened the top buttons of the girl's nightgown. 'Did you notice if she hit her head when she fell?' she asked Winnie.

'I don't think so, Sister. But she went down like a sack of spuds,' Viv said.

'Go and find Miss Beck,' she said. 'Tell her what's happened, and ask her to get a bed ready in the Infirmary.'

'I'm so tired . . .' Beth whispered.

'I'm sure you are, my dear.' Miss Coulter looked at her kindly as she cradled her head. It seemed like a tender gesture, but Winnie could tell the Home Sister was checking for wounds. 'Don't worry, you'll soon be tucked up safely. Then you can have a nice sleep.'

Miss Beck appeared shortly afterwards with two porters and a trolley, and within a few minutes they had taken Beth off to the Infirmary.

'Well done, both of you,' Miss Coulter said to them. 'You did exactly what you should have done.'

'It was Viv, Sister. She knew what to do. I just stood panicked.'

Winnie looked at Viv. She had turned as red as her shiny fingernails.

Chapter Forty-One

'Beth Bradshaw suffered a major convulsion,' Miss Beck said. 'She's resting comfortably now, but she's utterly exhausted.'

Helen frowned. 'What brought it on, I wonder? Is it epilepsy?'

'That seems the most likely to me. But the doctor is going to take a look at her, to make sure there are no other possible causes.'

'Poor child.' Helen couldn't remember seeing epilepsy mentioned in her medical notes, otherwise she would not have been accepted for training. 'What about the girls who were with her?'

'They're understandably shocked, of course, but they seem none the worse for it. Miss Coulter said they showed great presence of mind when dealing with the situation, particularly Trent.'

'Did she? I must say I'm surprised.'

'I'm not,' the Infirmary Sister said. 'I was very impressed with her work in the Infirmary.'

'I'm pleased to hear it.' It was a relief to know that her faith in the girl had not been misplaced.

'Indeed, Matron. I believe she has the makings of an

excellent nurse, and her actions this evening have proved it.' Miss Beck hesitated. 'There was something else I thought I should mention,' she said.

'About Trent?'

'No, Matron, concerning Bradshaw. When we were getting her into bed, I couldn't help noticing—'

'Where's my daughter?'

A shrill voice rang out from the other end of the corridor. The next moment a woman came flying round the corner, swathed in furs. Helen recognised her straight away, as did Miss Beck.

'Heavens,' the Infirmary Sister murmured, 'is that—'

'I believe it is, Sister.'

Helen turned to face the woman as she swept down the corridor. Celia Wells was every bit as glamorous as she was on the screen, with her platinum blonde hair and expensive mink. But she was shaking from head to foot and her beautiful face was ravaged by tears.

'My daughter!' she cried. 'I had a telephone call to say she's been in an accident?'

'Calm yourself, Miss Wells,' Helen reassured her. 'Your daughter hasn't been in an accident, but she suffered a convulsion earlier this evening.'

'A convulsion?' Celia Wells looked panic-stricken. 'Oh God, where is she? I must see her!'

She went to push past, but Helen put her hands out to stop her.

'A moment please, Miss Wells.' The woman's arms were thin and fragile underneath the thick fur coat. 'Can

I ask you, has Beth ever suffered a seizure before, to your knowledge?'

'What? No, of course not!' Celia stared at her. Close to, Helen could see the tear tracks down her thickly powdered cheeks. 'Now, where is she? I must see her!'

'Of course. Miss Beck will take you to her.' Helen motioned to the Infirmary Sister. 'But try not to tire her out, won't you? She's still exhausted—'

But Celia Wells was already gone, hurrying down the corridor, desperately searching for her daughter.

Helen returned to her office. It was almost seven o'clock, and she should have been off duty two hours earlier. Not that she had any plans. A long, lonely Saturday evening stretched ahead of her.

She gathered up an armful of paperwork she had promised herself she would tackle, switched off the lights and was just locking the office door when she saw Winnie Riley heading down the passage towards her with a very purposeful look on her face.

'Riley,' Helen greeted her pleasantly. 'What can I do for you?'

'I need to speak to you, Matron.'

'What about? Can't it wait until Monday morning?'

Winnie shook her head. 'I'd rather get it off my chest now, if you don't mind? Only I don't think I'll be able to stop thinking about it if I don't.'

Helen looked at the girl. Winnie Riley's blue eyes were troubled. She was a stoical sort of girl, not the type to come running with petty dramas like some of the others.

She looked down at the paperwork in her arms. It could wait a few more hours.

'You'd better come into my office,' she said.

Oh Winnie, what were you thinking?

The words repeated themselves over and over in Winnie's mind as she stood in Matron's office. It would have been so much easier to say nothing and mind her own business for once.

But then she thought about poor Beth, and those bruises, and the vacant look in her eyes, and she knew she couldn't let him get away with it.

Anyway, it was too late now. She was here, and the damage was already done.

'And what makes you think Bradshaw was assaulted?'

Matron regarded her calmly. Her expression and the tone of her voice gave no hint of any emotion.

'I saw bruises as she was getting into bed. Here,' she placed her hands around the top of her thighs through her skirt. 'They looked like they'd been made by fingermarks, pushing her legs apart—' She stopped speaking, not daring to say any more.

'And you say you know who carried out this assault?'

'I don't know for sure, but I think—' She took a deep breath. 'I think it might have been Mr Allenby.'

For the first time, Matron's face betrayed emotion. She stared at Winnie in shock.

'Mr Allenby? Are you serious?'

Winnie nodded. 'Yes, Matron.'

'And what makes you think he was involved?'

'He likes her,' Winnie said. 'He's always watching her in class. I've seen him. He finds excuses to be near her, to touch her. And he offered to give her private lessons.'

'They met in private?' Matron said faintly.

'Only once, as far as I know.'

Matron had turned as pale as her starched headdress. 'And why hasn't Bradshaw told me any of this?' she asked.

'She's too nervous. She thinks she'll get into trouble.'

'I see.' Matron picked up her pen and made a few notes.

Winnie hoped fervently that she had done the right thing. She didn't know what Beth would say about her speaking out, but she knew she couldn't keep quiet. If Mr Allenby had done anything to her, then he should be punished for it.

'And do you have any other reason to suspect Mr Allenby might be involved in this alleged assault?' Matron asked.

'I saw them together this evening, as I was closing the curtains in the nurses' home. Beth was standing outside, and Mr Allenby walked over to her.'

'And then what happened?'

'They talked for a minute or two, then they went off together.'

'Together? You're absolutely sure about that?' Matron's gaze sharpened.

'Yes, Matron. I saw them.'

'Did you see where they went?'

'No, Matron. But he had his arm around her.'

Matron made another note on the paper in front of her.

'She was so upset when she came back to the nurses' home,' Winnie went on. 'She didn't want to talk to anyone, she couldn't even look me in the eye. She said she had a headache and got into bed.'

'She might have been acting strangely because of the impending seizure?' Matron said.

'I thought about that,' Winnie said. She'd thought about all sorts of things, running them through in her head over and over again before she had finally decided she couldn't keep it to herself any longer. 'But what if it was the other way round? What if what happened to her actually brought it on?'

Matron stared at her in silence. Her dark gaze was unnerving, but Winnie met it fearlessly.

'These are very serious accusations,' Matron said at last. 'Are you sure you're prepared to stand by them?'

She could stop it now. Say she'd made a mistake, go back to her room and forget any of it ever happened.

But she'd done that once before, and the injustice of it still weighed heavily on her.

Winnie straightened her shoulders. 'Yes, Matron.'

'Very well,' Matron sighed. 'Let's see what Mr Allenby has to say for himself, shall we?'

Chapter Forty-Two

When Beth opened her eyes, the first person she saw was her mother sitting at her bedside, holding her hand.

She barely recognised her. Celia Wells's beautiful face was ravaged with tears, her green eyes red and swollen. It was an image the avid readers of *Picturegoer* would never believe, she thought.

Her mother broke into a watery smile when she saw Beth's eyes flutter open.

'Oh, thank God,' she breathed.

'What time is it?' Beth croaked out the words. Her throat felt thick and clogged.

'It's just past nine o'clock in the evening, darling.'

Beth snapped awake. 'Shouldn't you be at the theatre?'

'I've told them to let the understudy take over for tonight.'

'But it's the last night! This is important.'

'It's more important that I stay here with you.' She reached out and stroked the hair back from Beth's face. 'How are you feeling?'

'I – I'm not sure.'

She was still trying to put together what had happened to her. The events of the day were jumbled in her mind, like fragments of a jigsaw puzzle. But they all seemed so unreal, it was hard to make sense of them.

And in the middle of it all was a great blank hole that she could not fathom at all.

'What do you remember?' her mother prompted her gently.

A picture of Mr Allenby on top of her, grunting and pawing at her like an animal, came into her mind. Beth squeezed her eyes tight shut, trying to push the thought away. Why couldn't that part of her mind be blank, instead of what had happened afterwards?

'I remember going to bed,' she said. 'But then I don't remember anything else until I woke up on the floor.' She looked uncertainly at her mother. 'What happened to me?'

'You had a seizure, darling.'

'A seizure?'

'Matron thought it might have been brought on by the strain of the exams coming up.' She tenderly tucked a stray lock of hair behind Beth's ear. 'There's no reason to think you'll have another one, if it hasn't happened before.'

Beth thought of all the times when the world had frozen and people had stopped in their tracks for a few seconds before returning to life.

Beth had always thought she was daydreaming, except she had no memory of what she had been thinking about afterwards. The only thing she could ever remember was her sister, moving through the static landscape.

Another picture suddenly came into Beth's mind, of a different time and a different place.

'It has happened before,' she said.

Her mother leaned forward, her face urgent. 'When?'

'That day, on the boat.'

Her mother flinched, but for once Beth did not hold back. She had to get the words out, to pin down the elusive memory before it slipped away again forever.

'We were on the boat,' she said. 'Alison was shouting at me, telling me to turn the boat round and go back to the shore. And I was trying, I really was. But suddenly my head felt strange, and I had pins and needles in my arms. I thought it was just the effort of trying to row against the tide. Next thing I knew I was in the water and Alison was trying to get to me.' She closed her eyes, pushing herself to remember. 'It was exactly the same feeling as I had earlier. That lightness in my head, and the tingling in my arms. What if I had a seizure then, too? What if that's why I—'

She looked up and saw that her mother was crying. Actually sobbing, the kind of tears Beth had never seen her weep before, not even when Alison died.

'I'm sorry, I'm so sorry,' she kept saying, over and over again. 'I should have been there. I should have saved you both.'

Beth stared at her, trying to comprehend. 'But I was the one who made Alison take the boat out . . .'

'It would never have happened if I'd been there. But I wasn't. I'd taken myself off to bed with a wretched headache, thinking of myself as always. But I should have been there to protect you.' She looked at Beth, tears still streaming down her cheeks. 'And I've been cursing myself for it ever since.'

Beth stared at her mother. Could it really be true? All the time she thought her mother blamed her for what had happened, but all this time she had been blaming herself.

'I thought you hated me,' she said quietly.

'Hate you?' Her mother stared at her. 'How could you possibly imagine such a thing?'

'Because it was all my fault. And because Alison died and I didn't.' She raised her gaze to look into her mother's eyes. 'You've treated me differently since she died. You kept me at arm's length, never wanted to be with me. You just buried yourself in work all the time—'

'Only because I felt too guilty to face you!' Her mother's face was full of sorrow. 'I thought you hated me, too,' she said quietly. 'I thought you were keeping Alison's memory alive just to hurt me, to remind me of what I'd done, how I'd failed you both . . .'

'I wanted to remember her because she was my sister and I loved her!'

'I know. I loved her, too. And perhaps I should have shown it more, instead of taking the coward's way out, hiding her pictures away and keeping myself busy so I didn't have time to think. Perhaps then you might not have felt as if you had to sacrifice your own happiness the way you have.'

Beth stared at her in shock. 'What do you mean?'

'I mean all this!' Her mother gestured around the Infirmary room where Beth lay. 'Nursing was never what you wanted, was it? It was Alison's dream, not yours. You're an artist, Beth. That's your passion. But you threw it away for the sake of your sister. I wanted to be happy for you, I tried to show an interest. But all I could feel was angry that you were pushing yourself to be something you weren't. It was almost as if you were punishing yourself . . .'

'I was,' Beth said bleakly. She could see that now.

A life for a life. She had taken her sister's chance of happiness, so she had to give hers in return.

'It doesn't work that way, darling,' her mother said sadly. 'You making yourself miserable won't bring Alison back. If that was the case then I think between us we could have done it a long time ago.'

Perhaps we did, Beth thought. She remembered seeing her sister's frowning face around the hospital. *This is my place, not yours*, she always seemed to be saying. But what if she wasn't angry? What if this was simply her way of telling Beth that her sacrifice wasn't worth all the unhappiness she was bringing on herself?

'I wish I could have stopped you doing this,' her mother sighed. 'I should have spoken up, but I couldn't. I didn't feel I had the right, after what I'd done. But I hated this place,' she said. 'I couldn't even bring myself to come here on your first day. That's why I put that sketchbook in your suitcase, in the hope that you'd find your way back eventually.'

Dearest Beth. Never forget who you really are.

'You gave me the sketchbook? I thought it was Grace.'

'No, it was me. I hoped it would say everything I couldn't say myself. It's odd, isn't it?' she smiled sadly. 'I'm so used to speaking other people's lines, I don't know how to speak from my own heart any more.'

'Perhaps we should have both been more honest with each other.'

'Perhaps it's not too late?'

Beth met her mother's beseeching gaze. 'No,' she smiled. 'I don't think it's too late.'

272

'I'm glad.' Her mother stood up, gathering up her gloves. 'Now, I've spoken to Miss Beck and she agrees it would be best if you came home with me for a few days, just until you're properly rested.'

'And then what?'

'We can talk about that when you've fully recovered.'

A thought suddenly occurred to Beth. 'But you're flying to New York on Monday for a month!'

Celia shook her head. 'I've decided to step aside and give one of those little starlets a chance. I think I've been in the limelight long enough, don't you?'

'But you've always wanted to play Broadway . . .'

'I'm sure there'll be other chances. But for now I want to be with my daughter.' Her mother smiled warmly at her. 'I nearly lost you once, I'm not going to let it happen again.'

Chapter Forty-Three

'May I ask what all this is about, Matron?'

Miss Cheetham stood in front of Helen's desk, her face implacable as ever. Her body was perfectly still, but Helen could almost feel the tension that emanated from her.

Helen was surprised to see her there. She had summoned Mr Allenby to her office but Miss Cheetham had insisted on coming with him.

In contrast to the Sister Tutor, Mr Allenby seemed very relaxed. Either he was entirely innocent, or he was confident to the point of cockiness. Helen wasn't sure which, but there was something about him that irked her.

Winnie Riley was clearly bothered by him, too. She glared at him from where she stood in the corner of the room. Helen had sent her away the previous night and told her to sleep on what she had said. Deep down she was hoping she might have had time to reconsider.

But when Helen arrived at her desk on Sunday morning, Winnie was already there waiting for her. And from the shadows under her eyes, she clearly hadn't slept any better than Helen had.

'One of our students, Beth Bradshaw, suffered a seizure last night.'

'Poor girl,' Mr Allenby muttered.

'How unfortunate,' Miss Cheetham looked concerned. 'I hope she's all right?'

Helen ignored Winnie's snort from the corner.

'She'll recover,' she said. 'What's more distressing is the allegation that she had been assaulted earlier in the evening.'

'Assaulted?' Miss Cheetham looked confused.

'Good lord,' Mr Allenby murmured.

'And what has that got to do with us?' Miss Cheetham asked.

'It has nothing to do with you, Miss Cheetham,' Helen said. 'The accusation was made against Mr Allenby.'

Miss Cheetham gasped in outrage. 'I've never heard such nonsense!' She swung round to look at Winnie. 'Was it you? Are you the one spreading these wicked lies?'

Winnie flinched, and Helen stepped in. 'I've been told you've been giving Bradshaw private lessons?' she said to Mr Allenby.

'I'm afraid I did, Matron.' Mr Allenby looked rueful, not in the slightest perturbed by what was happening around him. 'I could see the poor girl was struggling, so I took pity on her. But Chris – Miss Cheetham – made me realise the error of my ways. She pointed out how my actions could be misconstrued, so we stopped.'

'And you're sure there haven't been any other clandestine meetings?' Helen asked Mr Allenby.

'No, Matron. I give you my word.'

'You were talking to her last night,' Winnie said. 'I saw you.'

Miss Cheetham shot her another venomous look, but Mr Allenby didn't even spare her a glance.

'Miss Riley is quite right, I did stop to speak to her,' he admitted. 'I was walking by and I noticed her near the nurses' home. She seemed very unsteady on her feet, so I went over and asked her if she was all right.'

'And then what?'

'She said she had a headache. I asked her if she needed an aspirin, but she said no. So I took her to the door of the nurses' home and left her there.'

'And what time was this?'

'Just after six o'clock, Matron. I remember because I was meeting someone at seven.'

'It was the students' afternoon off,' Miss Cheetham pointed out. 'Bradshaw could have met someone before then. A boyfriend, perhaps—'

'Beth doesn't have a boyfriend!' Winnie retorted. 'She spent the afternoon visiting her sister's grave.'

'Please, Riley.' Helen shook her head at her. 'You say you were meeting someone, Mr Allenby?' she said. 'I take it that means someone can vouch for your movements?'

Mr Allenby gave a nervous laugh. 'Why do I feel as if I'm on trial?'

His light-hearted attitude irritated Helen. 'These are serious allegations, Mr Allenby. If you could humour me—'

'He was supposed to be meeting me!' Miss Cheetham blurted out. Helen looked at her in surprise.

'Stephen – Mr Allenby – and I are in a relationship,' the Sister Tutor explained, blushing.

'I see.'

'It's not against the rules.'

'Indeed it isn't, Miss Cheetham. So you can vouch for him?'

Miss Cheetham opened her mouth to speak, but Winnie jumped in first. 'How can you believe a word she says? Of course she's going to stick up for her boyfriend, ain't she?'

'How dare you!' Miss Cheetham turned on her, her face flushed with rage. 'Are you calling me a liar?'

'I'm saying you know exactly what happened to Beth and you're covering up for him.'

Miss Cheetham turned back to Helen. 'Surely you're not going to let her speak to me like that, Matron?'

Helen glared at Winnie. She had sympathy for the girl, but she certainly wasn't doing herself any favours.

'Surely there's only one person who knows what really happened?' Mr Allenby spoke up. 'Have you spoken to Beth Bradshaw about it?'

'I haven't had the chance, unfortunately. Her mother has taken her home for a few days.'

'So she hasn't made any accusations herself?'

'No.'

'There you are, then.' Helen wondered if she had imagined the triumphant smirk that curled Christina Cheetham's lips.

'You know she won't say anything anyway, because she's too frightened!' Winnie broke in.

Helen turned on her. 'That's enough, Riley,' she said. 'I think it's best if you return to your room.'

'But—'

'I'm giving you an order, Riley. I suggest you do as you're told.'

Winnie looked mutinous, and for a moment Helen

thought she might argue. But then she flounced out of the room with a final dirty look in Miss Cheetham's direction.

'I've never heard anything like it,' Miss Cheetham said as soon as the door had closed behind her. 'I hope you're going to do something about her, Matron?'

'Please,' Mr Allenby stepped in. 'Let the girl be. She's a good student, she's just upset and worried about her friend—'

'She's a liar and a troublemaker. We don't need her sort here.'

'And what sort would that be?' Helen asked.

'Common.' Miss Cheetham spat out the word with distaste. 'You heard the insolent way she spoke to me.'

'She didn't express herself very well,' Helen admitted. 'But she came to me in good faith—'

'She came to stir up trouble!' Miss Cheetham's face was taut with anger. 'And I can't be expected to put up with students showing me so little respect.' She fixed Helen with a steely look. 'I mean it, Matron. Either that girl goes, or I do!'

Chapter Forty-Four

The following Monday evening, Dora took the bus up west to meet Millie and Helen at the Lyons Corner House on the Strand.

She was a few minutes late arriving at the grand Art Deco building and made her way quickly through the ground-floor food hall, with its delicatessen counter, glorious displays of flowers and mouth-watering cakes and pastries, and hurried upstairs to the first-floor restaurant.

Millie was already there, waiting for them. At first, Dora did not recognise the sophisticated middle-aged woman who sat at a corner table studying the menu over the top of her reading spectacles. Her blonde hair was short and beautifully styled, and her simple pale-blue wool dress was elegant and expensive-looking, finished off by a string of pearls at her throat.

It was only when she caught sight of Dora and let out a shriek of excitement, which drew everyone's attention, that Dora truly recognised her old friend.

'Dora!' Millie jumped to her feet, waving madly. 'Over here!'

Dora made her way over, already laughing. She had hardly reached the table before Millie swept her up in a hug that nearly lifted her off the floor.

'Oh, Dora. It's so good to see you,' she beamed. There were faint laughter lines around her china-blue eyes, but her smile was as warm and welcoming as ever.

'It's good to see you, too. You've hardly changed a bit.'

'Now I know that's not true!' Millie smiled impishly as they both sat down. 'I'm a terrible old country bumpkin now.'

'At least you're not old and grey like me.'

'You're not grey at all!' Millie protested.

'But you're saying I'm old?'

Millie laughed. 'We're all positively ancient, darling. Except Helen, of course. She's still as radiant as ever. Where is she, by the way?'

'I don't know. I thought she'd be here by now.' Dora looked around the restaurant, with its gilded ceilings and white tablecloths and uniformed Nippies hurrying back and forth between tables. 'Perhaps there's been an emergency at the hospital?'

'It's so strange to think of her being in charge, isn't it?' Millie handed her a menu. 'Shall we order something while we're waiting? How about some champagne, since it's a special occasion?'

'Oh, I don't know about that—'

'Please. It's my treat.' She held up her hand to summon the Nippy. 'And you mustn't look at me like that,' she added, as Dora stiffened. 'I know what you're like when your pride gets in the way. But we're celebrating and it would make me happy.'

'If you put it like that, I suppose I can't refuse.' But Dora was still wary. Millie was right, she was very prickly when it came to accepting what she saw as charity. It had taken her a long time to realise that Millie did not see it that way at all. Even though she was the daughter of an earl, she was not in the least bit patronising or snobbish. She was simply a very kind, open-hearted girl who treated everyone the same way, whatever their background.

It was one of the things Dora had always loved about her.

They placed their order, and Millie sat back in her seat with a happy sigh.

'Gosh, it's such a treat to come up to London,' she said. 'Whenever I come, I always wonder why I don't do it more often.'

'I don't think I'd ever miss the Smoke if I lived in the country like you,' Dora said.

'You're right, it is wonderful.' Millie leaned forward. 'But you must come and visit us at Billinghurst. Bring your family, of course. You can stay for the weekend.'

Dora smiled. She could only imagine what her Nick would say if she suggested they go and stay in a stately home. 'I'm not sure about that. You ain't met my lot!'

'Nonsense, the more the merrier,' Millie grinned. 'Anyway, how are you? I know we keep up with our news by letter, but it's not the same as a good chat, is it?'

She was quite right. Dora had been worried that they wouldn't have anything to say to each other after so long apart. But as they talked, it was as if the years had melted away and they were laughing together over the old times as if the last twelve years had never happened.

Somewhere along the line their champagne arrived,

but Dora scarcely noticed it as she told Millie all about her family, Nick's business, and how Walter had been called up for National Service.

'He'll be all right,' Millie reassured her. 'He sounds like a very bright young man. And if my Henry can survive two years in the military, I'm sure anyone can!'

Dora remembered the sweet, studious little seven-year-old she had last met at Helen's wedding. She knew from Millie's letters that he was studying medicine at Oxford.

'How's he getting on?'

Millie nodded. 'We're so proud of him. Will especially. He's very touched that Henry's chosen to follow in his footsteps. He says it makes him feel more like his father.'

'He was the one who brought him up,' Dora says.

Henry probably wouldn't remember his real father, Dora thought. He was little more than a baby when Millie's first husband Sebastian had been killed in the war.

Millie looked wistful for a moment. 'I'm glad they're so close,' she said. Then she turned to Dora and went on, 'I hear your daughter is following in your footsteps, too?'

'Yes, she's in the middle of PTS.'

Millie grimaced. 'God, I hope she's doing better than I ever did! I failed first time round, do you remember?' She lifted her champagne glass to her lips. 'I thoroughly deserved to fail, of course. I don't think there was a single rule I didn't break.'

'I don't think there was a single thermometer you didn't break, either!' Dora laughed.

'I was a walking disaster, wasn't I?' Millie shuddered.

'Do you remember the time Sister Holmes told me to clean the patients' false teeth, and I decided it would save time to stick them all in the same bowl and do them together?'

'And then you had to rush about trying to cram the wrong sets back in everyone's mouths before the consultant arrived to do his round?' Dora joined in.

'What a nightmare! I'm sure I did the medical profession a favour leaving when I did.'

'Nonsense. You were a very caring nurse.'

'Just not a very competent one!' Millie shook her head. 'Not like our friend Helen. Look at her now, Matron of the Nightingale. Who could have imagined it?'

'It seems strange, doesn't it?' Dora agreed. 'Although she was always the cleverest out of us all.'

'Oh yes, she was always capable,' Millie agreed. 'But when she married David, I thought she'd given up on her career. She seemed so happy and content working with him at the surgery, visiting patients around the village . . .' She looked at Dora. 'I suppose she told you they'd separated?' Dora nodded. 'It's such a shame. David's utterly devastated, poor lamb. He's lost without her. And we all thought they were so happy together—'

'Hello, you two!'

Thankfully, Helen arrived before Millie had a chance to say any more. Dora was glad. Even though she knew Millie was too nice to gossip, Dora didn't feel very comfortable talking about Helen's marriage behind her back.

'Sorry I'm late.' Helen slipped off her coat. 'There was a problem with the rotas.'

'You nearly missed the champagne.' Millie signalled to a Nippy to fill Helen's glass.

Dora watched Helen as she sat down. Was it her imagination, or did she seem to be avoiding her eye?

Millie, as ever, seemed to be oblivious to any undercurrents. 'Cheers,' she said, lifting her glass. 'Isn't it marvellous that we're all together again?'

'Cheers.' Once again, Helen did not look at Dora as she lifted her glass. Her senses were immediately on edge.

'Are you all right, Helen?' she asked.

Helen sent her a quick, nervous glance. 'I wasn't sure if you'd still want to talk to me, after everything that's happened,' she said with an uneasy smile.

Dora's blood ran chill in her veins. 'What are you talking about? What's happened?' she asked.

Helen frowned. 'Surely you must know?'

'I wouldn't be asking you if I did, would I?' Nerves made Dora's voice taut.

'I've had to suspend Winnie from training.'

'What?' It was Millie who spoke up as the words stuck in Dora's throat. 'Oh, lord.' She snatched up the bottle and refilled her own glass without waiting for the waitress.

'What's she done?' Dora asked.

Helen paused again, and Dora could see she was choosing her words carefully. 'She made certain accusations against one of the teaching staff at the nursing school.'

'What sort of accusations?'

'I can't say. It wouldn't be fair of me. But they were serious. As I understand it, she was speaking up on behalf of another girl, a fellow student.'

'So why has my Winnie been suspended?'

'Things got rather – heated, I'm afraid. Winnie was very disrespectful to the Head of the Nursing School. You must understand I had to take action,' she pleaded with Dora for understanding. 'Especially as these accusations don't have any foundation as far as I can see.'

'Did you speak to the girl?'

'No,' Helen conceded quietly. 'I haven't had a chance yet. She's still recovering at home.'

'Well, then,' Dora said. 'How do you know Winnie's not telling the truth?'

'I don't,' Helen admitted. 'But she was very rude to Miss Cheetham, so—'

'So my daughter got kicked out.' Dora took a gulp of her drink. But the champagne tasted like sour, fizzy vinegar on her tongue.

She knew it had all been too good to be true. Winnie settling down, actually doing well for once instead of getting into trouble. Why couldn't she just keep her nose out, instead of getting involved in everyone else's business and ending up in trouble?

'It's only until I have the chance to get to the bottom of what's happened,' Helen said. 'I intend to speak to Miss James, the Junior Tutor, but she is currently on holiday in Wales.' She looked apologetically at Dora. 'I'm so sorry. I thought you would have known about it by now.'

'No,' Dora said dully. 'No, I didn't.'

'It's only a suspension,' Helen went on. 'She hasn't been dismissed. As I said, I'm still waiting to investigate the matter—'

But Dora wasn't listening.

'When did you say this happened?' she asked Helen.

'She left the hospital yesterday morning.' Helen frowned. 'Surely she's come home?'

'No,' Dora said. 'No, she hasn't.'

So where was she?

Chapter Forty-Five

'She arrived yesterday,' Josie said, when she opened the door to Dora. She didn't seem surprised to see her, even though it was nearly ten o'clock at night. 'Very upset she was.'

'Why didn't she come straight home?' Dora asked.

'You'll have to ask her that, not me.'

She led the way into her sitting room. 'You wait here, I'll go and call her. She's barely come out of her room since she got here.'

Her room. Dora felt a pang at the words. This wasn't Winnie's home. She belonged in Old Ford Road, with the rest of them.

But perhaps she preferred it here? Dora couldn't blame her for that. She looked around at the neat room with its modern furnishings. Josie lived here all alone, and she could afford nice things. It was better than Dora could offer Winnie, sharing a room with her invalid grandmother in their chaotic little terrace.

Winnie appeared in the doorway, wearing a nightgown and that truculent look Dora knew so well.

'Sit down, love.' Josie ushered her to the settee opposite the armchair where Dora sat. 'I've just put some tea in the pot. I'll go and pour us all a cup, shall I?'

She withdrew diplomatically, sending Dora a warning look over her shoulder as she closed the door.

Be careful, she mouthed.

Dora bristled with offence. She didn't need Josie to tell her how to speak to her own daughter. She might be a head-teacher, but she had no kids of her own. She had no idea what it felt like to be a mother.

She looked at Winnie. 'What's all this I hear about you being suspended?' she said.

Winnie stared down at her hands. 'Who told you?

'I met Helen McKay today. But I would have preferred to hear it from you. Why didn't you tell me?'

Winnie shrugged her shoulders and said nothing. She still wouldn't meet Dora's eye.

Dora tried again. 'Do you want to tell me what happened? Helen said there was an argument with a tutor—'

'She was lying,' Winnie said. 'One of the other tutors attacked a girl, and she covered up for him.'

'Attacked?'

Winnie shot her a quick, embarrassed look. 'You know,' she said quietly. 'It was a man.'

Dora took a deep breath, forcing herself to stay calm. 'And did this other girl say anything? Did she report him to Matron?'

'No,' Winnie admitted. 'But only because she's too frightened to speak up—'

'So you decided to do it for her?'

'Someone had to.'

'But why did it have to be you?'

'Would you rather I'd kept quiet and let him get away with it?'

'I'd rather you hadn't got suspended!' Dora's rising temper got the better of her. 'Why did you have to get involved, Win? You were doing so well. You could have actually got somewhere for once, but instead you had to go and—'

'Mess it up? You don't have to tell me, I already know what a disappointment I am!'

Winnie jumped to her feet.

'Sit down,' Dora said, 'I ain't finished talking—'

'That's all you ever do, ain't it? Talk, talk, talk, like yours is the only opinion that counts. You never bother to listen, that's your trouble!' Winnie rushed from the room, slamming the door behind her.

Dora listened to the sound of her feet running up the stairs. She was about to go after her when Josie came in, carrying the tea tray.

'That went as well as I thought it would,' she commented dryly as she set the tray down on the coffee table. 'And you wonder why she didn't come straight home.'

'What was I supposed to do? Pat her on the head and tell her what a grand job she's done?'

'You could have listened, tried to understand her instead of laying into her straight away. And yes, perhaps you could have been proud of her. She stuck up for someone who couldn't defend themselves. Surely that's a good thing?'

'Yes, but why does it always have to be her who puts her neck on the line?' Dora said in frustration. 'Why can't she just mind her own business for once, instead of getting involved and landing herself in trouble?'

'Like mother, like daughter,' Josie said quietly.

Dora turned on her. 'I've got more sense than that!'

'Have you?' Josie's brows rose. 'Remind me, didn't someone just lodge a complaint against you?'

'That was different,' Dora muttered. 'I wasn't in the wrong. Gordon Roper was just angry that I'd confronted him—'

'Exactly. You confronted him with no thought for what the consequences might be for you. And that's what Winnie did, too.'

She was right, Dora thought. Everyone said how similar they were, even though she couldn't see it. And a lot of the qualities that Winnie had – her pride, her stubbornness, her passion – were qualities Dora struggled with herself.

'I'm not angry with her,' she said. 'I'm just – disappointed, that's all. I only want the best for her, Josie.' She looked towards the door. 'Perhaps I should go up and try to talk to her—'

'Not just yet,' Josie said. 'You won't get anywhere if you keep butting heads.'

'But I—' Dora was about to argue, then she realised Josie was right. Much as she hated to admit it, she was not the one her daughter needed at that moment.

'What should I do?' she said quietly.

'Just leave her for a couple of days. Give yourselves time to calm down, then you can talk.'

Dora looked back towards the door. It took every shred of her being to stop herself running up those stairs and taking Winnie in her arms. Not being able to comfort her was like a physical pain in her heart.

And there was something else, too. A look in Winnie's eyes, as if there was so much she wasn't telling her.

'You're right,' she said quietly. 'I'm the last person she needs.'

'Is that what you really think?' Her sister laughed incredulously. 'Why do you think she's so upset? She's mortified, Dor. She knows she's let you down and that's why she can't talk to you.' She shook her head. 'Don't you see? All she wants is to impress you and make you proud.'

'Of course I'm proud of her. She knows that.'

'I wonder if she does?'

Dora was about to reply, then stopped. She had never really expressed her pride in her children because that wasn't her way. She had always assumed they knew how much she loved them without a lot of gushing emotion. But now it started to dawn on her that perhaps it was what her daughter needed from her.

She stood up. 'I'd best go,' she said. 'It's getting late.'

'What about your tea?'

'I'll leave it for now.' Dora looked back towards the door. 'Give her my love, won't you?' she said quietly.

Josie smiled. 'Leave it a couple of days and you can tell her yourself,' she said.

'I hope so,' Dora sighed.

Chapter Forty-Six

'You've got a visitor,' Grace said.

Beth looked up in surprise from the watercolour she was working on. She was so lost in the narcissus she was painting that she hadn't even heard the knock on the door.

She was even more surprised when she saw Viv standing next to Grace. She was dressed to kill as usual, in a tight-fitting green dress and shiny stilettoes. She had taken to copying Bettie Page's famous hairstyle, and her long auburn tresses curled down her back, with a thick fringe at the front.

'I'll leave you to it,' Grace said, looking from one to the other. 'I'll bring you some tea, shall I?'

She left, and Viv gazed around the sunny orangery, with its vaulted glass ceiling and open view out on to the garden.

'Blimey,' she whistled. 'How the other half lives, eh? Bit different from my gran's house in Hackney, I can tell you!'

'I wasn't expecting you,' Beth said.

'I was on my way up west to see Roy, so I thought I'd drop in.' She nodded to Beth's painting on the easel. 'Did you do that? You're very talented.'

'I don't know about that.' Beth blushed as she set her

paintbrush back in the jar of water. 'So you've decided to make it up with Roy, have you?'

'I thought I might give him another chance.' Viv grinned sheepishly. 'To be honest, I miss him like mad, and I'm worried he's forgotten me.'

She went over to the window and looked out over the garden. 'How are you getting on?'

'I'm feeling much better, thank you.'

'You gave us all a bit of a scare, I don't mind telling you.'

'Miss Beck told me how you helped me,' Beth said quietly. 'Thank you.'

'That's what friends are for,' Viv shrugged. 'So when do you think you might be coming back?'

'I'm not sure . . .' Beth had been pushing the thought from her mind for the past three days. She knew she would have to make a decision sooner or later, but she couldn't bring herself to think about it.

She sat down at her easel and picked up her paintbrush again. The afternoon light was changing, and she wanted to capture it before it faded completely.

'Anyway, how is everyone in the set?' she said. 'I'm surprised Winnie didn't come with you.'

'That's one of the reasons why I'm here, as a matter of fact.' Viv looked over her shoulder at her. 'She's been suspended.'

'Suspended?' Beth stared at her in shock. 'Why?'

'Because of you.'

'Me? What have I got to do with it?'

'She went to Matron and told her what happened with you and Mr Allenby.'

The paintbrush fell from Beth's hand. 'How does she know what happened?' she blurted out without thinking, 'I never told anyone—'

'So she was right, then? She was sure something must have happened. I dunno how, but she just knew.'

Beth picked up her paintbrush again, but her hand was shaking so much she could barely hold it.

'I still don't understand why she got suspended,' she said.

'Apparently Matron hauled Allenby and Miss Cheetham in, and they denied everything. Hardly surprising, really. I told you they were in it together, didn't I? Anyway, there was a big row and I'm sure Winnie gave as good as she got. You know what she's like when she's got a bee in her bonnet!' Viv grinned. 'What wouldn't I have given to be a fly on the wall in Matron's office, eh?'

Beth stared at her half-finished painting, feeling sick.

'The upshot of it all was that Miss Cheetham got her knickers in a twist and demanded that Matron sent Winnie packing. Thank God she's only been suspended,' Viv went on. 'I s'pose she could have been out on her ear completely.'

She came over to perch on the arm of an antique brocade chair. 'Anyway, that's where you come in,' she said.

'Me?'

'You've got to sort this out, tell Matron what happened. She's bound to believe you, especially if you show her the bruises. You've still got them, ain't you?'

Beth flinched. She tried to keep her eyes averted from the hideous yellow-black marks when she undressed, because they brought it all back too clearly.

'I'm sorry,' she said, her head down. 'I just want to forget it ever happened.'

Viv stared at her in astonishment. 'That's all very well for you, but what about poor Winnie? You're the only one who can back her up.'

'I didn't ask her to go running to Matron, did I?' Tension made Beth snap.

She went back to her painting, but she could feel Viv watching her.

'So you're just going to let them get away with it, are you? And what about when it happens to someone else? Because it will, you know. Men like Allenby don't stop. He'll find another innocent kid to pick on, single her out for attention, make her feel special. And then, when she trusts him, he'll—'

'Stop!' Beth pleaded. 'I told you, I just want to forget it.'

'And what about Winnie? Where does that leave her? She stood up for you, don't forget. Why won't you do the same for her?'

Beth stared at the paintbrush in her hand.

'Winnie's worked hard to get through this course,' Viv continued relentlessly. 'It might not mean a lot to you, with your big house and your paintings and your housekeeper, but it means everything to her. And now she's going to have it all taken away, because you couldn't bring yourself to stand up for her. Call yourself a friend?'

Just at that moment, Grace came in holding a tray.

'Tea's ready,' she said brightly. 'And there's cake, too—'

'No thanks, missus. I ain't stopping.'

Viv turned back to Beth. 'Don't forget what I said, will you? Winnie's relying on you.'

'Well, she didn't stay long, did she?' Grace remarked after Viv had gone. 'What a curious girl. Is she one of your nurse friends?'

Beth looked at the watercolour. The picture that had seemed so bright and full of promise had withered and faded, just like the flowers in the vase.

'Not any more,' she murmured sadly.

Viv was still seething as she sat on the top desk of the bus, heading up Piccadilly. Usually she loved a good bus ride, especially up west. She would watch the people passing by on the street below, then crane her neck to catch a glimpse of the fancy types coming out of the Ritz. Once she thought she saw Dirk Bogarde going into Fortnum & Mason's.

But today she was too angry to notice anything as she puffed angrily on her cigarette in the back seat.

Who did Beth Bradshaw think she was? Winnie had stuck her neck out for her, but Beth was too selfish to return the favour when she needed it.

It wouldn't have cost her anything, either. From the way she was talking, Viv didn't think she would even be coming back to the nursing school. She had no reason to fear the wrath of Miss Cheetham, or Mr Allenby.

Winnie was a mug for ever getting involved, she thought. Catch her putting herself out for any of that lot!

And then she smiled. Wasn't that exactly what she was doing, taking a trip up to Kensington to try to help out Winnie? She took another long drag of her cigarette and shook her head. If she wasn't careful, she might actually start thinking of those wretched students as her friends.

She got off the bus at Piccadilly Circus and walked to Old Compton Street. As ever in the early evening, the street was already buzzing with the usual mixture of young and old. The ladies who plied their trade behind closed curtains during the day were starting to emerge on to the street corners, joining beatniks and bohemians, West Indian immigrants and musicians, and Brylcreemed Teds.

The Heaven and Hell was busy as usual, with youths crowding around the door. As Viv approached, the first person she noticed was Roy's best friend Pete. He was lounging outside the café, moodily smoking a cigarette. Even from a distance, Viv could tell he was in a foul mood.

'All right, Pete? You look like you've lost a bob and found a tanner.'

He looked up at her. 'Oh, it's you. I thought we'd seen the last of you?'

'Now where on earth would you get that idea?' She plucked his cigarette from his fingers and took a drag.

'Ain't seen you around much.'

'Yeah, well, you know what they say. Absence makes the heart grow fonder.'

'More like, out of sight, out of mind.'

'Don't be like that.' She handed him back his cigarette. 'Where's Bobby, anyway? You two had a falling-out?'

'You might say that. She's ditched me.'

'Has she now?' No wonder Pete looked so glum, Viv thought. Although she didn't blame her friend. She'd always thought Bobby could do a lot better for herself. 'So where is she?'

'In there.' Pete nodded towards the door to the café. 'With her new boyfriend.'

'She's found someone else, has she? Blimey, that was quick. Anyone I know?'

Pete squinted at her through the curling smoke from his cigarette. There was something about the way he leered at her that sent alarm bells ringing inside her head.

'I reckon you do,' he said.

Chapter Forty-Seven

'We didn't mean for you to find out like this, honestly.'

Viv stared at her. She still couldn't believe what she was seeing. Bobby, her best friend, so sweet and innocent with her big brown eyes and her butter-wouldn't-melt face, clinging to Roy's arm. Hanging off him like a limpet, as if she didn't dare let go.

She could feel the tears welling up inside her, but she would not allow herself to cry. She wouldn't give anyone the satisfaction.

Sandra Ellis's words came back to her. *I ain't the one you want to watch out for.* She could see now it was a warning. Sandra must have seen which way the wind was blowing, and had tried to let Viv know in her own way.

If only she'd listened to her. But Viv was so busy watching the left hand, she had no idea what the right was doing.

At least Bobby had the grace to look ashamed. Roy didn't even look sorry about it. If anything, he seemed bored by what was going on around him.

'Can I talk to my boyfriend, please?' Viv said, tight-lipped, her gaze still fixed on Roy.

Bobby clung on tighter. 'Anything you've got to say, you can do it in front of me,' she said. 'We're a couple now.'

'What's the matter?' Viv taunted. 'Frightened I'll steal

him while your back's turned? I'll leave that snakey behaviour to you.'

Bobby opened her mouth to speak, but Roy fished in his pocket for a couple of coins and handed them to her.

'Go and stick a few songs on the jukebox,' he said.

Bobby hesitated, and for a moment she looked as if she might argue. Viv hoped she would, knowing how well that would go down with Roy. He hated anyone answering him back, especially girls.

But then Bobby seemed to think better of it. She planted a defiant kiss on Roy's cheek and sauntered off. But her casual attitude didn't fool Viv for a moment. She caught the nervous look she gave her over her shoulder. Viv gave her a friendly little finger wave and she turned away sharply.

'So what's going on?' she asked Roy. She wanted to cry and scream, but she knew she had to keep her cool if she was going to get anywhere. Roy hated clingy girls. And he didn't take kindly to anyone putting pressure on him, either.

'Ain't you worked it out by now?' he sneered. 'And I thought you was meant to be the clever one!'

'I'm clever enough to know you ain't serious about her.'

'Says who?'

'Says me.'

'And how do you work that out?'

'Why would you swap a steak for egg and chips?'

He looked her up and down. 'You've got a point there,' he laughed.

'Well, then. What are you messing about with her for when you could have me?'

'Because she's here and you ain't.'

Viv stared at him. 'Is that it? You're ready to ditch me just because I can't be here every night?'

'If you're my girlfriend, I expect you to be by my side.'

'And what about all the times you've ignored me all night, or abandoned me to go off with your friends?'

'That's different,' he shrugged.

Viv glanced over to the jukebox, where Bobby was pumping coins in as fast as she could, while watching them out of the corner of her eye. 'It was only for a few more weeks,' she said. 'Three more weeks, Roy. Then I would have got through the exams, and—'

'And then what? More studying?' Roy shook his head. 'You used to be fun, Viv. We had a laugh. But since you started at that nurses' school . . .' He shook his head. 'You ain't the same. You're boring. All you ever talk about is studying, and exams.'

'That's not true!'

'You weren't even meant to be there that long,' Roy protested, not listening. 'You told me you'd probably get kicked out within a fortnight.'

'Yes, but that was before—'

'Before what?'

Before I realised how much I wanted to do it, she said silently. *Before I realised that it was something I might actually be good at.*

She didn't know when the feeling had crept up on her. Perhaps it was the first time Miss James had singled her out for praise in the class? Or it might have been when she helped Miss Beck in the Infirmary.

Or perhaps it was when she rushed to Beth's aid, and realised that she could be the difference between life and death.

'Don't you want me to be a nurse?' she said. 'Once I qualify, we'll be able to make plans. I'll be earning enough for us to get married, and—'

'I ain't interested in making plans,' Roy cut her off. 'I'm interested in having a good time now.'

Viv looked at him. He was so good-looking, it made her stomach curl. Roy was right, they didn't need to make plans. He was her only future, and she would do anything to keep him.

'And what if I could be with you all the time?' she said slowly.

Roy narrowed his eyes. 'What are you saying?'

'What if I gave up nursing? Would you still want to be with Bobby?'

He smiled slowly. 'Bobby who?' he said.

Viv went to the toilets to touch up her make-up. She still felt like crying, only this time for a different reason.

She was wiping away her smudged mascara with the edge of her handkerchief when Bobby walked in.

'I don't want a fight,' she said, holding up her hands.

'Very wise. Because you know I'd flatten you.'

Bobby kept a wary distance between them. 'Roy told me what you said – about giving up nursing?'

'Disappointed, are you?' Viv said. 'Looks like you've lost your new boyfriend already.'

'I am disappointed, yes,' Bobby said. 'But not in the way you think.' She took a step closer. 'I'm disappointed you're

302

thinking of giving up your future for someone as worthless as Roy Carter.'

Viv sent her a sideways look. 'If you think so little of him, why were you so keen to get your claws into him?' she asked.

'Do you think I'd be wasting my time with him if I had half the chances you've got?' Bobby's brown eyes held hers. 'Listen to me, Viv. Roy will never amount to anything, and neither will I. This is all we're good for, parading round the coffee bars and showing off. But you – you're different. You've been given the chance to make something of your life, to be someone.' She reached for her. 'He ain't for you, Viv. You're too good for him.'

Viv looked down at her friend's hand, resting on her arm. 'You know, I've got to hand it to you, Bob. Only you could steal my boyfriend and make it sound like you're doing me a favour!' she laughed.

'I'm serious, Viv. Whatever you do, don't give up your nursing for Roy. He ain't worth it. Look, I'll give him up, all right? I promise I won't see him again. Just swear to me you won't stop your training?'

Viv stared at her. Bobby sounded so earnest, for a moment she could almost believe her.

But then she realised, if it wasn't Bobby, it would be someone else. The only way she could keep Roy from straying was if she was there to keep an eye on him.

So that was what she had to do.

Chapter Forty-Eight

Helen barely recognised the girl standing in front of her desk.

Beth Bradshaw seemed to be at least six inches taller than the last time she had seen her. There was colour in her cheeks, her green eyes sparkled, and she seemed to be in remarkably good spirits for a girl who had just seen her future hopes cruelly crushed.

'You must understand our position,' Helen explained gently. 'If it had been just one seizure we might have been able to overlook it. But the fact that you've had at least one other major episode, and several minor ones from what I can gather, would seriously affect your suitability for nursing. It would be far too much of a risk to have you working on the ward.'

'I understand, Matron.'

Helen looked at her shrewdly. 'Why do I get the feeling this news hasn't come as a great disappointment to you?'

Beth smiled. 'I'd already decided nursing wasn't for me, I'm afraid.'

'I see.' Helen wasn't sure which of them was more relieved. From what she could gather, the girl hardly had a hope of passing PTS. And even if by some miracle she did manage to scrape through, Helen could not imagine her surviving for more than a few weeks on the wards.

But it always saddened her to see a girl leave. In the eight months she had been Matron, she'd had to shatter the dreams of several tearful would-be nurses. She had been dreading delivering the bad news, and she was glad to see it hadn't affected Beth as badly as she thought it might.

'Do you have any idea what you might do?' she asked.

Beth nodded. 'I'm hoping to get a place at St Martin's to study art in September,' she said. 'But before that I'm going to travel. My mother is contracted to film a movie so I'm going to Hollywood with her. Then we're hoping to travel through Europe in the summer.'

'How exciting,' Helen said. 'I wish you well with your future ventures, Miss Bradshaw.'

'Thank you, Matron.' Beth Bradshaw hesitated for a moment.

'Yes?' Helen prompted her. 'Was there something else you wanted to say?'

She knew very well what it was Beth wanted to say. She was about to ask the question herself, if Beth hadn't spoken up first.

She saw the anguish on the girl's face, a reflection of her inner turmoil.

'About that night . . .' she began uncertainly.

'The night you were taken ill?' Helen nodded. 'What about it?'

'Winnie came to see you. She – said some things.'

'Yes, she did.' Helen waited.

'The thing is . . .' Beth's eyes slid away. 'They were true,' she whispered.

'I see.' Helen regarded the poor girl. Just the thought of what she had endured had stolen the light from her eyes and reduced her once again to the sorry, shrunken creature she had been.

Helen hated the thought of making her relive what she had been through, but she knew she had no choice. And it probably wouldn't be the last time she did it, either.

'I think you'd better sit down, don't you?' she said gently.

She was still making notes half an hour later when her brother strolled in. As usual, he didn't bother to knock.

'Busy as ever, I see,' he remarked.

'Yes, I am.' Helen did not look up. 'I did tell my secretary I wasn't to be disturbed.'

'Yes, but I gave her one of my winning smiles and she decided to make an exception for me.'

'I'm sure she did.' William could charm the birds from the trees. He could certainly work his magic on the formidable Miss Pleasance. 'But I am rather busy, so, if you wouldn't mind—'

'It's all right, I can wait.' He took a seat in the chair opposite and stretched out, his feet up on the edge of her desk. Helen did her best to ignore him, but she was aware of him watching her.

'You're writing very feverishly,' he commented. 'Working on your memoirs?'

'More like detective fiction.'

'Oh?'

'A whodunnit.'

'Sounds intriguing.'

'That's not how I'd describe it. More sordid than intriguing.'

And probably an open and shut case, after what Beth Bradshaw had told her. But Helen knew she would have to gather more evidence before she could make her move.

'You'll have to tell me all about it. How about dinner tonight? My treat.'

She looked up at him in surprise. 'What's brought this on?'

'Do I need a reason to spend time with my little sister?'

Helen sent him a searching look, but William's bland expression gave nothing away.

'All right,' she agreed. 'But I'm too tired to go out. I'll come over to your flat instead.'

'Do we have to?' William looked pained. 'The cleaner hasn't been in for a while and my place is rather messy.'

'William, I'm well aware you live like a caveman. I grew up with you, remember?'

He sighed. 'Well, let's make it tomorrow night instead. Give me a chance to make the place look presentable.'

'Suits me,' Helen said. 'I'll likely be busy this evening, anyway. I've still got to get to the bottom of this.'

'Then I'd best leave you to it.' He swung his long legs off the desk and stood up. 'Get to it, Miss Marple!' he grinned.

Beth was glad their room was empty when she went up to pack her belongings, but it still felt strange to be there on her own. She had grown used to having the other girls around her, and she knew she would miss their bickering and their laughter. Having them there was almost like having Alison with her again.

They would be in the nursing school now, taking a Clinical Practice class. Beth shuddered at the thought. She didn't think she could ever have stepped inside that building again, not after what had happened to her.

Even so, she couldn't help feeling a brief pang of regret at the thought of leaving her friends. There had been good times as well as bad, but Beth knew she had made the right decision. Even if Matron had allowed her to finish her training, she didn't think she could have gone through with it.

She wished she could have spoken to Winnie before she left, to thank her for speaking up about Mr Allenby. Beth knew she would not have had the courage to do it herself.

She had hoped she would never have to say that man's name again, especially since she had already decided to leave. But Viv's visit had changed her mind. She knew she would have to find the courage to speak up, for her friend if not for herself.

In Matron's office, it had taken every ounce of her courage to tell her story. But now she was glad, because she knew she had done the right thing. The sordid chapter had to be closed completely before she could move on with her life.

The clock in the courtyard struck twelve. The other girls would be returning soon, on their way to lunch. Beth thought she might go down to the dining room to say goodbye to them before she left.

She pulled her sketchbook out from under her bed. It had been her sanctuary, her escape, but now she no longer needed it. She thought about it for a moment, then placed it carefully on Winnie's bed. She hoped it would be a nice keepsake for her when she returned.

She heard a sound behind her. Thinking it must be Viv returning to their room, she turned round to greet her but there was no one there.

She shrugged to herself, then turned back and finished her packing. As she closed the door behind her, she caught a glimpse of a fair-haired figure, sitting on what had once been her bed.

Alison no longer looked angry. Her sister was smiling the way she used to, almost with relief.

Beth smiled back. They had both found their place at last.

Chapter Forty-Nine

Winnie was taking in the washing from the yard when Helen McKay arrived.

After spending two days at her aunt's house, she had finally returned home the previous day at her mother's insistence.

'This is your home,' Dora had told her. 'It's where you belong.'

Winnie had made a show of reluctance, but if she was honest she really wanted to come back. Aunt Josie was lovely, but Winnie missed the noisy chaos of Old Ford Road and her family.

Not that there was much chaos going on. The whole family seemed to be treating Winnie as if she were an invalid, tiptoeing around her in a way she found quite unnerving. They hadn't talked about what had happened, but Winnie could tell her mother was struggling to understand what she had done.

She barely understood it herself. She felt guilty and ashamed that she had let herself and her family down. Her mother was right, she could never learn to keep her mouth shut. It had never helped her in the past, and it hadn't helped her now.

The atmosphere was charged, like the air before a storm.

She almost wished they could have a good old row and get it over with.

She headed back into the house, her arms full of shirts and vests. 'Looks like it's going to start raining again—' she started to say, then stopped at the sight of Helen McKay sitting at the kitchen table with her grandmother.

'Look who it is,' Nanna Rose beamed. 'Your mum's friend, Helen. Such a lovely girl. We've been having a nice little natter about old times, ain't we, love?'

'Indeed we have, Mrs Doyle.' Mrs MacKay looked younger out of her severe black uniform, but still tall and elegant in a camel coat over a tailored skirt and silk blouse. Her dark hair was tied back in a bun at the nape of her long neck.

'What are you doing here?' Winnie blurted out without thinking.

'Winnie!' her grandmother sounded shocked. 'That's no way to greet a guest.'

'I daresay she's just surprised. Aren't you, Winnie?' Helen smiled. 'But I wanted to come and talk to you myself, rather than sending an official letter.'

Winnie's heart plunged. *This is it*, she thought. This is where it all ends.

She had a sudden picture of her mother's face when she gave her the news. Dora wouldn't be angry, but her look of resigned disappointment would be more than Winnie could bear.

'. . . only been a couple of days, so you shouldn't have any trouble making up on what you've missed.'

Winnie snapped back to the present just in time to hear

the last words Helen was saying to her. They seemed to make no sense, unless . . .

'You mean I can come back?'

Matron frowned. 'That's what I just said. I've concluded my investigations into the matter, and I'm satisfied that you acted in good faith, so—'

'Did he do it?' Winnie interrupted her.

'I beg your pardon?'

'Mr Allenby. Did he – hurt Beth?'

Helen's face grew sombre. 'I've spoken to Miss Bradshaw and she confirmed an incident did take place,' she said. 'I've also spoken to Miss Beck, who reported seeing bruising, and Miss James, who raised some concerns of her own regarding Mr Allenby's behaviour with other students.'

'So he's done it before,' Winnie muttered. 'I knew it!'

'Needless to say, Mr Allenby has been removed from the teaching staff,' Matron continued.

'What about Miss Cheetham?'

Helen's expression tightened. 'She has also been moved to administrative duties outside the nursing school.'

'She should have been fired.'

She knew she'd gone too far when she saw Matron's expression darken.

'I appreciate you drawing the situation to my attention,' she said. 'But let me make it plain, I will not tolerate any further disrespect towards myself or the tutoring staff. Do I make myself clear?'

Her dark eyes blazed, and Winnie caught a brief glimpse of how stern she could be if she chose.

'Yes,' she said humbly. 'I'm sorry, Matron.'

'What's going on here?'

Her mother stood in the doorway, her shabby old rain-coat still over her district uniform. She took in the scene, staring from Winnie to Helen and back again.

'I heard you raising your voice to my daughter,' she said, and Winnie immediately recognised the tone in her voice. It was a tone that would have sent them diving under the kitchen table for cover when they were kids, and she nearly felt like doing it now.

'Mum, you've got the wrong idea—' she tried to say. But her mother was in full flow and would not be interrupted.

'You might be Matron of that hospital, but I won't have you coming into my home, laying the law down. For what it's worth, I'm proud of my daughter for what she did, and I won't have you coming here upsetting her.'

'Dora—'

'You've been too hard on her, suspending her for doing what she thought was right,' her mother went on. 'If she's made a mistake, then she'll apologise. But I'm warning you, if you even think about dismissing her then you'll have a fight on your hands—'

'Mum, she's said I can go back,' Winnie finally managed to get a word in edgeways.

Dora stopped her tirade and looked at her blankly. 'What?'

'You heard.' Helen's voice was taut. Winnie's heart sank. She only hoped her mother hadn't made her change her mind. 'So you see, there was no need to come in here snapping my head off!'

A blush rose in Dora's cheeks. 'I'm sorry,' she mumbled.

'I just came in and heard you telling her off, and I went off at the deep end.'

'So unlike you,' Helen sighed. But Winnie was relieved to see she was smiling when she said it. 'As it happens, I agree with you. Winnie should never have been suspended. I acted in haste and I'm sorry for that.' She turned to Winnie. 'But I look forward to welcoming her back to conclude her studies. If she'd like to come?'

'Of course she would,' Dora said, before Winnie could open her mouth to speak.

Matron gave Winnie a rueful smile. 'I can see where you get your impulsive nature from, Winifred,' she said. 'But let's hope we don't see quite so much of it in future!'

Chapter Fifty

There weren't many people who could get away with telling Dora off, but her mother was one of them.

'Well, you made a right show of yourself,' she said, when Helen had gone.

'I know,' Dora said humbly.

'You could have listened to what the poor woman had to say, before you jumped down her throat.'

'Why change the habit of a lifetime?' Winnie muttered. But Dora was relieved to see her daughter was grinning. It was the first time she had seen her cheerful in days, and it lifted her heart. Poor Winnie had been so downcast, Dora would have made a fool of herself ten times over just to put a smile on her face.

She shrugged off her coat and started to get dinner ready. Winnie and her mother helped her, as usual. But Dora noticed her daughter was thoughtful as she peeled potatoes at the sink.

'Did you mean what you said?' Winnie ventured finally. She had her back to Dora, her gaze fixed on the window. 'About being proud of me, I mean?'

'Of course I meant it. I wouldn't have said it otherwise.'

Winnie went back to peeling, her head down. 'I proved you wrong, didn't I?' she said in a small, choked voice.

'In what way?'

'You told Dad I wouldn't last five minutes.'

Dora frowned. 'I'm sure I never said any such thing!'

'You did! I remember every word. It was the night I told you I'd been accepted at the Nightingale.'

Dora stared at her daughter's turned back, searching her memory. And then it came to her. 'You mean when I went outside into the yard for a ciggie?'

'You do remember it, then?'

'I remember talking to your dad. And I remember saying those words, too, now I come to think of it. But I certainly didn't mean them in the way you think.' She put down the fork she'd been using to poke the sausages around the pan and turned to Winnie. 'I never doubted you could do it,' she said. 'I just worried for you, that's all. I know how hard nursing can be if your heart ain't in it, and I didn't want you to fail. You'd already lost your confidence after that business with your last job, and I wasn't sure if you could face another disappointment.' Winnie did not move, but Dora could tell she was listening to every word. 'I just wanted to protect you, Winnie. You'll understand one day when you're a mother yourself. Your children's happiness is more important to you than your own. But I should have had more faith in you. You're stronger than I gave you credit for, and you've surprised me. You're going to be a good nurse one day, Winnie.'

Winnie said nothing. She kept her head down, and Dora went back to her cooking.

A few more minutes passed. The evening paper arrived, and Dora's mother shuffled off into the parlour to look for her glasses so she could read it.

316

As soon as she'd gone, Winnie said, 'It wasn't my fault I lost my job at the town hall.'

'So you've said.' Dora looked at her daughter's turned back, and her neck began to prickle with a familiar warning sensation.

Don't say anything, she told herself. *Wait*.

But she had been waiting for a long time. Some dreadful secret had weighed heavy on Winnie's mind for months, something she couldn't share with anyone.

If Dora was honest with herself, she already knew. She had always known. But she had turned her mind away, not wanting to believe it.

'Something happened,' Winnie said quietly.

Dora took a deep, steadying breath. *Wait*. 'Do you want to tell me what?'

Winnie was silent, and Dora could tell she was searching for the words.

'Is it the same thing that happened to your friend Beth?' Dora asked.

She hoped she was wrong. Dear God, let her be wrong. But when Winnie finally turned to face her and she saw the bleak look in her eyes, Dora knew her worst fears had been confirmed.

'Who was it? Someone from work?'

Winnie nodded. 'Everyone knew what he was like. He – he'd tried it on with other girls. My friend Judith had to leave and get a job in Woolworth's because she couldn't cope with him leering and pawing at her all the time.'

Dora forced herself to stay calm, but her hand was

gripping the fork so tightly she could barely feel her fingers. 'Go on,' she said.

'And then he started on me. It was just suggestive remarks at first, and then he'd find any excuse to put his hands on me, just like he did with Judith. But it got so bad I couldn't bear to be near him. I told him to stop. I even went to Miss Wendell the supervisor about it. She knew exactly what he was like, but she did nothing. She just told me to stop being a troublemaker and get on with my work.'

Dora could feel the white-hot rage building up inside her, and it was all she could do not to let rip and tear the kitchen to pieces. She wanted to grab that supervisor woman by the neck and throttle her. But that was nothing to what she wanted to do to this man, whoever he was.

'And then what happened?' she prompted, even though she hardly wanted to hear it.

'One night, he asked me to stay late.' Winnie's voice slowed down, the words suddenly too hard to say out loud. 'I wanted to say no, but I didn't dare, because he was the manager and I was already in enough trouble. I didn't feel too bad about it because I knew Miss Wendell was staying late too. I tried to stay out of his way and to get everything done as quick as I could, but he cornered me in the office, and—'

She broke off, her head drooping. Her shoulders heaved, and Dora knew she was sobbing. She went over to her and put her arms around her. Tall and lanky and bolshy as she was, in that moment she was still her little girl.

'It's all right,' she soothed, even though she knew it wasn't, that it could never be. That memory would stay with Winnie forever, a little patch of tarnish in her bright, shining life.

'He didn't – do anything,' Winnie said. 'He would have done, but I fought back. I kicked him in the – you know.'

'Good for you,' Dora said. 'I hope you maimed him for life.'

'He was rolling about on the floor for ages.' Winnie smiled faintly. 'He'd locked the office door, but I saw where he'd put the key and I got out. I ran straight into the toilets, and that's where Miss Wendell found me.'

'And what did she do?'

'Nothing.' Winnie sniffed back tears. 'I told her everything that happened, what he'd done to me, but she wouldn't listen. She just washed my face and tidied me up, and told me to go home and not say anything.'

'Just like your friend?' Dora's blood ran cold. No wonder Winnie had been so upset.

Winnie nodded. 'I couldn't stand by and watch some-one else get away with it,' she said. 'I might not have been able to get any justice for myself, but I thought I could get it for Beth.'

'So this Miss Wendell didn't do anything about it?'

Winnie shook her head. 'She pretended it had never hap-pened, just like she always did. So I told her I was going to take it further. I said I was going to write to the Town Clerk and tell him exactly what happened. The next thing I knew, I'd been dismissed.'

A bad attitude, the letter had said. Just because she'd tried to stand up for herself.

'You should have written that letter anyway,' Dora said.

'What was the point? It was my word against theirs.'

Dora looked at the weary resignation on her daughter's face, and felt ashamed at how she had berated her over losing her job. Why hadn't she known, or at least asked questions, instead of assuming Winnie must be at fault?

'Oh love,' she sighed. 'I wish you'd told me.'

You should have known, a small voice said inside her head. She was her mother. She had sensed something was wrong, and she had done nothing about it. She had failed her own child.

'I was too embarrassed,' Winnie mumbled. 'I felt like it was my fault—'

'No!' Dora hugged her again, crushing her as if she would never let her go. She desperately wanted to protect her, and she couldn't bear the thought that she hadn't been there when her daughter needed her most. 'It wasn't your fault. If you don't understand anything else, you need to understand that. You did nothing wrong, all right? It was all his fault, this manager of yours – what was his name?'

'Everyone called him Roper the Groper,' Winnie gave a watery smile.

Dora went very still, her mind working.

'Roper the Groper, eh?' she said at last. 'Sounds like it suits him.'

Chapter Fifty-One

'Well, Miss Trent, I can't say I'm not disappointed.'

Helen regarded Viv across the desk. The girl still hardly looked like nurse material, with her tight jeans, bright red lips and rippling auburn curls hanging loose down her back. But the last few months had changed her. She had lost some of her bold, brassy edge, become more thoughtful and considered.

It was just a shame she wasn't giving more consideration to her decision.

'It's only two weeks until the PTS examinations,' Helen went on. 'It seems such a pity that you can't stay on and take them—'

'I'm sorry, Matron.' Viv shook her head. 'I've already made up my mind. The sooner I leave, the better.'

Better for who? Helen wondered. She surely hadn't imagined the wistfulness in the girl's face as she stood before her.

She had done her best to persuade her to stay, but Vivien Trent was adamant, so she really had no choice but to accept her decision.

'Very well,' she sighed. 'If you're determined to leave then I can hardly stop you. But should you change your mind between now and the final examinations, you are always welcome to return.'

Vivien's eyes widened in surprise. 'But I thought that was it? Once I'd left, there was no coming back—'

'Usually that would be the case,' Helen agreed. 'But I know you have the makings of a very able nurse, Miss Trent, and I'm very reluctant to lose you. You could be an asset to this hospital.'

She saw the idea register in the girl's mind. She had the feeling praise had not come Vivien Trent's way very often until she began her training at the Nightingale.

Then another thought seemed to assert itself, and Vivien squared her shoulders. 'Thank you, Matron,' she said stiffly. 'That's a very kind offer, but I don't think I'll be taking you up on it.'

'As you wish. But the offer remains, all the same.'

Matron's comments were still on Viv's mind as she returned to her room. It felt strange to think that this would be the last time she climbed those attic stairs. The room had become home to her over the past three months, far more than she ever imagined it would.

And now she would have to return to Granny Trent's house and face the music. If she would even have her. Viv hadn't told her grandmother about her decision, but she could imagine what she would have to say about it.

Perhaps she should have waited those last two weeks and taken the PTS exams? At least then she could have gone back to Granny Trent having kept her side of the bargain. And Matron was right, it did seem a shame to get this far and not see it through to the end.

She pushed the thought away. She had made up her mind

and that was that. Besides, she couldn't wait another two weeks. Roy certainly wouldn't, anyway. Viv had managed to get him away from Bobby with the promise of giving up her nursing, but she knew there would be another girl waiting in the wings, ready to try her luck. And Roy had proved he wasn't one to wait around.

She was expecting the room to be empty, so she was surprised to see Winnie there, unpacking her things.

'You're back!'

'So I am.'

They looked at each other, and Viv had to fight the urge to hug her friend. It wasn't usually her way and she knew it wasn't Winnie's either. So she hid her excitement behind her usual indifferent mask.

'I hope you noticed I've been keeping the place tidy for you?' she said.

'I should think so, too.' Winnie looked at the third bed. It had been stripped bare to the mattress. 'I see Beth's gone?'

Viv nodded. 'She left yesterday.'

'Poor thing,' Winnie said. 'She left me this.' She picked up a sketchbook from the bed and showed it to her. 'I'll miss her. But it's probably for the best, I suppose. At least she can do what makes her happy now.'

Viv watched her flicking idly through the sketchbook. 'She ain't the only one,' she said.

'What?'

Viv took a deep breath. 'I'm leaving.'

Winnie looked up sharply. 'Oh, Viv, you ain't?' She dropped the sketchbook back on to the bed. 'Why? What's happened? You ain't got yourself thrown out, have you?'

'No!' Viv laughed. 'I've just decided it ain't for me, that's all.'

She didn't mention Roy. She knew Winnie would never understand. She'd never had a boyfriend, let alone been in love. She didn't know what it was like to face losing someone.

But she might have known Winnie wouldn't be fooled.

'Is this about Roy?' she asked.

'No, it's nothing to do with him.' Viv looked away. She couldn't face seeing the disappointment in Winnie's eyes. 'I told you when I first came here, I was never going to be a nurse.'

'Tell that to the girl who saved Beth Bradshaw's life.'

'I didn't save anyone's life!' Viv shrugged. 'I only did what anyone with any sense would do, that's all. Anyway, it's done now. I've already told Matron I'm going, so—'

'I'll miss you,' Winnie said in a small voice.

Viv looked at her sharply. Was she mistaken, or were there actual tears in her friend's eyes?

Then she realised there were tears in her own. 'Go on with you, you soft ha'porth,' she said.

Chapter Fifty-Two

William was busy in the kitchen when Helen arrived. The deliciously rich aroma of tomatoes and garlic and wine greeted her as she walked in.

'Are you cooking?' she said.

'I invited you to dinner, didn't I?'

'Yes, but I only expected an omelette.'

It was a standing joke that eggs were the only thing her brother knew how to cook. He lived on them when he was in London. But thankfully the hospital canteen kept him well fed.

'Well tonight, Madame, I am serving boeuf bourguignon. Or beef stew, to you and me.' William appeared in the doorway to the kitchen, holding a wooden spoon. 'But it sounds better when you say it in French.'

'And since when have you been a cordon bleu chef?'

'I'm full of surprises.'

'I'll say.' Helen looked around. 'I see you've been cleaning up, too?'

'I couldn't let you walk into a pigsty, could I?'

'Why not? It's what you usually do.'

'Cheek! Take a seat,' he invited. 'I'll pour you a glass of sherry.'

'I'll pour it. You go back to your creation.' Helen crossed

the room to the small tray on the sideboard, where the decanter of sherry sat beside a cluster of glasses.

'How did you get on with your detective work?' William asked, as he disappeared back into the kitchen. 'Did you ever find out whodunnit?'

'Unfortunately, yes.' Helen grimaced as she sipped her drink.

'Unfortunately?'

She explained the situation with Beth Bradshaw and Mr Allenby. She told him how, after speaking to Beth, she had consulted Miss Beck and Miss James, the other Sister Tutor. As it turned out, Veronica James had a lot to say about her fellow tutors. And none of it made for pleasant listening.

'I'm surprised she didn't come forward earlier,' William said.

'I think she was scared,' Helen said. 'I get the impression Miss Cheetham had been bullying poor Miss James for years.'

'That wouldn't surprise me. Christina Cheetham can be a very forceful presence.'

'She also swore Miss James to secrecy about her and Mr Allenby.'

'I can't imagine why. Everyone knew about it.'

Helen frowned towards the open kitchen door. 'Did you know about it?'

'Of course. As I said, everyone did. It was the worst kept secret at the Nightingale, next to the Chief Medical Officer's hairpiece.'

Helen smiled. 'I wish you'd told me.'

'I thought you knew.'

Helen sipped her drink. The sherry was sweet and syrupy, not the kind William usually preferred.

'What I can't understand is why she let him get away with it,' she mused. 'It must have been incredibly hurtful for her, watching him flirting with all those young girls.'

'Perhaps she was just desperate to keep him?' William said. 'The way I understand it, Christina's always wanted to settle down and get married. She even tried to proposition me once, can you believe?'

Helen could believe it, only too well. There weren't many nurses who didn't have a crush on handsome Mr Tremayne.

'Even so, I can't understand any woman who would put up with that. Can you imagine, finding out the man you loved was capable of doing something so utterly cruel and degrading?' She shuddered. 'And then, worse still, trying to cover up for him?'

'I think she was more worried about covering up for herself,' William said.

'Well, it's ended badly for her, in any case. But at least Winifred Riley has been vindicated. Which is probably just as well. We've already lost two girls from this set – I don't think we could afford to let another one go.'

'Dinner is served.' William emerged from the kitchen, holding a dish aloft.

Helen sniffed the air appreciatively. 'If it tastes as good as it smells, I'm sure it will be delicious.'

'I just hope it's edible.'

As she followed him to the dining table, a flesh of red from under the settee caught Helen's eye.

'What's this?' She bent down to retrieve it.

'What?' William stuck his head around the door.

'This.' Helen held up the crimson silk scarf. 'Where did it come from?'

'It must be Millie's. I suppose she left it behind when she came up to meet you and Dora last week.'

He held out his hand. 'Here, give it to me. I'll make sure to take it home with me tomorrow night.'

'I'm surprised she hasn't missed it,' Helen said, running it through her hands. 'It's so beautiful. Hermès, isn't it?' She held it up to her face and breathed in. 'It even smells expensive—'

'Give it to me!' William snatched it from her grasp. Helen stared at him in surprise.

'There's no need to snatch,' she said.

'Sorry.' His smile was quickly back in place.

Helen watched him tucking the scarf in his pocket. Something tickled at the back of her mind, something that didn't seem quite right.

And then she remembered. Millie had been wearing a beautiful pale-blue dress the day they met. She would never have matched it with a bright red scarf.

Chapter Fifty-Three

Viv hauled her suitcase around the streets of Hackney for most of the afternoon until she felt it was safe to go home.

She sat in the Savoy café, nursing a coffee while she made her plan. She knew Granny Trent would be cleaning a solicitor's office on Dalston Lane between four and six that evening, so she waited until after five before she slunk back into the house.

She dumped her suitcase in the corner of the kitchen and looked around with a sigh. She had forgotten how dingy the house was, with its worn linoleum and thin curtains. But for all its shabbiness she realised she had missed the place. It was clean and well-kept, there was always tea in the pot and food on the table, and Granny Trent did her best to make it look cheerful, with her array of knick-knacks on the mantelpiece.

Viv had brought a bunch of daffodils with her. She knew how much her grandmother loved daffs, and she needed all the help she could get to win her over.

She searched in the cupboard under the sink for a vase, but she couldn't find one. In the end she filled a milk bottle with water and stuck the flowers in. She set it in the middle of the table and stood back to admire it. It wouldn't exactly make it into the pages of *Ideal Home*, but at least the bright splash of yellow cheered the room up a bit.

She had just finished making the tea when she saw Granny Trent hobbling down the road, a newspaper-wrapped packet of fish and chips tucked under her arm. It had been a while since she'd seen her, and it gave Viv a shock to realise how old and frail-looking she was. She'd always been such a forceful, indomitable presence in her life growing up, Viv had somehow never thought of her as getting any older.

Her grandmother didn't seem surprised to see her. She barely raised an eyebrow as she dumped her fish supper on the table and shrugged off her old coat.

'Well?' Viv said. 'Ain't you going to ask what I'm doing here?'

'Making yourself at home, by the look of it.' Granny Trent glanced at the suitcase in the corner. 'I take it this ain't a social call? What happened? Did they finally kick you out?'

Viv nodded. Sitting in the Savoy café, she had decided it would be easier to lie. But now, standing in front of her grandmother, she found the words wouldn't come as easily as she'd thought they would.

'What did you do?'

'Nothing, I swear. They just didn't think I had what it took, that's all.' The lie tasted wrong in her mouth.

'Well, more fool them.'

Viv stared at her grandmother in surprise. That certainly wasn't the response she'd been expecting.

'I ain't unpacked my stuff,' she said. 'Just in case you don't want me to stay?'

'Why shouldn't I want you to stay?'

'You said I wasn't to darken your doorstep again if I didn't—'

'I'm old, I don't remember half the things I say.' Her grandmother held up a hand. 'This is your home. You'll always have a roof over your head while I'm alive. Now, have you eaten?' Viv shook her head. 'I only got one lot of fish and chips 'cos I wasn't expecting company. But it should stretch to two with a bit of bread and butter.'

'Honestly, I don't want to put you out—'

'I ain't going to sit there and stuff my face in front of you, am I? Now fetch some plates, while I get the bread.'

They ate in silence for a while. Viv noticed how gnarled and swollen with arthritis her grandmother's hands were. She could barely hold her fork.

'So what will you do now?' her grandmother asked at last.

'I dunno. Go back to Clarnico's, if they'll have me.'

'They're bound to take you back. You were a good worker.'

Viv started at the unexpected compliment. She waited for the sting that usually followed, but for once there was none.

'You're taking this very well,' she said. 'I thought you'd go mad.'

'What choice have I got?' Her grandmother shrugged, helping herself to a chip. 'You learn to take life as it comes at my age. Besides, you did your best, didn't you?'

'Yes. Yes, I did.' That was the truth, at least.

'Well then, that's all I can ask for. And to be honest, you lasted longer than I thought you would.' She shook her head. 'I just think it's a terrible shame they wouldn't let you get to the end, that's all. A terrible shame,' she shook her head. 'And after all your hard work, too.'

Viv said nothing. She felt so ashamed of herself, she couldn't even look at her grandmother.

'Don't look so upset,' Granny Trent said. 'You did everything you could. You stuck with it when I thought you'd pack it in after a week.' She reached over and patted Viv's hand. 'You've got nothing to be ashamed of, as far as I'm concerned. You should be proud of what you've done.'

She sat back in her seat. 'Right, I think I'll go and have a little sit-down and listen to the wireless. You can finish those chips off, if you want.'

Viv looked down at her plate, the chips congealing in cold fat. Suddenly she had lost her appetite.

Chapter Fifty-Four

William lived in a mansion flat in Covent Garden, just off Drury Lane. The porters and wholesalers from the fruit and veg market were just packing up when Helen arrived in the early evening. She marched past them, barely noticing the rotting cabbages and potatoes strewn around her feet. She was too focused on what lay ahead of her.

She had not been able to sleep for thinking about that wretched red scarf. She knew it could not belong to Millie, but she also knew she had seen it before.

It had taken her a few days before she remembered where. Once she had, she could not get the picture of it out of her head.

She ran up the three flights of stairs to William's flat and knocked on the door. As far as she knew, he was catching the train back to Billinghurst that afternoon, so she wasn't expecting anyone to answer the door.

But if they did, she knew her worst suspicions would be correct.

No one answered. Helen knocked again, her heart hammering against her ribs. *Please let me be wrong*, she prayed. *Please, please let me be wrong . . .*

The door opened.

'Helen!' William stood there in his shirtsleeves. He looked as shocked to see her as she was to see him.

'I thought you were going home this evening?' she said.

'I couldn't get away. There was an emergency at the hospital—'

'Liar.'

She swept past him into the flat. 'Where is she?' she demanded.

'Who?'

'You know very well who. The girl with the red scarf. The one I saw you with at the hospital that day.' She went into the kitchen and looked around.

'What girl? I don't know what you're talking about—'

He stopped speaking abruptly as Helen held up two glasses.

'There are two plates here, too. And one of these glasses has lipstick on, so please don't insult my intelligence by telling me they're both yours,' she said. 'Is that how you learned to make boeuf bourguignon? For your secret mistress?'

'Helen, I can explain—'

'So where is she?' Helen said, looking around. 'Hiding in the bedroom, I suppose?'

'I'm not hiding, Madame.'

She swung round. There, in the bedroom doorway, stood a young girl of about eighteen years old. She was slightly built and exquisitely beautiful, like a blonde Audrey Hepburn with her elfin cap of pale hair and her luminous brown eyes. She was barefoot and dressed in a pair of men's silk pyjamas.

Helen turned back to Will. He was standing there, mute and red-faced.

334

'How could you?' she snapped. 'How could you do that to Millie and the children?'

'Please, if you'd just give me a chance—'

'I thought you'd changed. I thought you'd grown up.'

'Helen, stop. I can explain—'

'I don't want to hear your excuses! I'm disgusted with you, Will. And with her! For Christ's sake, she's young enough to be your daughter!'

'She is,' Will said quietly.

'What?' Helen stared at him.

'That's what I'm trying to tell you, if you'd give me the chance to speak.' He turned to the girl in the doorway. 'Helen, I'd like you to meet Catrine Villeneuve – your niece.'

Chapter Fifty-Five

'My niece?'

Helen looked from one to the other. She could scarcely believe what she was hearing. 'Is this some sort of joke?' she asked. 'Because if you're lying to me—'

'I'm not.' William was smiling, the tension gone from his face. 'I'm telling you the truth, I swear.'

'But how – you're her father?'

'It was as big a surprise to me as it is to you, I promise you.' He turned to the girl in the doorway. 'Catrine, can you pour your aunt Helen a brandy? She looks as if she could do with one.'

Helen sank down on the couch and watched as the girl crossed to the drinks cabinet and poured three large measures of brandy. She certainly seemed to know her way around the flat.

'I don't understand.' She shook her head. 'How long have you known?' She thought of all those 'emergencies' that kept him in London, the way he had been discouraging Millie from coming up to town.

'I knew nothing about it until Catrine literally arrived on my doorstep six months ago.'

'After my mother died,' Catrine said. She downed her brandy in one gulp.

Helen turned to Will. 'Who was her mother?'

'A girl I met while I was stationed in France at the start of the war. Romy was a nurse at the air base, and we fell in love. But then I was sent back to England. We promised we'd write to each other, but we were both very young, and the passion soon faded once we were apart.'

For you, perhaps, Helen thought. Poor Romy had obviously been left with more than a pleasant memory.

'So this affair wasn't going on when you and Millie—'

'God, no!' William looked appalled at the thought. 'I adore Millie, you know that. I'd never do anything to hurt her.'

'*Maman* became ill,' Catrine took up the story. Her English was flawless, with a touch of a husky accent. 'She was worried for me. We had no other family except each other, and she knew there would be no one to care for me. After she died, I found a letter she had written to me, telling me all about my father. And there was a photograph . . .'

She went to the bureau and fetched it from a drawer, then gave it to Helen.

There was no denying the resemblance between her and her mother, she thought. And there was no denying it was her brother with his arms around her.

'So she never told you anything about your father while she was alive?'

'She never told me his name. She said he was a British pilot. She said he was the love of her life and that he broke her heart.'

Catrine glanced at Will when she said it, and Helen wondered if she had imagined the spark of resentment she saw there.

'I truly had no idea,' Will said, in answer to Helen's unspoken question. 'If I'd known she was pregnant with my child, of course things would have been different . . .'

Different how? Helen wondered. But she could not allow herself to think about that. There were more pressing matters at hand.

'So you tracked him down?' she said to Catrine.

'She's a very resourceful girl,' William said with a touch of pride. 'But you can imagine my shock when she appeared and said she was my long-lost daughter. Of course I knew her straight away. She's so like her mother.'

Helen looked at the photograph again. They looked so young, Will and his French lover. Romy could not have been much older than Catrine was now. They looked identical.

'And what did you do?' she asked.

'What could I do? I couldn't turn her away. She's my flesh and blood.'

'So you've been keeping her hidden away here?'

He looked offended. 'Not hidden away, exactly.'

'Then what would you call it?' She remembered that day at the hospital. Catrine must have gone to visit him there. Clearly he hadn't been happy about it, from the way she'd fled in tears.

If only Helen had rounded that corner a few moments earlier, she might have caught them together . . .

'I assume Millie doesn't know about her?'

'No,' he admitted quietly.

'And you lied to me?'

'I was going to tell you. I just couldn't find the right time.'

'And when are you going to tell your wife?'

He looked wretched. 'How can I?' he asked. 'It's not exactly the sort of thing you can just blurt out at the breakfast table, is it? I'm still waiting for the right moment.'

'Well, you can't keep her a secret forever.'

'I know that!' William ran his hands through his hair, a sure sign he was agitated. 'I just don't know what to do, Helen.'

'I should go back to France,' Catrine said. 'I have brought too much trouble, coming here . . .'

'No,' William said straight away. 'I won't hear of it. You must stay.'

'And you must tell Millie,' Helen said.

'I know,' William sighed. 'I just don't know how.'

'However you tell her, it needs to be soon. If I've had my suspicions, then I'm sure your wife has them too.'

Chapter Fifty-Six

Gordon Roper headed home up Vallance Road, carrying his string bag of shopping.

It had been a good day at the office. A pert little blonde had just started in the Accounts department, and Gordon was sure she liked him. She was always friendly and smiling, and when he'd sneaked a little pat on her backside that morning she'd given him a wary look but she hadn't said anything about it.

He might be in there, he thought. He'd have to ask her to work late one night, to go over some figures. Although it was only her figure that he really wanted to go over . . .

He'd have to be a bit careful about it, though. Especially with Miss Wendell watching him. He couldn't understand it, she'd always turned a blind eye in the past. Boys will be boys, and all that. But lately she'd been a bit tetchy about it. Once or twice she'd even stopped the girls from staying late.

She probably fancied him herself, Gordon thought, smoothing his sparse strands of hair across his bald head. Not that he would ever look at a dried-up old spinster like her. She must be forty if she was a day. He much preferred them young and fresh, like that gorgeous little blonde piece . . .

He was still smiling as he let himself into the house.

'Is that you, Gordon?' Almost immediately his mother started calling down to him.

'Bloody hell, woman! Let me get my foot in the door,' he cursed under his breath.

She was beginning to get on his nerves. Why wasn't she dead by now? He'd thought that last bout of rheumatic fever was going to finish her off. It might have done, once upon a time. But thanks to the miracle of the National Health Service, she'd been nursed back from the grave.

He was sure she was only staying alive to spite him.

He thought about the new district nurse, Miss Garvey. She seemed all right. She was so busy, she never really stopped to notice what was going on. She couldn't wait to get out of the door half the time. Not like that other interfering cow . . .

'Gordon, love?'

'Give me a minute, Mother,' he called back through gritted teeth.

He should move out, he thought. His sister had made herself scarce quick enough, moving to Harlow. She might think she'd got one over on him, leaving him to take care of their mother, but she'd be laughing on the other side of her face when the old woman finally died and left him the house.

'Hello, Gordon.'

She jumped at the sound of the voice behind him. Turning round, he was shocked to see that district nurse, Dora Riley, sitting in his parlour. She looked right at home there, relaxing in his favourite armchair, a cup of tea and two of his favourite garibaldi biscuits on the table in front of her.

'What the hell are you doing here?' He stared at her in confusion. 'Where's the other one?'

'Nurse Garvey's been and gone. You know what she's like. Rush, rush, rush everywhere.' She smiled at him. 'But I've just made a cup of tea for your mother and made her comfortable. I'm sure she'd like to see you, though. Just for a little chat. You know how lonely she gets, on her own all day.'

She looked at the string bag dangling from his hand. 'Pilchards, eh? I hope there's enough to go round, because according to your mum you ain't been feeding her very well lately—'

'You've got no right to be here!' His shock subsided, and outrage took its place. 'You've been told, I complained about you—'

'And we all know why, don't we? Because I know how you treat your poor mother. No wonder you wanted me out of the way. But I've made up my mind, I'm going to start visiting her again,' she said. 'Not as her nurse, but just for a friendly chat, to keep her company.'

Gordon gasped. 'I won't allow you in my house!'

'It's your mum's house, Gordon. Not yours. Look, she's even given me a key so I can pop in and out whenever I want.' She dangled it in front of him tauntingly.

'Get out,' Gordon snapped.

'Ooh, hark at you.' Dora Riley looked at him consideringly. 'You're a bit of a bully, ain't you? But never anyone your own size. Just old ladies – and young girls.'

He stared at her, shocked.

'You think I don't know about what you get up to?' she smiled. 'You've got quite a reputation at that town hall,

Gordon. Roper the Groper, they call you. They laugh about you behind your back, did you know that? They think you're a pathetic, dirty little man, getting his thrills by touching young girls who are too frightened to fight back.' Her face grew serious. 'But some of them don't laugh. Some of them end up having to lose their jobs because they just can't take your pestering and pawing.' She stood up, her eyes level with his. 'You know who I'm talking about, don't you, Gordon?'

He stared into her face and realisation began to dawn on him. Pieces slid into place in his brain, locking together to make a picture . . .

'She's your daughter,' he murmured.

'Bingo. Give that man a coconut.' She took a step closer, and Gordon instinctively staggered back, putting distance between them. 'That's right. Winnie Riley is my daughter. The girl you forced to leave a perfectly good job, the girl whose life you nearly ruined!'

'It was only a bit of fun,' Gordon said feebly.

'Fun?' She was so angry, her green eyes seemed to be sparking fire. 'Do you think it was fun for her when you had her pinned down on a desk, trying to rape her?'

He flinched. 'I – I didn't—'

'Only because she fought back, like I taught her to. I hope she did you some damage, Gordon. Because by God, I feel like doing you some damage now!'

She took another step towards him and Gordon backed off, colliding with the arm of the chair. He held up his string bag to fend her off.

'What are you going to do, hit me with a tin of pilchards?'

Dora Riley laughed in his face. 'You really are a poor excuse for a man, ain't you? Let me tell you something, Gordon. If it wasn't for your poor old mum sat upstairs, I'd tear you limb from limb myself!'

She meant it, too. He could feel the rage coming off her like heat. 'You – you can't threaten me,' he stammered. 'I'll call the police—'

'You do that, Gordon. And when they come, I'll tell them what you did to my girl.'

She had him cornered, but he still tried to defend himself. 'You've only got her word for it.'

'You think if I went down that town hall I couldn't find half a dozen girls willing to stand up and tell the police what you've done?'

'Is – is that what you're going to do?'

She gave him a pitying look. 'Oh no, Gordon. The police will be too easy on you.' She shook her head. 'I've got something much worse in mind for you.'

'What's that?' he squeaked. He could feel the sweat prickling on his brow.

'I'm going to tell my husband.' She leaned closer. 'You might have heard of him – Nick Riley? He was a local heavyweight champion when he was a kid. But he's more famous for the fights he got into outside the ring, if you know what I mean?' Her voice was menacing in its softness. 'He's calmed down a bit now he's older. Unless any dirty little sod lays a finger on his daughter, of course. I can't even imagine what he'd do then, but it ain't going to be pretty.'

Gordon gulped, but his throat was too dry to swallow. 'You're not going to tell him?'

'That depends,' she said. 'On whether you lay a finger on another girl at that town hall, and whether you start treating your mother right.'

'Gordon?' As if on cue, a faint voice called from upstairs.

'Looks like she could do with another cup of tea,' Dora smiled. 'Perhaps you could stop for a chat with her, too? She gets ever so lonely.' She tapped his chest. 'Anyway, I'll be dropping in every couple of days to keep an eye on her. And you, of course,' she said. 'And if I find out you've been doing anything you shouldn't . . .' She drew her finger across her throat. 'I'll be watching you, Gordon,' she said. 'And if you ain't very careful, my old man will be watching you, too.'

Chapter Fifty-Seven

PTS Finals

'They're coming!' Bernie cried.

They all crowded around the common room window to watch as the four unsmiling ward sisters made their way up the path from the main hospital building. It was a chilly March morning, and their navy-blue cloaks were whipped by the wind.

'They don't look very friendly, do they?' Maya said, her brown eyes wide with fear.

'I feel sick,' Peggy groaned. 'I can't remember a single thing, can you? I don't think I'll even be able to write my name on that test paper.'

Winnie knew exactly how she felt. They had been preparing for this day for three months, and yet now it was finally here, she wasn't ready for it at all.

The dreaded PTS Finals consisted of two days of hell. The first day was a practical and oral test, followed by a written examination consisting of various papers on anatomy, physiology, public health and nursing care.

For days, they had been taking each other's temperatures and pulses, dressing limbs and checking their blood pressure. Urine tests and different dietary requirements dominated every conversation.

Winnie had been awake most of the previous night poring over her notes and trying to cram everything into her brain. But she'd woken up this morning only to find she could remember even less than she had started with.

It didn't help that Miss James had arrived at the nurses' home that morning for what was supposed to be a pep talk. Instead, she ended up fluttering around them like a nervous mother hen.

'Make sure you arrive promptly for each of your tests,' she had said. 'And don't address the examiners unless they speak to you first. And remember to bring at least one clean apron with you, just in case. And do something about your hair, O'Dowd, it looks like your cap is perching on a bird's nest. And don't forget to relax,' she smiled at them bracingly.

'After all that? Not a chance!' Alice whispered.

They watched as the ward sisters followed the path that skirted past the nurses' home, heading for the school building.

'I suppose we'd better go,' Lou said. 'They'll be waiting for us.'

They all looked at each other, but no one moved.

'This is ridiculous!' Camilla huffed. 'I don't know about you, but I can't wait to get this over with!'

They left the nurses' home, still huddling together like sheep.

'Can anyone remember how much urine you put into

Benedict's Solution to test for sugar?' Phil asked in a desperate voice.

'If you don't know it by now, you never will,' Bernie replied.

'Eight drops to five ml of solution,' a chirpy cockney voice behind them said.

Winnie swung round. 'Viv!'

She grinned at them. 'Surprised to see me?'

'What are you doing here?'

'Come to take the test, same as you lot.'

'But you can't!' Camilla cried. 'That's not fair. You left two weeks ago.'

'Yeah, well, I changed my mind. Thought I might as well finish what I started.'

'But you can't just walk back in!'

'Matron says I can,' Viv shrugged. 'Why don't you go and ask her if you don't believe me?'

Camilla stared at her, open-mouthed for a moment. Then she turned on her heel and marched off towards the nursing school.

'It's not often you see her lost for words, is it?' Silent Susan piped up, and everyone stared at her in astonishment.

'I never thought you'd come back,' Winnie said, as they followed Camilla up the path to the nursing school.

'Neither did I, believe me.'

'What changed your mind?'

Viv was silent for a moment. 'My gran,' she said finally.

'What did she say to you?'

'Nothing,' Viv said. 'That's the point.'

'Eh?' Winnie stared at her, mystified.

'It doesn't matter. I'm here now, and that's the main thing.'

They reached the nursing school. The others were already gathered around the door, too nervous to go in.

'Come on, then, girls, what are we waiting for? Viv winked at Winnie. 'In for a penny, in for a pound!'

Chapter Fifty-Eight

'Oh God, no! I can't bear it!'

Millie burst into noisy tears, and Helen looked accusingly at her brother.

Why had she ever agreed to this? William had insisted that she should be there when he told his wife about Catrine, and now Millie was heartbroken and Helen was stuck in the middle and feeling extremely awkward.

'I'm sorry, darling, truly I am.' William took his sobbing wife in his arms. 'I know how much this has hurt you—'

'I'm not crying for myself, you idiot!' Millie pulled away from him. 'I'm crying for that poor girl. Why didn't you bring her straight home to Billinghurst?' She wiped away her tears with the back of her hand. 'God only knows what it must have been like for her, arriving in a strange country, meeting a father she's never known, who promptly shuts her away as if she's some horrid, dirty little secret!'

'It was only my flat,' William argued limply. 'Hardly a nunnery.'

'I insist you bring her home straight away,' Millie said, not listening. 'She needs to meet Henry, and Lottie and Tim. And the dogs. Oh, this is awful. What must she think of us?'

Helen and William looked at each other, and he gave her a rueful smile. *This is why I love her so much*, his look said.

'That's very kind of you, darling,' he said. 'But there's just one problem.'

'What's that?'

'She's decided she wants to stay in London.'

Millie stared at him, appalled. 'You see? She hates us already. This is all your fault—'

'No, it's not that. Catrine seems to have decided she wants to follow in her mother's footsteps and become a nurse.'

Helen already knew what he was going to ask, even before he turned to her, and said, 'What do you think, Hel? Would you consider taking her on at the Nightingale?'

'What a wonderful idea,' Millie said, her face brightening.

'Is it?' Helen was sceptical. 'Does she have any experience?'

'Apparently she's done a pre-training course at a hospital in France. Go on, Helen. What do you say?'

'It doesn't sound as if I have much choice, does it?' Helen sighed. 'But she mustn't expect any special favours, just because we're related,' she warned William.

'I'm sure she won't. I mean, I'm your brother and I don't take advantage, do I?'

'Like now, you mean?' Helen said.

'Well, I think it's the perfect solution,' Millie declared. 'Helen can keep an eye on her. And Henry will be starting his medical training at the Nightingale soon, so the whole family will be there. Won't that be fun?'

Helen looked at her sister-in-law's smiling face. Sometimes she wished she could be more like Millie, and only see the good in every situation.

Because from where she was standing, it looked like a recipe for disaster.

Chapter Fifty-Nine

Results Day

Lil Trent was working her way through her basket of mending when Viv came home.

She had been waiting all afternoon, one eye constantly on the old mantelpiece clock. But even though she was on tenterhooks, she was determined not to give herself away.

'There's tea in the pot,' she said.

'Ta.'

'Might be a bit stewed, though.'

'I'll stick some water on it, it'll be fine.'

Lil tried to gauge her granddaughter's mood as she lit the gas under the kettle, but as usual, Viv's face gave nothing away.

Finally, as the kettle came to the boil, Viv said, 'I took my nursing exams.'

Lil did her best to look surprised. 'How did you manage that? I thought they'd chucked you out?'

'They didn't. I left.' She shot her a defiant look as she said it.

'You mean you lied to me?' How Lil kept a straight face she had no idea. She shocked herself sometimes.

Viv sent her a sideways look as she added water to the pot. 'Anyway, I changed my mind, so I went back and took them,' she said.

'And how did you get on?'

'I passed.'

Relief surged through Lil, but once again she gave nothing away. 'That's nice,' she said, digging into her basket for a spool of thread.

'Top marks, actually.'

'Good for you.'

Inside, Lil wanted to jump up and down for joy. But she didn't want to startle her granddaughter. Viv was like a nervous horse, likely to bolt at any moment if she made a wrong move. And besides, Lil knew her arthritic limbs would never take it.

She always knew her strategy would work. Viv was like her mother, contrary to the end. If Lil Trent had made a fuss and begged her to go back and take those exams, she knew full well Viv would never have done it.

It was the same with that awful boyfriend of hers. If Lil tried to lay the law down and stop her seeing him, Viv would probably elope to Gretna Green just to spite her. Better just to keep quiet and hope that her granddaughter's good sense prevailed in the end, as it was now.

'So what happens next?' she asked. She held up the needle to the light, squinting to find the hole. But her old eyes weren't up to it.

'Here.' Viv took it from her and threaded it. 'I can sign up for another three years and get properly qualified, if I want to.'

'And is that what you want?'

353

'Dunno. I might. I'll have to see.'

Lil Trent willed herself not to say the wrong thing. 'Well, it's up to you,' she said. 'If not, there's always Clarnico's.'

'That's what I thought.' But Viv didn't sound too thrilled at the prospect, Lil was pleased to note. 'I'll keep my options open.'

'Just as you like.' She paused. 'You going out later on?'

'Probably.'

'With him?'

She could have kicked herself when she saw Viv's face flicker. No matter how hard she tried, Lil could not hide her distaste for Roy Carter. As far as she was concerned, the sooner her granddaughter was shot of him, the better.

'Not tonight,' Viv said. Then she added, 'As a matter of fact, some of the girls from my set are going out to celebrate. They've asked me to go with them.'

Lil's heart jumped in her chest. 'Well, that'll be nice.'

'If I go.'

'If you go. But it's up to you.'

'Yes,' Viv said. 'Yes, it is.'

Lil Trent smiled to herself as she went back to her mending. It was like a game between them, this back and forth.

And she had been playing it a lot longer than her granddaughter.

'Now you're sure about this?'

'For crying out loud, Mum, I ain't signing up for the Foreign Legion!'

Helen looked at the girl sitting across the desk from her. It was nearly six months since Winifred Riley had first come

354

into her office with her bolshy attitude and her conspicuous lack of references. But now she was so glad she had decided to take a chance on her, because she had turned out to be easily one of their best students.

And the reason she had taken a chance on her was the woman who now sat at her side, hovering at her elbow.

'Your mother's right, Winnie. This is a big commitment you're making, and you need to be sure about it.'

'It's three years of your life,' Dora chimed in. 'And it ain't no picnic, I can tell you. If you thought PTS was hard—'

'What's the matter? Don't you think I can do it?'

Winnie looked at her mother, and Helen could see the light of challenge in her eyes.

'I think you can do anything you set your mind to,' Dora said.

'Like mother, like daughter?' Helen smiled.

Dora grinned back at her. 'Like mother, like daughter,' she agreed.

Acknowledgements

Since I wrote my last Nightingale novel in 2017, readers have been asking me constantly when the next one was coming out. And even though at the time I had no intention of writing another one, I always said 'Never say never', because in the back of my mind I knew one day I would be returning through those hospital gates to see what the girls were up to.

Anyway, I'm very grateful to my agent, Caroline Sheldon, for keeping the faith and making it happen. And to Selina Walker and the wonderful team at Century for welcoming me back so warmly. Honestly, when I walked back into that building it was as if I'd never been away (except the office has got even posher since I left). It was wonderful to see so many familiar faces, and lots of new ones, too. I look forward to getting to know you all.

In particular I'd like to thank Katie Loughnane, my new editor, for making the whole process of reacquainting myself with the Nightingales so easy and fun. It was very strange to be picking up the reins again after so long, but knowing I had Katie in my corner really helped.

Massive thanks to Amy Musgrave for bringing the Nightingales to life with a brilliant new cover, and for her

357

painstaking research into 1950s nurses' uniforms. I hope you agree, her efforts were totally worth it.

Thanks, too, to Katya Browne for shepherding the whole project through from start to finish, and being very understanding about my schedule clashes, even when I'm sure she was secretly tearing her hair out. As I write this, I'm about to deliver my proofs, so hopefully she'll be just as understanding with my erratic proofreading . . .

More thanks must go to marketing maven Hope Butler, for making sure everyone knows the Nightingales are coming. By the way, if you haven't signed up for the Penny Street newsletter, then what are you waiting for?

Honestly, I could go on and on, thanking all the people who have contributed to the book you now hold in your hands. From production to publicity, editorial to sales, there's just no room to name them all. But just know I really, really appreciate everything you've done (and are doing) to make the Nightingales sing again.

Last (but not least), thank you to my husband Ken, my daughter Harriet and the rest of my family for being there when I need them – and knowing when to make themselves scarce when I'm in deadline mode . . . !